D0389333

TROUBLETWISTERS

— BOOK FOUR —

THE MISSING

TROUBLETWISTERS

— BOOK FOUR —

THE MISSING

GARTH NIX
— AND —
SEAN WILLIAMS

SCHOLASTIC PRESS · NEW YORK

Library of Congress Cataloging-in-Publication Data Available

ISBN 978-0-545-25900-2

10 9 8 7 6 5 4 3 2 1   14 15 16 17 18

Printed in the U.S.A.   23
First edition, May 2014

The text type was set in Sabon.
Book design by Christopher Stengel

To Anna, Thomas, and Edward
and all my family and friends
— *Garth*

To my wife, Amanda. With
thanks to Finn, our soccer expert
— *Sean*

TABLE OF CONTENTS

CHAPTER ONE

What the Earth Contains

With a roar and a thundering crash, a large chunk of jagged bedrock dropped heavily into the truck grumbling impatiently on Watchward Lane. Jack Shield, brown-eyed, brown-haired, and possessing legs that seemed to be mostly shin, glanced up from the makeshift goal he was defending and, too late, covered his ears.

A soccer ball caught him in the stomach, throwing him heavily onto his back.

"Hey!" Jack cried out.

"Sorry." Jack's sister, Jaide, was instantly by his side, helping him up. "It was meant to go past you, but I got distracted. It's so noisy!"

Jack nodded, dusting himself off. He didn't have the heart to argue, although the ball *had* seemed to move much faster than a normal kick would allow. Perhaps it had received a helping boost from Jaide's Gift. . . .

"I wonder when Grandma will come out to tell them off again," he said.

They both looked to the front door of the big, rosy-bricked house they lived in, half expecting it to burst open that very instant. Three seconds passed and there was no sign of their grandmother, but they knew it wouldn't be long. Her temper was on a short fuse when it came to civic disturbances of any kind. Jaide possessed a similar temper, leading Jack to frequently wonder if Grandma X's hair had been red, too, before it had turned white.

Jack and Jaide looked completely different, but they were, in fact, twins. They and their mother were living in the small town of Portland because of Gifts the twins possessed — Gifts they hadn't known anything about until they'd accidentally destroyed their house in the city. Even worse, it was dangerous for their father to come near them, lest his own Gifts further disrupt theirs. Hector Shield was a Warden, like their grandmother, and the twins were troubletwisters, doomed to whip up mayhem until their Gifts were firmly under control.

Jaide's Gift gave her power of the air, and she had indeed used a careful puff of wind to give the soccer ball a secret push toward the goal.

Now she looked back over the fence, to where the yellow, toothy head of the front-end loader was turning with a snarl to find another chunk of stone. Perhaps if she could deliberately time the next kick with another crash, Jack would be distracted again and she would have better luck.

"What are they doing in there, anyway?" her brother asked. "I thought they were supposed to be fixing the old place up, not tearing it down."

"Tara told me they're building an underground garage big enough for three cars." Tara was Jaide's best friend, and the daughter of the developer who had bought the property next to their grandmother's home. The two buildings were identical — three stories high, with wide windows and a widow's walk circling the roof. The only difference was that one had been left to go to ruin.

Jack retrieved the soccer ball and moodily bounced it on the ground in front of him. "Did Tara say why it has to be so noisy?"

Jaide shrugged. "Garages don't dig themselves."

"Well, I don't like it."

Jaide wondered if he was thinking of the time a bull-dozer had attacked them when they had first moved to Portland. It had been driven by a hideous creature made of rats and other animals taken over by an evil intelligence known only as The Evil — a nameless, amorphous power from another dimension that was always trying to insinu-ate itself into anything and everything on earth, starting with small things like bugs and moving its way up to people and inanimate objects like bulldozers. The Evil was the ancient enemy of the Wardens, which was why being a troubletwister was so important. One day Jack and Jaide would graduate to become Wardens, and join the great fight.

"Just ignore it," Jaide said, snatching the ball from her brother's hands and running away to the other side of the yard. "I'm up five goals to two. You're never going to catch up!"

Jack narrowed his eyes and crouched between the posts, ready to defend his goal.

"Do your worst!" he cried back to her.

"What does that even mean?"

Jack didn't know, exactly. He'd read it in one of his father's old novels. It was a challenge of some kind, and he needed to do something to turn back his sister's powerful kicks. Perhaps a flicker of shadow across her face would distract her, at just the right time . . .

With a cough, the front-end loader fell silent. The absence of sound seemed to ring in the air.

Jack breathed a huge sigh of relief, then lunged too late for the soccer ball, which zoomed past him so quickly he practically heard it sizzle. It ricocheted off a tree twenty feet behind him and startled a large ginger cat who had been sleeping with one eye half-open, waiting for careless birds.

"Yowl!"

"Sorry, Ari!" Jaide was contrite, but not very. Aristotle was one of Grandma X's Warden Companions, and he was supposed to be umpiring. "That'll teach you to pay attention."

He sniffed the ball and poked it with one of his claws. His whiskers wiggled. "It's hot. Is that allowed?"

"Yes," said Jaide.

"No," said Jack.

"This is why cats don't play sports," said Ari with a yawn. "Fighting is much more interesting when there aren't so many rules."

"Don't listen to him," said an elegant gray-blue cat coming around the side of the house. Kleopatra was the second of Grandma X's Warden Companions. "Without rules, we'd be nothing but wild animals. Humans and cats alike."

Ari rolled his eyes and moved back into his favorite sleeping position. "Shush. You're scaring off the birds."

"If there are any left after that racket . . ." Kleo ran up to join the twins, her tail swaying high above her rump. "I came to see why the noise has stopped."

"We don't know," said Jack, reaching down to rub her chin. "Maybe it's their lunch hour."

"I can hear people shouting," said Jaide, whose hearing was particularly good during daytime, when her Gift was strongest. "I can't make out what they're saying, though . . . sounds like they're under the house."

All four of them looked up at the sound of footsteps running along Watchward Lane toward them. Ari opened both eyes and watched with interest as the owner of the footsteps appeared in the arched entrance to the garden.

It was Tara, looking dusty under a hard hat decorated with decal flowers.

"We need you next door," she said, slightly out of breath.

"How long have you been there?" Jaide asked. "I didn't know —"

"I wanted to call you, but Dad said we were just dropping in for *one minute* on the way home and, anyway, my phone was out of charge." Tara shook her head. "That doesn't matter. You have to come."

Jaide glanced at Jack, wishing they'd never lied about being interested in architecture. Tara's dad probably just wanted to show them an interesting piece of drywall. Besides, she was winning at soccer.

"You go on ahead," said Jack. "My ears still hurt. I don't want to go any closer in case they start up again."

"They won't," said Tara. "That's why I'm here. They've stopped for a reason. I couldn't call over the fence because they'd hear me. You know I can't . . . you know . . . because . . . you know."

She mimed a zipper across her mouth and waggled her eyebrows in frustration.

That awoke the twins' interest. Tara, along with another boy from school named Kyle, knew all about Wardens and The Evil, but had been bound by their grandmother never to speak of it in public. They literally *couldn't* speak, write, or even draw anything that might reveal the troubletwisters' secrets.

If she was having trouble talking now, that meant something connected to The Evil had happened next door.

"What is it?" asked Jack urgently.

"They've found something," she said, coming closer and leaning in to whisper.

"What kind of something?" asked Jaide.

"That's why I want you to come and look." Now she was tugging both their arms. "I don't remember what it's called, but I've seen one of them before."

Reluctance turned to intense curiosity, and the three of them hurried out of the garden and up the lane, soccer ball forgotten, followed closely by the two cats.

Parked diagonally across the entrance to the house next door was a white van emblazoned with the name MMM HOLDINGS. That was Tara's father's, but he was nowhere to be seen. They ran past the massive truck into which the rock from under the house was being loaded, past the inert front-end loader, past all manner of construction equipment, all lying idle. There was no sign of anyone on the ground level of the construction site.

An earthy ramp led down into the house's foundation under the living room, right next door to the location of Grandma X's secret blue room, where she maintained the wards that protected Portland from The Evil and taught the troubletwisters their magical lessons. It was a repository of old things, many of them imbued with magical properties through their long proximity with Wardens. It was also a kind of armory or quartermaster's store, though the twins suspected even Grandma X didn't know half of what was in there, particularly as their father and other Wardens delivered new old things there all the time, to be investigated and redistributed to other Wardens who might need whatever powers had ended up in the antiques.

The house next door seemed to have no such space.

"Dad?" called Tara.

"Down here, darling," floated back a familiar voice. "I wondered where you'd gotten to."

Tara waved for the twins to follow her as she descended the ramp. It looked dark down there to Jaide's eyes, but Jack's soon adjusted. There were four men standing at the far side of the roughly hewn space, where the wall wasn't yet fully dug. They all had on hard hats, and one of the men was holding a flashlight. The beam of light danced across something Jack couldn't quite make out until he was closer.

It was a long, brass tube, not unlike a cannon in size and proportions. One end poked out of the wall. The other was still buried. It was covered in dirt, apart from one spot where one of the men had rubbed at it, exposing the metal. When the light hit that patch, it shone.

"Hello, kids," said Martin McAndrew, Tara's father. He was a short man with a personality as broad as his too-white smile. "This is a construction site. You really shouldn't be down here without proper headgear."

"We won't be long," said Jaide, peering past him to get a better look at the object in the earth. Tara was right: It did indeed look like something they had seen before. But what? "We just wanted to check out what you found."

"Well, sure, I guess." He blinked in surprise at the cats coming down the ramp, sniffing the dusty air. "Everyone's curious, eh? Not surprising. We think it might be something left behind after an old battle. Or part of a broken machine. It might even be valuable. Does Portland have a museum?"

As Martin and the workers discussed this, Tara and the twins jostled closer. Jaide's Gift was tingling, so she knew the object had *something* to do with the Wardens. Perhaps it was an artifact they had read about in the Register of Lost and/or Forgotten Things. There might even be a reward!

Jack's mind was off on a similar tangent. Their father was an expert at finding lost objects once important to the Wardens. He really should be here, looking at this thing. Perhaps they should give him a call . . . ?

"It looks just like one of those things . . . you know . . . that your friend the professor built. . . ." Tara managed to force out.

"Of course," said Jaide, kicking herself for not seeing it sooner. It was still mostly buried, and there was a dent in it that might have been caused by one of the digging machines, but it did look very much like a cross-continuum conduit constructor. She hadn't recognized it straightaway because it had a slightly more modern look, like their grandmother's new car. It wasn't brand-new, but it wasn't three hundred years old, either.

"I didn't know there was another one," breathed Jack.

Jaide wasn't worried about that. "How did it get down here?"

"What are you going to do about it?" asked Tara.

"I'm getting your grandmother," said Kleo.

By then the three kids were ear to ear, just inches from the long, brass tube. Jack leaned in for a closer look at the end of the tube, and a coil of bright white light whipped between him and the exposed metal. A stinging shock went through him, into Tara, who felt nothing, and jolted Jaide in turn. She gasped in surprise.

Suddenly her Gift was amplified. A spiraling gust of wind kicked up around her feet, raising a thick cloud of dust. Jack staggered back, coughing and struggling to contain his own Gift. The flashlight went out, and the light coming down the ramp dimmed as though a cloud had passed across the sun.

"A cave-in!" Tara's dad tried to pull all three of them away from the wall. But the twins resisted. They knew that this was no ordinary event, and the dust was just dust. Their Gifts had been woken by something — or was it the other way around?

There was a whooshing noise. Flickering golden light danced through the shadows and clouds of dust. Something papery fluttered in Jack's face, and he brushed it away with one hand, only to find that it stuck to him and wouldn't let go. He shook his hand, and it wriggled up his sleeve to his elbow, where it clung on tight. Trying to dislodge it with his other hand only repeated the process up that arm.

Jaide, meanwhile, felt a thud as though something had dropped to the ground right in front of her. There was a chittering noise that sounded like insects. *Lots* of insects, all rustling and clicking at once. The hair on the back of her neck stood up as dozens of tiny white dots winked into life through the gloom.

She knew what they were. They were eyes. But not ordinary eyes.

++We have found you, troubletwisters,++ said a terrible voice directly into her mind. ++We have found you!++

Jaide raised a fist above her head and swung it about in a tight circle. Her Gift responded to her sudden urgency, sweeping the dust away in a tight circle around them and revealing the creature that crouched before her. It was as big as a medium-size dog, but made entirely out of insects. The legs and antennae of each bug gripped each of its neighbor's, creating a rippling, ever-changing mass that, even as she watched, raised up in front of her and unfolded four spindly tendrils to clutch at her face.

Ari flashed past her, a ginger cat enraged, fur on end and claws unsheathed. The Evil scattered and fell back as Jaide gathered her Gift around her before it could regroup.

Jack wasn't oblivious to his sister's predicament, even as he wrestled with the clinging, living parchment that had worked its way up to his shoulder and was threatening to envelop his face. Keeping it at bay with one hand, he took all the shadows around him and wove a protective cloak around the workers and Tara's father so that they couldn't see The Evil and it couldn't see them, either. He looked for Tara, and found her tugging a length of timber from an exposed beam and testing its weight as a club.

The Evil raised itself up and confronted two trouble-twisters, one girl, and a cat united against it. Hundreds of tiny white eyes glared with unflinching malevolence.

++Join us,++ The Evil said. ++It is your destiny!++

"You don't frighten us," said Jaide, telling herself to believe it. The Evil couldn't have been at full strength, or she would have felt its terrible presence battering at her mind.

"Four against one," added Jack, who had the living parchment caught tight in his hand now. It wriggled and squirmed but couldn't get free.

++We are one,++ said The Evil, ++and we are many.++

With a terrible ripping noise, The Evil split into quarters and leaped in four directions at once.

Jaide whipped up the wind to blow her quarter away, but it broke down even further into individual insects, and each unfurled two pairs of tiny gossamer wings. Humming loudly, the swarm was buffeted by the wind but not greatly slowed. Jaide covered her face as hundreds of buzzing, stinging bugs converged on her at once.

Tara swung the plank of wood like a baseball bat. It sailed right through her bug creature, squashing maybe a dozen or two but having no effect on the rest. She nearly tripped backward over Ari, who was doing his best to swipe at his portion of The Evil, and finding it difficult to do more than punch holes that quickly healed over.

Jack tried something he had never attempted before, which was to send shadows into the white eyes of The Evil insects. If he could put out that awful glow, maybe that would kill The Evil, too. But the light was unquenchable. No matter how many shadows he threw at the bug creature lunging at him, its eyes still glowed white. His frantic gesturing only set free the parchment, which renewed its quest to smother him. With two rippling leaps it reached his neck, and with a third it clapped tightly over his eyes, blinding him.

The bugs saw their chance and took it. Feathery wings and prickly legs tickled his face and neck, buzzing and biting.

++Yes, yes,++ gloated The Evil. ++Come closer and together we will open the way for good.++

"Blow the man down!"

The cry came from behind Jaide. She ducked as a pair of royal blue wings flapped overhead, scattering the insects that were attacking her. A curved black beak snapped at the clumps bothering Tara and Ari. With a snap of her wings, Cornelia the macaw swooped to help Jack, who had staggered backward into the earthen wall, struggling against two attacks at once.

Before Jaide could rally her Gift, a beam of silver light shone down the ramp, issuing from the moonstone ring of a stiff-backed, white-haired woman dressed in jeans, a white linen shirt, and cowboy boots, with Kleo, her Warden

Companion, trotting at her feet. The light scattered the insects crawling over Jack, and sent them swirling in a panic.

"Grandma!" Jaide ran to her side and hastened to explain. "It wasn't our fault. The Evil came out of nowhere. I don't know how —"

Grandma X shook her head. "Let's deal with it first. We'll talk after."

++You will never defeat us,++ The Evil intoned. The swarm had taken on the shape in which it had first appeared, and it rose up on three spindly legs and spread its arms wide to face this new challenge.

"It's not our job to defeat you," said a soft voice. "Just to contain you."

Jack felt a firm, wooden hand come down on his shoulder. "Rennie?" he said.

"I'm here," she said, and some of Jack's panic evaporated, even though he still couldn't see. The living parchment absolutely refused to come away from his face. When he tugged at it, it stretched like rubber, then snapped back exactly as it had been.

Jaide watched the Living Ward of Portland, one of four wards charged with keeping The Evil at bay, do something with her one human hand. A translucent bubble formed around The Evil, turning the whiteness of its eyes to myriad tiny rainbows. The Evil reached out to pop the bubble with one bug-claw but it only bulged slightly, spreading circular ripples out in waves.

Rennie's hand moved again, and the bubble began to contract.

++We will return,++ The Evil vowed. **++We have found a way. We are coming.++**

The bubble shrank and the bug-thing crouched to avoid

touching it. Eyes blinked and rolled as The Evil folded in on itself, becoming a shapeless swarm confined to the size of a basketball, a football, a tennis ball. . . .

++We are coming!++

Soundlessly, the bubble collapsed to nothing, and the eyes went out. Instantly, the swarm was released, unharmed, and the air was full of buzzing insects.

Jaide grinned in relief and Tara clapped her hands.

"What's going on?" asked Tara's father. He and the workers, released from the gloom Jack had cast over them, swatted at insects and looked at the sudden crowd on the work site with suspicion. "It wasn't a cave-in, was it?"

"Termites," said Grandma X, raising her moonstone ring a second time. "You called Rennie here for a second opinion."

Rennie, in her former life, had been the town's handyperson.

"Looks bad," she said. "You'd better go call an exterminator."

Martin McAndrew blinked three times and nodded.

"You're right," he said. "That's a good idea."

He reached in his pocket for his mobile phone.

"You'll want to do that somewhere else," said Grandma X, with an unbending gleam in her eye. "Reception is bad down here."

Tara's father and the workers headed obediently up the ramp.

"A little help here?" said Jack, his voice muffled by the parchment.

Jaide hurried to him, horrified that she hadn't noticed that he was still under attack. She had simply assumed that all of The Evil had been expelled by Rennie and Grandma X.

"What is it?" asked Tara, as together Grandma X and Rennie helped Jack peel the living parchment from his face. Cornelia circled above, offering encouraging squawks.

"I think . . . yes." Grandma X held up the parchment by it its top corners while Jack and Rennie held the bottom two. "Okay, easy," she told it in a reassuring voice. "We have you now."

The paper became still.

"It's a message," she said, "of a kind that Wardens send one another sometimes. Living mail, if you like, only I've never seen one as determined as this. It must have been sent a very long time ago, and held up somehow, desperately trying to get through."

"What does it say?" asked Jack, eyeing the paper resentfully. It had better be something really important, given it had almost smothered him in its quest to make sure it was noticed.

The paper seemed blank at first. Then ink swirled around the edges and sent fine filaments across the page. Letters formed, then words, written in an unsteady hand.

We're here and we are trapped. Please help us!

It wasn't signed.

"What does it mean?" asked Jaide. "Who's it from?"

"Where are they?" asked Tara.

"How do we help them?" asked Jack. Cornelia landed on his shoulder and cocked her yellow head.

Grandma X's face had gone very pale. She folded the parchment into four and clutched it tightly in her hand.

"Tell me how you came by this," she said.

They explained about the brassy tube buried in the

bedrock under the house and the mysterious way their Gifts had woken as they came near it.

"It's a cross-continuum conduit constructor, isn't it?" said Jaide.

Grandma X nodded.

"And these aren't really termites," said Tara, pulling one of the wriggling bugs from her hair. It had four wings, five body segments, and no less than ten legs.

"Did they come from the same place as the message?" asked Jack.

Grandma X nodded.

"How?" asked Tara.

"The cross-continuum conduit constructor opened a small hole inside the wards," said Rennie. "That's how it got into Portland. The Evil followed the message through."

"So it was our fault," said Jaide, feeling a pang of guilt.

There were many places in the world where The Evil tried to break in, places where the fabric of reality was weak. Each was protected by four wards, and each ward had a different nature, as depicted in a simple rhyme that every troubletwister learned by rote:

SOMETHING GROWING
SOMETHING READ
SOMETHING LIVING
SOMEONE DEAD

The Something Read Ward was a piece of romantic graffiti scribbled on the town lighthouse by Jack and Jaide's parents. Rennie was Something Living. What the other two wards were, the troubletwisters didn't know. The Evil was always trying to get around the wards and the Wardens who maintained them. Jaide hated the fact she had helped it find a new way in.

Grandma X stirred from her deep thoughts.

"It wasn't your fault," she told Jaide in a firm voice. "Don't ever believe what The Evil tells you. It only means to frighten you or put doubts in your head. It saw an opportunity, that's all . . . an opportunity the message provided."

"Does that mean the message came from the same place as The Evil?" asked Jack.

"From the Evil Dimension?" asked Jaide.

Instead of answering, Grandma X crossed the room to study the cross-continuum conduit constructor. The parchment went into her pocket, but she kept one hand pressed against the pocket as though keeping its contents safe.

"Tara," she said, turning away from her examination, "thank you for bringing this to our attention. Please tell your father that I would like to buy it from him for a price we'll settle later. I would also like his expertise in freeing it from the earth. I need to get this home as soon as possible, so I can examine it."

Tara nodded and headed up the ramp.

Grandma X turned to the twins.

"Whatever you have planned for the rest of the day," she said, "I'm afraid it's canceled."

"Why?" asked Jack, exchanging a worried glance with his sister.

"What does this mean?" asked Jaide. She had never heard their grandmother sound so serious.

"I don't know what it means. That's why I'm going to do something that's only happened once before in my lifetime. I'm going to call a Grand Gathering and ask them the question that for the life of me I cannot answer on my own: Why do I recognize the handwriting on that note?"

CHAPTER TWO

A Warden's Duty

Two hours later, in an opulent palace far away, a hall full of glass came to gleaming life. Hundreds of candles flickered in massive crystal chandeliers that hung suspended on long cables from a painted ceiling far above. Down one wall hung a bank of well-polished mirrors that were famous around the world. Down the other wall, tall windows reflected the light dim yellow back inside. Outside it was the dead of night. No one near the Palace of Versailles noticed the unusual light flickering inside, or the people it illuminated.

Meanwhile, in Portland, Jack and Jaide were in the blue room, peering into a much less elaborate mirror. This mirror was lying on its side and resting on two chairs, whose backs supported its heavy weight without complaint. The mirror, which normally reflected images in a perfectly ordinary fashion, now acted as a window to the famous Hall of Mirrors, where they could see Wardens from all over the world assembling for the historic Grand Gathering of the Glass.

Grandma X was pacing on the other side of the blue room, out of the mirror's sight, one hand pressing on the pocket where the note still sat. She had revealed nothing more since the discovery of the cross-continuum conduit constructor, but she was muttering silently to herself, which was in itself more worrying than anything she could have said. Jaide and Jack waited with impatience for the Gathering to begin in the hope that they would learn what on earth was going on.

Perched silently in her cage, Cornelia watched closely with one black eye, taking in everything and saying nothing.

"Were you at the last Grand Gathering?" Jack asked Custer, a local Warden who was watching with them in the blue room. He was a middle-aged but somehow ageless man with high cheekbones and long blond hair. His most striking feature was the ability to turn into a saber-toothed tiger at will. He had tried to teach the twins to shape-shift, but neither seemed to possess Gifts that worked that way. Everyone assured them that they *would* have other Gifts, possibly soon, but there was no way to tell what they would be. It was just a matter of waiting to see.

"I was present at the last Grand Gathering," Custer replied with a formal inclination of his head. "It is good that such terrible times are long behind us."

Grandma X shot him a look that Jack couldn't interpret. Perhaps she was warning Custer not to give away too much. There were supposed to be no secrets between her and the troubletwisters anymore, not after the last time The Evil had attacked, exploiting knowledge that had been kept from them, supposedly for their own good. That the twins were present for the Grand Gathering suggested that this compact was being honored, but they knew there were limits nonetheless. They were troubletwisters and they were kids. It didn't come easily to grown-up Wardens to treat them like equals.

"Look, there's Dad!"

Jaide had spotted Hector Shield in a reflection of a reflection. He was peering out of another mirror, just as floppy-haired and crumpled as he usually looked. His glasses sat on a slight angle, and she wished Susan, her mother, was there to straighten them for him. Susan wasn't a Warden, but like Tara and Kyle she was aware of the twins' training. It was her job, she said, to make sure everyone remembered there was an ordinary world out there, too, full of things like homework and chores. She was an aero-ambulance paramedic who worked three-day shifts outside of Portland, and although the twins missed her, it also meant she was usually away when they were exercising their Gifts. It worked better that way.

Hector waved, waggling all ten fingers of both hands and beaming in welcome, but it was impossible to talk to him. A loud buzz of voices issued from the mirror as Wardens from all over the world joined the vast assembly through mirrors of every shape and size. Faces peered out of bedrooms, closed shopping malls, dressing rooms, and airports. Every age, race, and culture was represented. Some of the Wardens had clearly been woken from deep sleeps to attend and were still in their pajamas. One appeared to be underwater, peering into the reflection of her goggles. All of them were adults. Look though he might, Jack saw no other troubletwisters.

Sometimes Jaide could make out fragments of what they were saying to one another. It seemed to be variations on a single question: *What's going on?*

An imposing figure stepped into the Hall of Mirrors, a man wearing a dark gray suit, with broad shoulders and a full, bearded face. His hair was yellow and thick, and stood out like a mane. The twins had never seen him change shape, but nothing would have surprised them less than learning that he could turn into a lion.

His name, they knew, was Aleksandr, and the few times they had met him he had seemed to be in charge, as he appeared to be now. With ringing footsteps, he walked down the gallery to its center and stood there alone, staring at the mirrors surrounding him.

When silence didn't fall immediately, Aleksandr raised his left hand and snapped his fingers.

Jack and Jaide held their breaths. There was suddenly no sound at all. It was as though the air in the blue room had vanished, replaced by a feeling of great significance — of history, even.

"The Warden of Last Resort calls us," Aleksandr said, "and we have come, the Grand Gathering of the Wardens of Earth, only summoned in times of direst need. We await the reason for our summoning."

He paused, and his deep voice echoed off marble and glass, rolling and rumbling for a full second.

"It had better be good," Aleksandr added before the last of the echoes had faded away.

Before Jack could ask Custer who the Warden of Last Resort was, a clear strong voice spoke out in reply.

"She's alive," said Grandma X.

Jaide jumped several inches in the air. She hadn't noticed her grandmother coming up behind her. Grandma X put her right hand on Jaide's shoulder, pressing her back into her seat. In her other hand she held up the note.

"*Who* is alive?" asked Aleksandr.

"My sister."

"Impossible."

"I have proof!" said Grandma X over a rising hubbub. She tried to explain about what the twins had found, but too many voices shouted her down. Aleksandr raised his hands for calm, but even he couldn't bring order. All he could do was wait until everyone's surprise and shock — and no little outrage, it seemed — had been vented.

"The message was from Lottie?" Jack asked Grandma X in a whisper, while he had the chance. He and Jaide had been hunting for information about their missing great-aunt, Grandma X's twin, for months now, and had turned up nothing except that she'd disappeared long before they were born. They had assumed her dead at the hand of The Evil, but they had never been able to prove it. It was incredible that news of her had turned up like this.

If the note had been written by Lottie, and had come from the same place as The Evil, that meant Lottie was in the Evil Dimension. They had received the merest glimpse of that place the day their Gifts had woken, and it had been horrible. To be trapped there . . . Jaide shuddered at the thought, and Jack hugged himself.

Grandma X glanced down at the troubletwisters. She had heard Jack's question, but for a moment she didn't seem to see her grandchildren. Her gray eyes were full of grief and anger. This wasn't a secret that had been kept from them, Jack understood. No one had known, not even Lottie's own twin sister.

Grandma X sighed, nodded, and seemed to grow suddenly impatient with the racket. When she spoke again, her voice was like thunder, and it drowned out anyone who tried to speak over her, even Aleksandr.

"My sister is alive," she said, *"and you know what that means."*

The twins didn't know. They waited breathlessly for silence to fall, in hope and dread of finding out.

"We abandoned her," Grandma X said in her ordinary voice. Custer reached up to take her hand but she shook him off. "We left her to die, all of us, even me — *but she didn't die.* She has endured horrors we cannot imagine. Yet she lived in hope. all these years. She sent us a message, and she waited and waited for rescue, and we didn't come. She is still waiting for us, even now, after all we have *not* done for her."

"She might be dead —" said Aleksandr.

"She is not. The living-mail charm dies with the user."

"Then it is a trap, set by The Evil to sow dissent among us."

"She would never fall."

"How can you say that? No one is entirely immune here, let alone *there*, where The Evil's power is strongest."

"Lottie would die first," said Grandma X. "I was the weak one, not her."

Jack was horrified to hear his own fears coming from his powerful, confident grandmother's mouth. The Evil often claimed that of every set of troubletwister twins one would turn to its side. Their father's twin brother, Harold, had done exactly that, and there had been moments when The Evil's power had been almost too strong for either Jack or Jaide to resist. Each time, they had been saved, but maybe it was a matter of time, and when their time ran out, the weaker would fall.

If Grandma X was the weak one, thought Jaide, how strong must Lottie have been?

"We must rescue her," said an elderly Warden from the far end of the Grand Gathering. "Lottie and any others who remain with her."

"We cannot," said Aleksandr.

"It must be possible," said a Warden peering through a shaving mirror. "By what means was the message received?"

Grandma X briefly explained about the discovery in the grounds next door.

"The artifact lay dormant until exposed by happenstance," she concluded. "The presence of the troubletwisters activated it, and a Bridge briefly formed."

Jack and Jaide felt the combined attention of the Grand Gathering fall upon them, but not for long. Their role in the events of that day was a crucial but small one.

"*Another* Improbable Conglobulator?" said a Warden incredulously. She was one of several in a fun house, her image twisted into an impossible shape. "It surely cannot be the one Lottie herself used."

"It must be," said Grandma X. "Lost but not destroyed, as we thought it had been."

"Could we use it to send someone after her?" the twisted Warden asked.

"That would be extremely dangerous," said Aleksandr. "Any conduit to The Evil flows both ways. Was there an incursion in Portland?" he asked Grandma X.

"There was," she said. "A small one, and it was contained."

"Possibly because the conduit was open only long enough to allow the message through. A more significant breach, one large enough to send a whole person, might wreak a terrible toll, perhaps even destroy the wards." He shook his head gravely. "We learned forty-five years ago what meddling with the realm of The Evil can do. This device must never be used again."

"You would have us do nothing?" asked a Warden gazing into the reflection of a perfectly still pool.

"Lottie and her friends acted recklessly and without forethought," said Aleksandr in a deep warning voice. "Their willfulness cost the lives of many other Wardens, Wardens who sacrificed themselves to seal the breach between Earth and the realm of The Evil that she opened. Reopening that breach will undo their valiant efforts to save this world. It will put us all at risk. And . . ."

Here Aleksandr hesitated. He seemed to be considering

the wisdom of his words, and the twins wondered if he was about to change his mind.

"There is something I must tell you," he said. "It will be news to most of you, because the information has been kept secret for fear of The Evil's spies learning of it. A great work is being undertaken, even as we speak. Its existence will explain why I said that we *cannot* rescue Lottie, rather than *will not*."

He paused for dramatic effect.

"The relic of Professor Olafsson, inventor of the cross-continuum conduit constructor, Improbable Conglobulator, Bifrost Bridge — call it what you will — has been recovered. With his knowledge and the professor's original notebooks, we have discovered a way to neutralize the threat of The Evil once and for all. When Project Thunderclap is put into effect, the realm of The Evil will be barred from our world forever. I expect this to happen in a matter of days."

The hubbub this announcement provoked was even louder than the first one, although this time the twins didn't understand why. Among renewed cries of "Impossible!" Jaide heard several voices shout "Madness!" or "Insanity!" A Warden in a turban called out, "Isn't this what led to the Catastrophe in the first place?" Those Wardens who remained silent, she assumed, were already in on the plan.

"They really found the professor?" Jack whispered to Custer.

"So it would seem."

That at least was good news. They had discovered the animated death mask of the long-dead Warden in Rourke Castle six months ago. He had helped them and become a rather peculiar friend until he had been snapped in half and stolen by one of The Evil's spies.

"The Hawks have clearly been busy," Custer added.

"The who?" Jaide asked.

"There are factions among the Wardens. The Hawks advocate taking the fight to The Evil, rather than merely defending ourselves from it. The Doves want us to try to negotiate with The Evil, to arrange a peace. They have always argued. Ever since the Catastrophe, the Hawks have been in ascendance. Lottie's actions —"

"Lottie kept her own counsel," said Grandma X. "And she never entertained the possibility that she might be wrong."

"Why *wouldn't* we want to cut off The Evil?" asked Jaide. "Anything to make the world safe, right?"

Custer indicated the mirror, where Aleksandr had raised his hands for calm. The Gathering was settling. Hector was no longer smiling.

"I will tell you everything in a moment," Aleksandr said. "Let me just say now that the success or failure of Project Thunderclap rests entirely on surprise. Tip our hand too early, and we will fail. Leave it too late, and the same thing will happen. Even if we succeeded in rescuing Lottie without alerting The Evil to our plans, we could not trust Lottie to keep this secret. Therefore, I ask all of you to put aside thoughts of Lottie or anyone else trapped with her. She made her choice long ago, and the weight of it must rest heavily on her shoulders alone."

"You want us to ignore another Warden's cry for help?" asked Hector, his expression appalled. "Once the realm of The Evil is sealed, she will be permanently out of our reach."

"Yes." Aleksandr's expression was grim, but unflinching. "That is the way it must be. We have each of us taken oaths binding us to a single great duty: to save the world from The Evil. To serve that greater good, we must sacrifice our individual concerns, just as we must sometimes sacrifice ourselves."

A new hush filled the Hall of Mirrors, one of nervous anticipation. Aleksandr was talking to Hector, but all knew to whom he was really addressing his words. The twins looked up at Grandma X and could tell by the clenched muscles in her jaw that she knew best of all.

"Will you promise me," Aleksandr asked her, "not to attempt a rescue?"

Everyone's attention was on Grandma X, who stood stiff-backed and silent in the face of their combined regard. The twins waited for her to speak, knowing that she would never agree to such a terrible thing. Jaide tried to imagine what it would be like if Jack was the one in the realm of The Evil. She would stop at nothing to get him back, no matter what he had done. Jack felt exactly the same way. They were twins. They were troubletwisters. It was hard-wired into them to help each other in times of serious need.

There wasn't a person in the Grand Gathering not feeling that way, they were sure. So why would Aleksandr ask the impossible? Grandma X couldn't possibly agree.

"Promise me," he said again, and this time it was an order, not a request.

Jaide could practically hear her grandmother's teeth grinding.

"Yes," she finally said. "I will do as you ask."

The twins were aghast.

"You can't!" blurted out Jaide.

"But she'll die!" said Jack.

"Lottie has been dead to those who loved her for many years," Aleksandr said.

"So?" said Jaide. "This is wrong, and you know it. You're wrong to ask Grandma to do this."

"There must be another way," said Jack. "We have to help Lottie get back."

"Silence!" ordered Aleksandr.

"Hush, troubletwisters," their grandmother said.

The light flickered in the blue room. A gust of wind sent Custer's long hair dancing.

"How would you feel if *your* twin was stuck in the Evil Dimension," Jack asked Aleksandr.

"Or you," added Jaide. "What did Lottie do that was so bad, anyway?"

"Remember your training," said Custer, but it was too late. The twins' Gifts were awake and responding to the anger they felt. Shadows stretched and deepened until the darker corners of the blue room became impenetrable black holes. The gusting wind picked up speed as it circled under tables, along bookcases, and around the light fixtures, moaning as it went.

"Control yourselves, troubletwisters!"

They did try, but the angry boom of Aleksandr's voice only worsened the force of their Gifts. And the chaos wasn't confined only to the blue room, either. Just as the mirror could send their images and voices to the rest of the Grand Gathering, so too could it send their Gifts. One by one the candles in the Hall of Mirrors turned black and shed no light. The giant chandeliers began to sway. Wardens wearing hats clutched them tightly to their heads as the gale picked up strength.

Jack and Jaide tried their best to control their Gifts, but the presence of so many Wardens made them restless and seemingly keen to show off. A miniature hurricane did a wild jig around Aleksandr, while thin tentacles of shadow tried to tie themselves in knots in his hair and beard.

"Jack, Jaide, not here."

Their father's voice cut gently but firmly through the crowd. The soft reproach brought blushes of embarrassment to both twins' cheeks, and sufficiently dampened their anger at Aleksandr so that their Gifts began to creep back through the mirror. The light of the candles returned.

Aleksandr tried to put his hair in order, but it stayed standing up in patches.

"This is inexcusable," he said. "All troubletwisters are immediately expelled for the remainder of the Gathering."

"They mean well —" Hector tried to object.

"They are a disruption and an irrelevance. They will leave at once!"

Jack and Jaide looked shamefacedly at their grand-mother, who nodded, not unkindly.

"Thank you for trying," she said, "but there's nothing more to be done now. Go on."

"But, Grandma —" Jaide started to say.

"Wait outside. I'll come to you when it's over."

The twins reluctantly made their way through the clutter and the tapestry that led to the top floor of the house via the secret door that linked the main house to the blue room with an impossibly short stair created by their great-grandfather, a Warden with a Gift for architectural magic. Jack's face felt hot the whole way, while Jaide bit sharply down on her tongue to stop herself from saying something she might regret. As the door closed behind them they heard Aleksandr calling the Grand Gathering to order.

"What happened?" asked Ari, appearing at the top of the stairs with eyes round in surprise. "Is it over already? I thought you'd be at it for hours."

Jaide freed her tongue. "*They* might be, but not with us. They kicked us out!"

"Don't feel bad," said Kleo, padding up the stairs past Ari to give Jaide a head-bump. "Warden Companions weren't allowed, either."

"No . . . that's not it . . . oh!" Jaide flapped her hands at her side, and nearly succeeded in actually flapping herself right up to the ceiling. "That man's such a pain."

"Which man?" asked Ari.

"Aleksandr," said Jack, taking over the explanation, as he sensed his sister was close to another explosion. "He wants to trap Grandma X's sister in the Evil Dimension forever. And she's going to let him."

"That doesn't sound like her," said Kleo.

"Maybe she doesn't really mean to," said Ari. "Maybe she's going to do something about it behind his back."

"What can she do?" said Jack. "She can't take on The Evil all on her own."

"That would be very unwise," agreed Kleo.

"They kept talking about some catastrophe forty-five years ago, when Lottie was lost," said Jaide. "Do you know what that was?"

Both cats shook their heads.

"You could look it up in the *Compendium*," said Ari. The *Compendium* was the pooled records of every Warden's dealings with The Evil, and it also provided valuable information on the Wardens themselves, when the information could be understood.

"We could do that, if the *Compendium* wasn't in the blue room," said Jack. "Maybe later, when it's all over."

"Is that you, kids? Are you done?"

Their mother's voice floated up from ground level.

"She cooked dinner for you," said Kleo.

"How bad is it?" asked Jaide.

"It looks . . . edible," allowed Ari.

"On our way!" Jack called back. Susan Shield's meals were notoriously bad, but his stomach was empty and the very thought of food temporarily put all other concerns from his mind.

Jaide followed her brother down the stairs with feet as heavy as her heart. How could Grandma X even *pretend* to abandon her sister like that? Whatever Project Thunderclap was, it wasn't ready to go just yet, or Aleksandr wouldn't be warning people off. There was still time, so why wasn't Grandma X insisting they use it?

Halfway down the stairs, the lights flickered. Jack looked up, but didn't think anything of it. The house was old. An electrician had once come to put extra outlets in the twins' room, but after an hour inspecting the wiring declared his amazement that anything worked at all.

"What's the Warden of Last Resort?" Jack asked.

The cats exchanged a look.

"Why do you ask?" Kleo wanted to know.

"It was just something Aleksandr said at the beginning of the Gathering. He said it had been called by the Warden of Last Resort. He wasn't talking about Grandma, was he?"

The lights flickered again, this time accompanied by a prolonged crackling sound.

Jack looked up at the bulb above his head. Its color had changed from a soft yellow to a harsh blue. Tiny sparks shot from it and discharged harmlessly into the air.

"That's weird."

"Jack . . . ?"

It was Jaide who spoke. She had fallen behind without him noticing. He turned and saw her standing five steps above him, balanced precariously in mid-step with a hand touching a banister on either side, as though afraid she might float away.

Every long, red hair on her head was standing on end.

"Jaide! Are you all right?"

"Yes," she said, nodding quickly. "But I think —"

The crackling sound came again. This time the lights flared green, and bright sparks ran down Jaide's arms into the stairs.

"Jack, I think something's coming!"

CHAPTER THREE
CATS AND DOGS AND TROUBLETWISTERS

What is it, Jaide?" asked Jack, staring up at her in alarm. "What's happening?"

Jaide couldn't have explained it even if she'd tried. It felt like the air just before a thunderstorm broke, only inside her, building up in every nerve and fiber. She felt full of energy, and it was tugging her, pulling her forward. . . .

"Outside," she said, trusting suddenly that instinct to move, hoping it wouldn't let her blow up or anything. Tiny, glowing balls of blue light appeared on her first step. They followed her as she ran down the stairs, past Jack and the cats, to the ground floor.

"There you are," said Susan, appearing in the hallway with an oven mitt on her right hand. "I was just about to —"

She stopped in amazement as Jaide rushed past her, glowing purple all over and trailing a spray of orbs and bright sparks. Jack, Kleo, and Ari raced after her in a clatter of feet and paws.

"I don't know, either," Jack answered her unspoken question as he hurried by. Susan followed, tugging off the oven mitt and picking up a walking stick from the umbrella stand by the front door.

Outside, it was dark and starless. Jaide came to a halt in the front yard and spun around once. She looked up at the weathervane, but it was motionless, pointing stolidly west in accordance with the wind, as normal weathervanes did. She ran along the side of the house to the backyard, which was dominated by a single tall tree that was known, on occasion, to change species. Currently it was a giant sequoia with thick roots clenched tightly just under the yard's lumpy surface. There Jaide stopped. Above her, faint lights danced among the branches of the tree and thick black clouds roiled. There was no rain or wind, just the steady flashing of sheet lightning.

"Is it Dad?" Jack asked, sudden hope blossoming in his chest. Maybe he had come to make them feel better about being kicked out of the Grand Gathering. Maybe he had been kicked out, too.

"*Is* it Hector?" asked Susan, holding the walking stick upraised, like a club. The cats looked around them, tails swaying from side to side.

"I don't know," Jaide said, trying to take the measure of this strange new feeling. It was like being filled with electric lemonade and told not to burp. The sensation was building so fast it was almost painful. "It feels like him, but . . . different."

"I think you should come inside," said Susan, eyeing the clouds with misgiving. "It could be dangerous."

Jaide was inclined to agree, although the strange feeling in her body didn't want her to move. She took a step forward. Sparks flared and spat. She took another step, fighting the feeling with every inch. Her hair whipped and flailed about her head, glowing like lava.

She raised her foot to take a third step and a thick bolt of lightning struck down from the heavens into the earth just behind her. The sound of it was immense, a physical thing that threw her off her feet and into Susan, who dropped the walking stick and caught her in her arms. They both went down, leaving only Jack and the cats to see what happened next.

The lightning bolt didn't vanish, as they normally did. This one stayed anchored to the earth, whipping and cracking all along its length, thin horizontal channels rippling up and down, connecting to the house, the tree, even Jack himself. He flinched but it had locked onto him before he could move, sending a weird fizz of energy down his body, from his ears to the soles of his feet. It lasted a second and left him smelling faintly of fireworks. Ari batted at it with his foreclaws, but the lightning was undeterred. Kleo stood stiff-legged and stiff-tailed, with eyes tightly closed, and shivered when it had passed.

There was a boom so loud it made the ground shake.

Then the lightning was gone, leaving a long purple afterimage from the top of Jack's vision to the bottom.

"Jaide!" said Susan. "Are you all right?"

Jack was at his mother's side instantly, helping Jaide upright. She brushed the hair from her eyes and blinked rapidly.

"I'm fine," she said. "In fact, that was almost fun."

"*Fun?*" said Susan. "You're lucky to be alive. Inside, this minute, both of you."

"I agree with your mother," said Kleo. "The weather looks highly irregular."

Behind them came the sound of a clearing throat.

"Hello? A little help here?"

They spun around. Jack's vision cleared just enough to make out a teenage boy standing in a blackened circle in the center of the yard. His hair was dark and tightly curled, and although it was hard to tell exactly how old he was, or even how tall he was, he seemed about the same age as the twins. His legs were buried to the knees in the soil, which still sparked and shimmered with the force of his arrival.

"How did you —"

"Where did you —"

The twins stopped as their mother pushed forward. "Let's get you out of there before that happens again."

"Don't be silly," the boy said. "I have everything perfectly under control."

"Yeah, it looks like it," Jaide said.

"I've heard of raining cats and dogs," said Ari with poorly concealed amusement, "but this is ridiculous."

Jaide took one arm while her mother took the other. Jack's hands went under the boy's armpits.

"One, two, *three*," said Susan. Together they lifted.

"Ow, that hurts," the boy complained. "Stop or you'll leave my feet behind!"

"Hmm," said Susan, letting go. "What's your name?"

"I am Stefano Battaglia, master of lightning!"

"Well, Stefano Battaglia, you are firmly stuck in the dirt." She scratched her head. "We might have to dig you out. Let me go find a shovel."

Jack inspected the soil around Stefano's knees. It was tightly compacted, and oddly crystalline after the lightning strike, but it looked as though it would shift if he pushed here . . . perhaps dug out that divot there. . . . Dimly, he heard Jaide talking.

"This is Jack and I'm Jaide," she said. "I thought you were going to be our dad. He likes to travel this way, too."

"Hector? Oh, no. I'm fully qualified to bolt on my own. It's quite easy when you get the hang of it."

"You know Dad?"

"Of course I do. He's my mentor." Stefano studied her with his head to one side. "You really don't know who I am?"

"Sorry, no."

"How odd. And I've studied with him for a year, too." Stefano looked up at her. "He didn't tell me there was another lightning wielder in the family."

Jaide blinked. "Do you mean me?"

"Of course. How else did you know I was on my way to you?"

She could only gape at him. This was too many surprises at once. First, Hector had a protégé he had never mentioned, and now her second Gift might be the same as his, giving her power over lightning and the ability to travel by thunderstorm. Gifts did occasionally run in a family, but she had never dared dream of this.

"Or maybe," Stefano added with a slight curl to his lip, "you just got lucky."

The return of Susan, armed with a shovel, a trowel, and a gardening fork, was all that stopped Jaide from telling him what she thought of that idea.

"Here we are," said Susan, glancing at the sky. "I don't think it's going to rain, but let's get a move on, just in case."

Jack sat back, wiped his dirty hands on his jeans, and looked up at everyone. He had been thoroughly involved in what he was doing. It occurred to him that he had missed something.

"What?" he said.

"We're going to dig him out," said Susan, handing him the trowel.

"Uh, I think I've done that already," he said, pointing at the loosened earth. "Try moving your legs."

Stefano tentatively raised his right knee, and it came cleanly out of the soil. Jaide and Susan helped him lift his left leg out and step up to ground level. Once released, he was surprisingly tall.

"Finally," he said, instead of saying thanks. And instead of helping Jack to his feet, he reached for a small satchel lying nearby and slung it over his shoulder. "If you show me to my room, I'd like to freshen up."

"*Room?*" said Jack and Jaide at the same time.

"Are you sure you've come to the right place?" said Susan, looking as perplexed as the twins felt.

"He has," said Grandma X from the back porch. "I was going to tell you all earlier, but . . . recent events being as they are . . ."

She stepped out of the pool of light shining from the doorway, into the night. Both twins were struck by how old she looked, as though the Grand Gathering had drained her of her usual vitality. Above them, the clouds were dispersing and the stars coming out. Not even a full moon peeking around the Rock could bring out the usual sparkle to her eyes.

"Hector has asked me to take in Stefano here for special training," she explained. "He's a troubletwister, just a little more advanced in his experience."

"What kind of special training?" asked Jack. He had never met another troubletwister before. No one had ever told him that they could be taught different things.

"Don't worry about that. Let's get our guest inside and make him feel welcome. Come on, Stefano, make sure you wipe your shoes thoroughly. They're quite amazingly muddy."

The twins and their mother followed Grandma X and Stefano into the house and up the stairs. Stefano simply nodded as the basic layout of the house was explained to him. He seemed more interested in the cabinets of oddities that filled the corridors and the unusual paintings hanging on the walls. Once, he stopped to examine the frame of a map depicting in some considerable detail a continent Jaide had never heard of. "Fake," he said with a sniff, and continued on.

Only on seeing the twins' room on the second floor did he exhibit any signs of appreciation.

"This looks very comfortable!" He shouldered his way into the room, taking in the four-poster beds, the generous chests, and the chandelier. "A bit messy, though."

"Actually, you're through here," said Grandma X before the bristling twins could respond. She guided him to a door that neither of them had seen before, which opened into a much smaller room just next door. It contained a narrow cot, a single chest of drawers, and one lamp. There was just one miserly window, high up on the wall. It looked as though it had never been opened.

"Well," Stefano said, looking down the length of his nose, "I suppose this will have to do."

"Freshen yourself up and then come downstairs," Grandma X told him. "Susan has prepared a meal for us all, I believe."

"Oh, yes," said the twins' mother, remembering her politeness. "You're very welcome to join us . . . to stay, I mean . . . please, just feel welcome. It's not your fault Hector didn't tell us. I'll talk to him later."

The four of them bustled out, leaving the stranger to settle in on his own.

"What the —"

"How can —"

Grandma X silenced the twins with a finger to each of their lips and ushered them all downstairs. Kleo sneezed as they entered the kitchen. The air was hazy with smoke.

"Oh, no, the piecrust!"

Susan whipped open the oven and removed a pot pie. It had turned black around the edges. One ornamental leaf seemed to actually be on fire.

"No problems," she said, producing a large carving knife. "I reckon this can be salvaged."

While she hacked away the portions of the piecrust that had turned most thoroughly to charcoal, Grandma X answered the twins' many questions, most of them concerning how long she had known, and who was Stefano, anyway? She explained that the role of mentor was a perfectly ordinary one because troubletwisters always found it problematic to be around their Warden parent while learning their Gifts. That was exactly the role Jack and Jaide shared with her and Custer, although they had never had it described that way before. Hector had asked her to take on Stefano just that morning, and she would have told the twins that afternoon had she not been distracted.

"Where's Stefano's twin?" asked Jaide. "He does have one, doesn't he?"

"Santino's still with Hector," Grandma X explained. "They're working on something secret, Hector said . . . although I can probably guess what that is, now that I come to think of it. . . ."

"Project Thunderclap?" asked Jack.

"Your guess, Jackaran, is as good as mine."

The twins waited for her to say more, but her face had become stony, and they knew better than to push her when she used their full first names.

"Is it going to be a permanent arrangement?" asked Susan. "With Stefano, I mean."

"No," Grandma X said. "A fortnight or two should do it. I don't imagine it'll take me any longer than that to teach him what he needs to know."

"Right, well," Susan said, "we'll have to think about school. How old is he?"

"Fourteen," said Grandma X.

"Only a year older than the twins, then. They could introduce him to Tara and Kyle and their other friends. I'll call Mr. Carver in the morning."

Jack rolled his eyes at Jaide, who made an anxious face back. They had nothing against new kids at school — they had recently been new kids themselves, as had Tara — but not when the new kid barged into their home and acted as if he owned the place. Besides, Tara and Kyle were their only real friends. They didn't have any others to share.

"What is that *smell*?"

Stefano was standing in the doorway, his face twisted in an agonized expression.

"That's dinner," said Grandma X, as though burned pot pie was perfectly ordinary fare. And it was, Jack reflected, all too often.

"These will need to be washed." Stefano hefted his muddy trousers.

"Put them in the laundry and I'll show you how to use the washing machine later." Grandma X indicated a seat. "Come in and join us."

Stefano did so, his nose screwed up in distaste. But for the contortion, he might have been handsome, Jaide thought. His dark hair was curly and hung down to his shoulders. His eyes were a surprising blue. He had freckles.

Susan served up vigorously revitalized and irregularly shaped portions of the pot pie, declaring it to be chicken. Jack might ordinarily have made his skepticism known, but in front of Stefano he felt too bad for his mother to say anything other than "Delicious!"

"Tell us where you're from," Susan asked Stefano.

"My brother and I were born in Ravenna, Italy," he said around a mouthful of pie that he seemed to be having difficulty swallowing. "Our father is a carpenter, and we grew up with him until our Gifts awoke."

"You don't have much of an accent," said Jack.

"Mama was English. Besides, I've spent the last two years traveling the world. It rubs off on you."

For all her reservations, Jaide was impressed. "Traveling with Dad?"

"Yes, with Hector. He is a very good teacher. We would have nothing but the best."

"What kind of things do you do with him?" asked Susan.

"Ordinary stuff," he said with an expansive wave that almost knocked Ari off the kitchen counter. "Last year we retrieved the Crown of Clowns from the underground city of Ortahisar and fought an outbreak of The Evil in Stockholm. And then there was the rescue of Professor Olafsson from the minions of The Evil, of course. That was quite a scene."

The twins leaned in eagerly.

"You found him?" asked Jaide. "Where was he?"

"Oh, we helped in a small way. It was all in a day's work."

Jack didn't know whether to be jealous, amazed, or suspicious. Why wasn't *he* having adventures like that, instead of being stuck in an old house in Portland? It wasn't as if they hadn't had their fair share of blow-ups, some of them rather awful, in fact, but none of them sounded as excellent as this. Could it be true?

Jaide was having similar thoughts. Perhaps when she became a proper Warden she would be able to do these kinds of things. If only they could do them with their father *now*, without their Gifts going haywire . . .

"I'm glad Professor Olafsson is safe," she said. "Where is he?"

"It's not really him. It's just a relic."

"His relic, then."

"In Beacon Hill, with Aleksandr."

"Where's that?" asked Jack.

"Don't you know? It's where all the important Wardens like Aleksandr live. I've been there often."

"Have you, Grandma?" Jack asked, hoping she would say something to outcompete what was obviously a wild boast.

"Not for a very, very long time," she said, wrenching herself from what looked like a very deep thought. "I have no reason to leave Portland."

"And of course, you can't," said Stefano.

"Can't what?" asked Jaide.

"Leave Portland," Stefano said as though stating the glaringly obvious. "If she does, the wards will fail. While she's the Warden of Portland, she can't leave. She's stuck here until she retires."

Jaide stared at Grandma X, knowing instinctively that what Stefano said was true. She and Jack had often wondered what would happen if Grandma X ever left the wards — indeed, she had gone to great lengths not to in the past — but they had never known it was so clear-cut. She was trapped in Portland until someone came to relieve her.

"I didn't know Wardens retired," said Susan with a raised eyebrow.

"It's a polite way of saying *dies*," said Grandma X, with something of her usual spirit. "Now, there's another matter

I need to talk with you three about. It was decided only an hour ago, so it'll be news to you all."

Susan got up and started clearing plates. No one had eaten very much.

"I won't tell you why Stefano is here," Grandma X told the troubletwisters. "That's between him and me, although if he wants to tell you himself, he may. However, one thing Hector did ask me to do was to submit him to an immediate Examination. I'm telling you this, Jack and Jaide, because I've decided that you should be Examined also. The process will begin tomorrow and conclude Saturday. Do you have any questions?"

Jack looked at Jaide, and both of them looked at Stefano. He had gone pale, which was worrying.

"What's an Examination?" asked Jack. "I presume you're not talking about anything to do with school."

"Hardly. The Examination tests your fitness to advance to the next degree of proficiency," Grandma X said. "I have heard it described as 'going up a level.'"

That sounded promising. Among the things the twins had learned about Wardens was that there was a definite hierarchical structure in the otherwise fairly loose society. The lowest rung on the ladder was, of course, to be a troubletwister, a youngster just coming into their Gift. How many steps there were, they didn't know.

"If we pass does it mean we'll be Wardens?" asked Jack hopefully.

"No, but you will be one very important step closer."

"What kind of test is it?" Jaide asked. "Multiple choice?"

Stefano uttered a strangled sound that didn't sound as though it had ever been a word.

"No," said Grandma X. "It's not that kind of test."

"Rats," said Jaide, who was convinced that *B* was her lucky letter.

"Will it be dangerous?" asked Susan. Sometimes she wished she had never pushed to know more about what her children got up to with their grandmother. Knowing even a little left her in a constant state of anxiety.

"It will be . . . trying," said Grandma X, "or else it wouldn't be a test. Jack and Jaide have tonight to prepare. I have arranged for the Examiner to attend them at eight thirty. The process will entail missing a small amount of school."

Normally, Jaide would cheer that news. "Don't forget we have soccer tryouts in the afternoon!"

"How could I?" Grandma X offered her a smile that was reassuring on that score. The coming weekend was a long weekend, thanks to a public holiday on that Friday, and Portland was hosting a regional soccer match, something that had been on the twins' minds the whole month. Mr. Carver hadn't picked the under-15 team yet and they were both hoping to be on it. "I can assure you that you won't miss out."

Stefano's gaze was darting from Jack to Jaide, and back again. "I play soccer also. If I must attend school, do you think I could join the tryouts as well?"

"I don't see why not," said Grandma X. "In fact, as Hector told me that you have already sat the first round of Examination, you will be going to school in the morning. I'll send the twins on when they're done."

Weirdly, and worryingly, Stefano actually looked relieved at the thought of going to school.

"Won't you tell us anything about the Examination?" asked Jack.

"You know all you need to know," said Grandma X.

"But we don't know anything!" said Jaide. "How can we prepare if we don't even know what to prepare for?

"You have been preparing every day since you became a troubletwister. The Examination will tell us how far you have come. That is all."

CHAPTER FOUR

THE BLUE ROOM IS LOCKED

The twins spent the remainder of the evening hiding out in their room, avoiding Stefano while fretting about the Examination and grilling the cats for information. Kleo's lips were sealed, as they ever were when it came to information Grandma X wanted to keep hidden from the troubletwisters. Ari was more likely to let secrets slip, but even he had little to offer.

"I only know what I hear other Wardens talk about," he said, "and there have been no Examinations since I became a Companion."

"None at all?" asked Jaide. "I assumed there were lots of troubletwisters before us."

"No. Your grandmother has been alone as long as I've known her."

"Apart from us," Kleo pointed out.

"And the Living Ward, I guess," Ari added, "although you'd have to say a giant mutant axolotl probably wasn't the best company. She certainly didn't have it around for tea."

Jack felt a pang of sadness for his grandmother then. Until the twins had arrived to stay with her, she'd had no contact with them, or Susan, and rarely Hector. Her sister, Lottie, had been lost in the Evil Dimension. Her husband and parents were dead. The only other person who had seemed to be friendly with her was Rodeo Dave, who owned the secondhand bookstore on the corner of Watchward Lane. He had once been a Warden himself, and fancied Lottie to boot, but he had had his memories erased a long time ago and didn't know anything about Grandma X's secret life. No wonder she had seemed so scary when they'd arrived: She just wasn't used to having people around.

"Lights out in half an hour," said Susan, sticking her head around the door. "Last chance to do your chores."

"I've done mine," said Jaide smugly.

"I'll check on Cornelia now," said Jack. It was his job to make sure she had enough seed and water, and to clean her cage once a week. "I'll get the *Compendium* while I'm there."

"Don't get your hopes up," said Kleo. "The Wardens wouldn't leave any clues right out where you could find them."

"Maybe this is part of the Examination." Jack didn't really think that, but he had other leads to follow, anyway. There was the Catastrophe from forty-five years ago, for starters, and the Warden of Last Resort. Grandma X might not be actively keeping secrets from them anymore, but there was still an awful lot left to find out.

He was shocked to reach the door to the blue room and find it locked. The secret panel clicked but wouldn't open. He pushed it a couple of times, then knocked.

"Hello?"

The panel clunked and slid open to reveal Grandma X. She looked flustered and bedraggled.

"Jack, of course. You want to say good night to Cornelia. Come on in. But don't linger. Stefano and I are hard at work."

Jack hadn't even known they *were* working. He passed through the tapestry, keen to see what they were up to, but nothing looked out of order. The big mirror was back where it belonged, and there was no sign of the cross-continuum conduit constructor. It had been taken somewhere safe, he presumed. Stefano glowered at him from one corner of the room, angry at the interruption. He didn't say anything, and Jack didn't say anything back.

Cornelia was asleep already, clicking her beak and muttering softly to herself. Jack distinctly heard her say "Charlie? Your porridge is getting cold!" but figured he would never understand the dreams of birds. Her water and seed tray were fine.

"All done?" asked Grandma X.

He felt as though she was trying to get rid of him.

"Can I borrow the *Compendium*?"

"Of course." She got it for him, a fat binder full of loose pages she kept on a mahogany desk on the landing, and put it safely into his hands. "Don't stay up too late. You'll need to be alert for tomorrow."

"Okay. Good night, Grandma. Good night, Stefano."

Stefano just grunted. He seemed to be sweating and his eyes looked slightly crossed. Jack hadn't noticed it before, but Stefano was holding a short iron rod that was the spitting image of one Hector Shield carried. This one was shiny and new, however. As Jack stared at it, a faint spark shot out and ground into an old ashtray, which let out a puff of smoke.

"Off you go, Jack," said Grandma X, practically pushing him up the stairs. "Good night."

Once he'd gotten to their room, Jaide listened with interest to her brother's account of Stefano's odd behavior, but had no explanation for it.

"Maybe she's teaching him how to use his lightning Gift, as she taught Dad," she suggested.

"But she wouldn't have taught Dad, would she?" Jack said. "Troubletwisters are taught by other Wardens because parents make their kids' Gifts go crazy."

The cats professed not to have any idea, but Jaide caught a knowing look in Kleo's cool gaze, suggesting that she did know but just wasn't telling. *Later,* Jaide promised herself. They had other things to search for now.

As Ari had suggested, there was nothing in the *Compendium* to even hint at the process of Examination. No matter how fixedly the twins concentrated on the concept, holding the *Compendium* in both hands and closing their eyes, when they opened the folder it always landed on the same notice.

Examination will be conducted at regular intervals to ensure the safety of troubletwisters and to maximize the likelihood of their survival.

"That's worrying," said Jack.

"But it's not telling us that the Examination *itself* is dangerous," said Jaide, hoping that was true. "Let's move on. I want to know about the Catastrophe."

Asking the *Compendium* that question produced a wealth of information — too much, in fact, to take in all at once. Dozens of Wardens had written reports on the subject, but not many of them actually talked about what had happened. The reports seemed to be part of a larger argument that had raged for many years between the two factions that Custer had mentioned that day: the Hawks, who wanted to take the fight to The Evil, and the Doves, who wanted to declare peace, or a truce, or something like that. What they actually wanted wasn't very clear, except that they wanted the fighting to end. When the two sides weren't shouting at each other, they spent very little time actually talking about what had happened forty-five years earlier.

There was one page that looked like a newspaper article, which was weird because something like this would never have been reported in a real newspaper, and neither twin was aware that the Wardens had a paper of their own. It was dated from January the same year as the Catastrophe, and said:

Bifrost Bridge: A Device to Cross Dimensions and Bring Peace?

In a new development, representatives of the Harmony Party approached the High Warden Council with a plan to open diplomatic relations with The Evil. Spokeswoman Lottie Henschke testified that the state of unceasing war between Wardens and our ancient enemy is unsustainable. "An alternative must be found," she said. "Opening a Bridge to its realm is the first step in achieving that goal."

Chief Speaker of the Progress Party, Aleksandr Furmanek, replied that such a Bridge was indeed in development but would not be used to "appease the monster that has terrorized humanity for so long."

"Do you think that Bridge was the one we found?" asked Jaide.

"I don't know," said Jack. "If it was, what was it doing right next door?"

Before the twins could find any hard facts, Susan

returned to turn the lights out. No matter how much they pleaded, she wouldn't give them even an extra five minutes. They hadn't even asked about the Warden of Last Resort. She took the *Compendium* away from them, shooed the cats outside, and tucked them in.

"Mom, do you know what happened to the house next door?" asked Jack.

"It's always been like that," she said. "The one time I visited while I was dating your father, there was some talk of renovating it. Apparently, your grandfather had always meant to do it before he died, but never got around to it."

"You mean Grandma and Grandpa used to own it?" asked Jaide.

"I think so. It was a long time ago. I could be remembering it wrong."

"What was Grandpa like?" Jack knew very little about his father's father. Every time they brought him up, Grandma X changed the subject.

Susan smiled fondly, even though she was sure the twins were just stalling now.

"I never met him. He died long before I was on the scene."

"Would we have called him 'Grandpa X'?"

"I don't think so. His name was Giles or James or something like that. Now," she said firmly, "enough questions. You'll need your sleep if you don't want to make any mistakes tomorrow."

They couldn't argue with that. But when the lights were out and the door almost closed, Jaide whispered, "Lottie Henschke."

"What?"

"In that article about the Bifrost Bridge. It said Lottie *Henschke*. We have her last name now."

"And Grandma X's, too." Jack was astonished. He'd been concentrating so hard on the Catastrophe that he had missed that important tidbit.

"She might have changed it when she got married," said Jaide. "But, yeah. That's going to make them much easier to find."

"Are we still going to look? Even though we know Lottie is stuck in the Evil Dimension?"

"The *Compendium* is being difficult about how she got there, so I think we should. And we still don't really know much about Grandma. We don't even know her birthday!"

That was true. Susan had bought her a cake one day in March, but Grandma X had been quick to inform them that, while she was touched by the gesture, her actual birthday was something she kept to herself, along with her age. Jaide found that both weird and old-fashioned, which summed up her grandmother pretty well.

"All right," said Jack, reminding himself to be glad they were missing school the next morning. Mondays were the worst. Mr. Carver always made them describe any dreams they'd had over the weekend, and insisted on trying to interpret them. Once, he'd gone on for half an hour about how something Miralda King had dreamt meant that Portland's mayor, her father, should grant planning approval for a school obelisk on the grounds that it would align his students' chakras.

Jack closed his eyes, and within moments his breathing became regular and slow. However hard Jaide tried, though, she couldn't get to sleep. It had been a long and eventful day. She kept thinking about Professor Olafsson and Lottie and everything else that was going on that she could do nothing about. It was only by concentrating on what Stefano had suggested earlier that finally settled her mind. What if she *did* have the same lightning Gift as her father? That would be wonderful beyond belief. And if Jack had it too, they could duel each other with lightning bolts . . . something she was sure neither their grandmother nor mother would ever allow. . . .

The Examiner was a fussy, sixtyish man with very short silver hair who walked into the kitchen unannounced while they were eating breakfast. He was wearing a light overcoat and a shirt with no collar or tie, done right up to the neck.

"Ah, Alfred!" Grandma X declared, making a space for him at the table and offering him a cup of coffee.

"No need, no need," he said with a slightly odd accent, which the twins couldn't place, particularly as it seemed to shift around a bit. "Good morning to you all. I'm not too early, am I? The beams are recalcitrant this morning."

The twins wanted to say, *Yes, give us another week* — and also, *What beams and what do they have to do with anything?* But instead they said hello and introduced themselves. Stefano just nodded and fiddled with the sleeve of his shirt, looking nervous. Clearly, he and Alfred the Examiner were already acquainted.

"Very good," he said. "I'm pleased to be here, Jack and Jaide, to test your fitness to advance to senior troubletwister status. Your grandmother assures me that you have been ready for some time. We will find out shortly if she is correct."

"Am I ever wrong, Alfred?" Grandma X asked.

"We are all wrong sometimes," he said with one eyebrow upraised.

"Yes, sir," said Stefano, unexpectedly. "Is it time for school yet?"

"I suppose so," said Susan. "If you're that keen I can drop you off early. Kids, your grandmother is coming with me. We're going to have morning tea at the fancy new place by the marina. There are sandwiches by the stove for lunch if you're done by lunchtime."

"They will, as you put it, be very much done by lunchtime," the Examiner said.

The twins were afraid to ask what that meant, and anyway, the kitchen had dissolved into chaos. Dishes were collected, washed, and put away. Grandma X went upstairs to change her around-the-house cowboy boots for her going-out cowboy boots. She had many pairs of cowboy boots, and some system that decided which ones were to be worn for different occasions. The ones she wore when she came back down were crocodile or alligator skin, and had very sharp points.

"Are we ready? Good." She kissed the twins on the cheeks, something Jaide let her do in front of Stefano only because she was feeling so nervous suddenly. She wished Grandma X and Susan weren't leaving. "Don't let Ari have any of your lunch: He's getting fat."

"I am not!" protested Ari, emerging from behind the door. His ears flicked as Grandma X and the twins looked at him with disbelieving expressions. "Or not that much. Besides, it is a mark of distinction among cats to be a little heavy. . . ."

"No human food," insisted Grandma X. "We'll return when Alfred calls us."

Susan looked just as unhappy as the twins felt as Grandma X bustled her out the door. Stefano was already out by the car, a 1955 Austin 1600 with bright red-and-yellow flames painted down the hood. This car had replaced the yellow Hillman Minx that had met its end at the bottom of the river. Jack and Jaide stood on the veranda and waved them off, feeling absurdly — they hoped — as though they might never see them again.

When the car had vanished up the lane, they turned to go inside.

"Where did he go?" asked Jaide. "I thought he was right behind us."

Jack blinked rapidly as a sudden gust of wind threw dust into his eyes.

"I don't know," he said, stepping into the hallway. It was empty. "Hello? Did you see where he went, Jaide? Jaide?"

He spun around on the spot and was shocked to discover that he was alone. Not only was Alfred the Examiner missing, but so, too, was Jaide. It was as though she had vanished into thin air.

"Come on, this isn't funny."

He spun around one more time, in case he had missed something completely obvious, and in doing so he brushed against the long shadow cast by the open doorway across the entry hall rug. Suddenly, darkness consumed his vision. The house vanished. The world vanished. And he was gone, too.

Inside the kitchen, Ari felt the hand holding him by the scruff of his neck relax. He immediately leaped from Alfred's lap, where he'd been held prisoner, and ran to the front door. Looking around, he saw no one except Kleo, padding regally around the corner, shaking her head.

"You were told to stay away," she scolded him.

"Not told as such," he said. "It was more a suggestion. Anyway, I just wanted to see —"

"Curiosity is not a survival trait," said the Examiner from the kitchen. Ari shook his head. The man had the hearing of a cat!

Faintly, as though from an exceedingly distant place, Kleo thought she heard someone calling for help. She cocked her head, but the cry was gone as quickly as it had come. She hadn't even been able to tell which troubletwister it was.

"Stay right here," she told Ari. "They'll need us when they come back."

"If —"

Ari's mouth clapped shut at a look from Kleo that said as clearly as words: *Don't say it.*

CHAPTER FIVE

GIFTED

Jaide was utterly lost. She didn't know where she was or even *what* she was. Everything around her was confusing and strange, a blur of movement and light that never ceased changing. But what was most disorienting was not knowing how she was experiencing it. She couldn't feel her arms and legs. She couldn't blink her eyes. She didn't seem to *have* eyes. She felt as if she was tumbling and flailing and screaming, but there was nothing she could do to stop it.

Is it The Evil? she wondered. *Have I been attacked?*

That was nonsense, she told herself. Alfred the Examiner had been there. The Evil would never have gotten past him.

But what if he's one of them? What if he's an Evil minion and Grandma never suspected?

She reminded herself of all the times she had doubted Wardens before. First her grandmother, who she had thought was a witch. Then Custer. Then Rodeo Dave. They had all turned out to be good, trustworthy people, firmly on her side.

Don't forget Uncle Harold. We trusted him, and look what happened!

Jaide told herself to ignore that panicky internal voice. It wasn't helping. Evil attack or not, she needed to find out what was going on and get herself out of it, somehow. She needed to breathe slowly, even if she didn't appear to have any lungs, and calm the frantic beating of the heart she no longer had. Whatever was happening to her, she wasn't dead yet.

"While there's life," her father always said, "there's hope. And Brussels sprouts." Unlike most sensible people, Hector Shield loved Brussels sprouts.

His optimistic mantra didn't help Jaide at all when she was sucked into an engine and torn violently to pieces.

Jack willed his eyes to open, but they wouldn't. He could tell that there was light out there, but he couldn't see it. He couldn't feel anything either. For all his groping and fumbling, he might as well have been in deep space. He couldn't even feel his hands. Soon he began to doubt they even existed.

If he didn't have hands, what about the rest of him? He couldn't feel his feet, either, or his head, or his heart. . . .

Stay calm. There has to be an explanation.

Jack did his best to forget an old book he'd read about people who had been buried alive. Being trapped underground had always been something that frightened him, and his experiences in the sewers under Portland hadn't helped that fear. But he would know if that had happened to him. This was something else, some kind of trick. Perhaps by The Evil. It had attacked them yesterday. Why not today as well?

We've beaten The Evil before. We can do it again.

But how, he wondered, could he fight something he couldn't even see?

The first step, he told himself, was to find himself. All he had to do was touch something and he would know where he was. That was easier than it sounded, but it was something to aim for. He might not have hands, but he still existed. And if he existed, he had to be *somewhere.*

He could tell that he was moving, tumbling and rolling through spaces he could neither see nor sense. But weirdly, he could tell that these spaces weren't infinite. There were boundaries and edges, and somehow, without eyes or hands, he could glimpse what those shapes were.

Was that a chair? Or a table?

Just as he was beginning to make sense of it, a giant's boot heel came down and crushed him.

Jaide screamed, and the fact that she was still able to scream was oddly reassuring. She wasn't dead. She was still herself. But where was she now? The engine was roaring and rumbling around her, and she was violently gusted from side to side without warning. The pitch of the engine kept changing, like someone was working a gas pedal in a car. It made her think of Mr. Holland, the town butcher, who drove through Portland like he had never heard of a brake pedal.

A lightbulb went off in her mind. What if she *was* somehow in the engine of his car? The only way that could be possible was if she had somehow, madly, impossibly, become *the air.*

That made a weird kind of sense. Her main Gift was the wind, and she might have a hint of her father's lightning Gift, too. If she had been turned into air, a car engine might be just the kind of thing she would be drawn to. But what did that mean? And how was she going to get back? She couldn't imagine what Alfred the Examiner was thinking.

If she'd had a hand, she would have smacked herself in the forehead. Of course. This *was* the Examination. He had put her into the wind somehow and now it was up to her to get out again.

She was being buffeted by fans and deafened by the rapid fire of pistons. Understanding was one thing. Doing something about it was something else entirely.

And what about Jack? she wondered. Was he undergoing a similar trial?

There was nothing she could do for him. She had to find a way back to herself before Mr. Holland drove out of town or the wind took her somewhere even more uncomfortable.

Jack squished out from under the giant's heel like an orange pip squeezed between two fingers and shot off along a long, rectangular space. At the end of the rectangle, he bounced around a larger shape that reminded him of a large cushion, then down another long space that kinked in the middle, like someone holding up his hand to wave.

Exactly like that, he thought suddenly. Too exactly to be anything *other* than that.

He was in a person's shadow.

No, he corrected himself. He knew what being in a shadow felt like. He could see things, for starters, and he could feel things, too. This was very different. Instead of him slipping into a shadow, this felt like a shadow had slipped into him and taken him over.

He *was* a shadow.

And if there was one thing he had learned in his months of being a shadow-walker, it was that even on the sunniest of days, all shadows were connected.

He didn't know where exactly the person's shadow led him. It could have been a tree, or a sign, or perhaps a traffic light, but he didn't stay there long. He bounced off one edge of that shadow into another without any way of slowing himself down or controlling his movement. What if he kept bouncing and bounced far enough to leave the wards? Would he ever get back to his body?

Another concern struck him. Jaide had just disappeared. Maybe he had, too. Was this supposed to happen? Was this something Alfred the Examiner had planned to do to them the moment Grandma X and the others left the house?

No wonder Stefano seemed worried. He must have been through this before.

Thinking this made Jack both angry and slightly relieved. Stefano had known what would happen but hadn't said anything. But *he* had survived, so why couldn't Jack?

There had to be a way to get out of the shadow maze. All he had to do was find it.

Jaide was struggling to get anywhere at all. She might have become the wind, but it wasn't doing anything she told it to. If anything, it did the opposite. When she told it to take her *that* way, it went in the other, and when she tried to go back, it only took her somewhere else. She was beginning to despair of ever getting out of the engine, let alone getting home again.

She wondered how long she had been trying. She wondered when Alfred the Examiner would bring her back, once it became clear that she had failed. She wondered what would happen if she became permanently lost and couldn't ever find her way back. She wondered if "failing" the Examination was another euphemism for dying, just like "retiring" was.

But she wasn't going to give up. She could control the wind when she was in her body, so why not now?

Perhaps Jack was doing better than her, she thought. She wished there was some way she could ask him. If he was, he might be able to help her . . . even if it was technically cheating.

Jack was experimenting with willing himself to bounce back the way he had come every time he hit an edge. He didn't think it was going well. Normally when shadow-walking he was acutely aware of where his body was, and the farther he went, the more he was pulled back to it. With practice he had managed to go as far as school, although that still took a great deal of effort.

Now, he had no actual way of knowing, but he felt that he was only getting farther from where he wanted to be, not closer. Whatever he was doing, he was doing it completely wrong. The harder he tried to become the shadows he wanted to, the worse he did.

He needed help, and there was only one person that he would call, if he could just figure out how to do it. Grandma X did it. Aleksandr did it. Even The Evil did it. Why couldn't he?

Barely had he formulated the plan when a faint voice called out to him from impossibly far away.

++Jack? . . . hear me?++

He recognized Jaide's voice immediately, and right away part of him knew how to respond. It was like finding a muscle that had always been there but that he had never used before.

++Jaide, I'm here! Are you all right?++

++. . . very faint . . . hardly hear . . .++

He tried to shout, without really knowing how.

++I'M RIGHT HERE!!++

++Ouch,++ she said. ++No need to deafen me.++

Jaide felt rather than heard Jack laugh in relief.

++How are we doing this?++ she asked.

++I don't know. Maybe it's a twin thing.++

Either way, now that the connection was open, it seemed easy and natural. She felt better about it being there but that didn't change the basic fact of their situation.

++I'm lost,++ she confessed.

++Me too.++

++But I feel like I know where you are.++

++Yeah, you're . . . *that* way.++

This was something else hard to define. Jaide just knew that Jack was over *there*, wherever *there* was. In fact, now that she knew that, she could feel herself moving in that direction. As long as she didn't try to push, it seemed the wind was happy to take her. The moment she hurried things along, she was tossed and tumbled again.

With a roar and a feeling of being blown out in a hot rush, Jaide emerged from the car. By the exhaust pipe, she assumed. Now she bobbed and swayed through a blurry field of light that could have been anywhere.

++This is some test,++ said Jack.

++It's awful. I can see why Stefano would rather go to school.++

++Do you know where you are? I think I'm underground somewhere, hopefully not in the sewers again.++

Jaide confessed that she had no idea. ++How are we going to get home?++

++I don't know. Let's get ourselves together first, then we'll try to think of a way.++

++What if we don't?++

++Don't think like that. We will.++

Jaide could tell that he was trying to be positive despite

being as worried as she was. Some of his thoughts and feelings were leaking in, too, along with the words. She was grateful for his effort and resolved to do the same. Whatever happened to them, at least they had each other.

On the doorstep of the house on Watchward Lane, Ari was dreaming of mice. Big, fat mice dancing right in front of his nose. They smelled delicious, but their eyes were glowing white, and he knew what would happen if he ate them. The Evil made everything taste awful. . . .

He jerked awake as a sudden eddy sprung up out of nowhere, swept him into the air, turned him over three times, and dropped him unceremoniously on his head. For once, the cattish ability to land on his feet utterly failed him.

That wasn't the only strange thing. The shadows cast by the morning sun were swinging wildly from side to side.

"Kleo!" he yowled, righting himself indignantly. "Kleo, something's happening!"

The gray cat and the Examiner hurried from the kitchen into the hallway behind him.

"Ah, yes," said Alfred. "Now, the question is *where* . . ."

The earth rumbled. Kleo looked down at her feet as though the floor was affronting her.

"Is that supposed to happen?" she asked.

"Sometimes." The Examiner peered all around him, looking under the cabinets and in the cupboards. "Troubletwisters, as you know, are profoundly unpredictable."

There was a heavy thud from behind them, and there was Jack, curled on his side on the floor as though he had dropped from the sky.

No, thought Kleo. *Dropped from one shadowy corner of the ceiling, where the light was most dim.*

Ari ran to him and poked him with a paw.

"Ow," Jack said, rubbing his head. He would have a bump later, but it was good to have hands to know that, and even better to have a head that hurt at all.

A crackle and bang came from the living room, followed by a wild cry for help. Kleo was the first on the scene, where she found Jaide clinging to the chandelier, swinging helplessly from side to side.

"Get me down!" Her eyes were wild and her red hair was in disarray, but behind her desperation not to fall she felt only triumph. They had done it! They had made it home!

Alfred the Examiner moved a couch under the chandelier and Jaide dropped into it.

"Jack?" she called. "Jack?"

"I'm here," he said, emerging from the hallway, looking as bedraggled as she felt. He tapped the side of his head. "I can't hear you in here. Must be because we're back to being ourselves again."

They rarely hugged anymore, but she decided that this time was an exception. She pulled him to her and he didn't resist. In fact, he held her briefly but tightly and was smiling when she let go.

"Congratulations," said Alfred the Examiner, standing to one side with his arms folded. "You have passed."

The twins beamed at each other, and basked in the admiration of the cats, who rubbed against their legs, purring loudly.

"Better late than never," said Jack. "Where are Mom and Grandma? We must have missed lunch by ages."

"Oh, no," said Jaide. "The soccer tryouts!"

"What do you mean?" said Ari. "You've only been gone for a short nap."

"One hour, forty-five minutes, and twenty-three seconds," the Examiner proclaimed, with a wry glance at Ari.

"That's short for me," Ari said.

The twins looked at each other. Getting back to the house had seemed to take *forever*.

"Let's put this couch back in its place," said Alfred, "and then you can tell me how you did it."

Over hot chocolate in the kitchen, Jack and Jaide on one side of the table, Alfred on the other, the cats sitting silently in a patch of yellow sunlight by the window, they recounted their story. With no bodies and no proper senses, there had been no way to tell how long it took to do anything. If they had to guess, the twins would have said that their bumbling journey to find each other had lasted several hours, and when they had done that, the real challenge lay ahead of them.

"It was hard just staying together," said Jaide, frowning at the memory of the trials they had so recently endured. "Jack was in shadow and I was wafting around in the air. We couldn't really see anything except for each other. How were we going to find a *house*?"

"Eventually it hit us," said Jack. "A house was exactly the wrong thing to look for. I mean, we hadn't gotten together that way — by looking for something that was a *thing*, if that makes sense. We had found *each other*."

"So that's what we decided to do," said Jaide. "We decided to look for some*one*, not some*thing*."

Alfred nodded. "Who?"

"Well," said Jack, "first we tried Grandma, but we couldn't find her. We guessed that was deliberate so it would be harder for us."

Alfred nodded again. "Then you tried the cats."

"We did," said Jaide, "but we couldn't find them, either."

"For the same reason," Alfred explained. "Ari here was asleep and Kleo was with me. However, I did not sense you looking for me. It must have been someone else."

"Cornelia," Jack said. "That's who we followed. It took a while to find her, but when we did we followed her home." He looked around. "Where is she? I haven't seen her all morning."

"In the blue room," said Kleo. "She's been acting weird again."

"How weird?"

"Just . . . weird."

Cornelia had come to live at Watchward Lane when her former owner, Old Master Rourke, had suddenly died. For several days she had been afraid of the twins, but eventually she had come to trust them. She had been friendly ever since, although sometimes it was hard to understand her. No one knew exactly how old she was, but her frequent use of pirate talk suggested that she was very old indeed. Jaide wondered if birds suffered from senility, then decided that was unkind. Cornelia was allowed to be a bit odd, as long as she wasn't unhappy. She had just saved the twins from being lost forever, after all.

"How did we manage to talk to each other?" she asked Alfred. "Is it a twin thing?"

"It is," he said. "And it is something that all troubletwisters learn, if they are compelled to." His cool eyes regarded them both for a disconcertingly long time. "Your task now is to refine that ability, to enable you to communicate with others. Wardens are all twins, after all. That is how it works."

They nodded, understanding instinctively that anything Alfred said wasn't something they should lightly ignore.

"Tell me now about the rest of the test," he said, folding his long, well-manicured hands on the table. "What did you experience?"

Jaide described how it had felt like she was the wind, and Jack followed with his experiences as shadow.

"*Like* the wind?" Alfred echoed back at them. "*As* shadow? There is no *like* or *as* in the Examination. You became what you became, and that is all there is to it."

"I don't understand," ventured Jack somewhat nervously. He didn't want to look foolish but at the same time he didn't want to miss something important. "So I really *was* a shadow?"

"No. You became your Gift."

"How?" asked Jaide, frowning. "Is that even possible?"

"It is, but it's very difficult to explain. The short answer is that this is one of *my* Gifts," Alfred said with a tight smile. "I predict that you found yourself unable to control your movements, in wind and shadow respectively, until you let your natures have their way. Is this correct?"

"It was exactly like that," said Jack, remembering how he had bounced around until he had found Jaide, and then later when they had found Cornelia. "It was horrible."

"You must remember this," said Alfred, leaning forward over the table. "Your Gifts are not your friends. You think you control them, but you do not. They will fight you at every turn, unless you have . . . wooed them correctly. While you have made some important steps forward in this process, understand that it will never be complete, even if you pass all your Examinations. Your Gifts will be willful your entire lives. It is a constant battle."

That was somewhat disheartening. Jaide had imagined that it was just a matter of practicing and practicing until everything worked perfectly.

"Why?" she asked. "Why is it like this?"

"That is one of the mysteries," said Alfred, but unlike with Grandma X, Jaide didn't sense that this was a stalling tactic.

"Is it like soccer?" said Jack. "Even the best players miss a kick sometimes."

"Perhaps." Alfred leaned back. "The other thing you must understand is that this was only your first Examination. There are four. The second will take place tomorrow evening. I will talk to your grandmother and she will ensure that you are ready."

The twins nodded obediently, although all feelings of accomplishment had fled. Nothing could have prepared them for the first test. What was the second going to be like?

"What about Stefano?" asked Jack.

"He will be Examined, too. That is why he is here."

"I thought it was to learn something special from Grandma," said Jaide.

Alfred inclined his head the tiniest fraction. "If that is what she said, I am sure it is so."

In the living room, a clock chimed twelve. Jack's stomach, immune to nerves, awoke at the merest suggestion of lunch. He got up and found the sandwiches and put them on the table. Ari pricked up his ears. His eyes followed every slight movement of the food.

"Would you like mine?" Jaide said to Alfred. There wasn't one for him, and she wasn't feeling especially hungry.

"Thank you for the offer," he said. "Please don't mind me. I will be leaving shortly."

Jaide nodded but didn't immediately open the wrapper. The thought of school and Stefano filled her with no small amount of dread, even if there was soccer to look forward to later. She had been practicing for weeks for this day. She wasn't going to miss it for anything.

A small nudge at her hip indicated that Ari had noticed her hesitation and was giving her a hint.

"No," she said. "Grandma told us not to."

"And you always do what she says?"

"I try to."

"And we should encourage that behavior, Aristotle," said Kleo sternly.

"Aww, give a cat a break." Ari rolled theatrically on his back, exposing his stomach. "I've been sitting here all day. Don't I get a reward?"

Jack made a choking noise and pieces of sandwich sprayed across the table.

"It's all very well for you to laugh at my predicament —" said Ari.

"No, look!" Jack pointed to the chair opposite him, where Alfred had been sitting. "He's gone!"

Jaide whipped around and Kleo jumped up onto the table. Sure enough, the seat was empty.

"I was looking right at him," Jack said. "His eyes were closed, and then he opened them, and then . . . whoosh!" There was no other word for it. "He went straight down."

Ari touched the wooden floor under the seat with his nose, sniffed tentatively. "Warm. That's how he did it."

"He went through the *floor*?" exclaimed Jaide.

"Floor*boards*," said Jack, smacking his palm into his forehead. "That's what he meant earlier. But how can anyone travel that way? Surely he wouldn't get very far."

"Not just through floorboards," said Kleo, "but vegetation of all kinds, including roots, grass, and moss. You might think it unglamorous, but I'm sure it's very effective."

Despite the fact that it seemed old-fashioned, the twins were impressed. Was there no limit to the inventiveness of the Wardens? Or was it the Gifts? Jaide was confused now. Maybe later she would look it up in the *Compendium*.

"Eat your lunch," Kleo told her. "Then off to school. The excitement is over for today . . . hopefully."

Ari's pink tongue darted out while no one was looking and scooped up a tasty-looking crumb from the many Jack had spat out. Kleo always added *hopefully* when she said something like that. Ari understood. With troubletwisters around, it didn't pay to be too cocky.

CHAPTER SIX
A PEST PROBLEM

Tell us more," said Miralda, with a flutter of her eyelashes.

Jack rolled his eyes and slid even farther down in his seat. Jaide poked him. If he slumped any more, he'd fall to the floor. Stefano's description of his hometown had started off well — Ravenna had been the capital of various ancient empires, invaded and conquered many times over — but once he had left the fighting behind, it had soon become boring.

"Well," said Stefano from where he was holding court at the front of the class, a hand under his chin as he pretended to think, "Lord Byron lived in Ravenna for a while. He fell in love with a local woman, a contessa, but she was married so they were doomed to part. Later, T. S. Eliot wrote a poem about a pair of newlyweds he saw there. Oscar Wilde wrote a poem about the town itself."

Striking a pose, Stefano recited:

O how my heart with boyish passion burned,
When far away across the sedge and mere
I saw that Holy City rising clear,
Crowned with her crown of towers!

Jack looked around the room. Half the girls and some of the boys had glazed looks he normally associated with people looking at pop stars. Even Tara was on the brink of succumbing. He could tell because the ball of her pen hung unmoving above a doodle of a flower with seven petals that she'd only half finished. Kyle was slumped over his desk, snoring faintly.

"Excellent," said Mr. Carver, Jack's unexpected ally in interrupting the monologue. "Thank you, Stefano, for that vivid picture of the town you live in. You may sit down now."

A dozen pairs of eyes tracked the boy back to his seat at the front of the class. The girl sitting next to him looked as if she was about to faint. Jack kicked Kyle under the table, waking him with a snort.

Mr. Carver took Stefano's place. He was dressed in shorts and a soccer jersey that looked five sizes too big for him, with the emblem of a team that Jaide was pretty sure didn't exist anymore. His sneakers were brown.

"Tonight, for homework, I want you all to write a poem about Portland. Meditate upon the Rock and Mermaid Point, the river and the bay, the willows and the, um, fish markets, and conjure an image of our town for someone who has never been here. What's special about it? What can you find here but nowhere else? But no monsters," he added, specifically for Kyle. "We've had quite enough stories about them."

"What about ghosts?" Kyle asked, now wide-awake.

"Ghosts, too," said Mr. Carver. "Although I'm not aware that we have any."

"My dad says there's a woman in white who comes out on the full moon and —"

Kyle stopped in mid-sentence as though his throat had closed over. The only people who knew why were Jack and Jaide. The ghostly white woman was probably Grandma X in her spectral form, looking the age she was when she became a Warden. Kyle was forbidden to talk about anything to do with her in public, even if he didn't know he was.

"Yes, well, the Portland Peregrinators are valued members of our community," said Mr. Carver with a puzzled look, "and your father has a vivid imagination, but let's please keep the imagery to the realm of the actual rather than the fantastical.

He clapped his hands, which made Jaide jump. "Now! To the oval! It's time for the soccer tryouts."

The class erupted into life. Mr. Carver led them outside and then, in a brisk, high-stepping jog through the playground, to the oval next to the school. Stefano was surrounded by a gaggle of admirers, answering question after question about what he was doing in Portland and how long he would be staying. He was charmingly vague on both points.

There was a mound of equipment in the middle of the oval, including a net full of soccer balls. Recent rains had made the turf lush and full, ready for the rip and tear of eager cleats. Two new goals had been put up in the last week, one with the banner of a sports company from Scarborough, the other the logo of Tara's dad's development firm.

Scarborough always won, Jack and Jaide had learned in the weeks leading up to the match. The competition was for who came second. Dogton, a nearby town of similar size, was Portland's main rival. There were plans for tents and temporary stands, even a small farmer's market on the Friday morning before the games started. It was going to be the biggest event since the Portland Players' performance of *Peter Pan*, the twins were assured. That had seemed tame by city standards but had kept the small town buzzing for weeks afterward.

Instead of a whistle, Mr. Carver had a small flute around his neck. He piped it to get the class's attention, but no one heard it. He blew harder, producing a strangled squeak that made nearby dogs hide under furniture.

"Now, children, if you'll take a ball and form three lines, we'll get started."

Predictably, the longest line formed where Stefano chose to go, requiring a reshuffle before the groups were equal and they could begin. First they practiced ball skills, like juggling, passing, and blocking, and then they practiced running around and between orange cones Mr. Carver had laid out across the oval. Singly and in pairs, students ran up and down the field, taking potshots at the goal while randomly chosen goalkeepers did their best to knock the balls away. Mr. Carver threw balls to see who could head the best, and then divided the class in two, ignoring the pleading of those desperate to be on Stefano's team. A scrimmage ensued, the conclusion of which was obvious to anyone who had been watching.

Stefano was easily the best player in the class. He handled the ball with easy grace, passing it smoothly to the teammates around him and snatching it with blinding speed from those who got in his way. His long, tanned legs took him up and down the field without any sign of exertion, zigzagging, nutmegging, and pinching at every opportunity. Once, he performed a bicycle kick, a move that Jack had never seen in real life before, kicking the ball backward over his own head. Kyle, acting in a defensive position and theoretically responsible for stopping the ball, could only stare in amazement as it whizzed through the goalkeeper's outstretched hands and into the top right corner of the net.

"Score!" said Mr. Carver from the boundary, both

arms shooting up into the air before he composed himself and pulled them back down. "Um, that is well played, Stefano. It's not whether you win or not but that we all do our best. Gather round, children. I think I've seen enough to make my decision."

Jaide was feeling confident as the class clustered around their teacher. She had gotten in a few good kicks, not once by using her Gift, and she had hopes of being a striker. Jack, she was less sure about. He had spent too much time watching Stefano's moves and trying to copy them, and had missed some critical shots. He wasn't the worst in the class by any means — several balls had vanished into the back-yards of homes on neighboring Crescent Street, kicked clear off the oval by eager but inexpert feet — but that might not be enough for him to make the team.

Surprising no one, first Mr. Carver offered Stefano a center midfield position. From there he could roam wher-ever he wanted to go and do whatever he wanted to do.

"You *will* still be in Portland this weekend, won't you?" asked Mr. Carver, fiddling nervously with his flute.

Stefano bowed. "I wouldn't dream of leaving."

"Then I think we can count you as a student," he said with a relieved grin. "Dogton won't know what hit them. I mean, your contribution to the team will be gratefully appreciated. Next . . ."

He made Miralda captain, which made sense only in the light of the obelisk funding request that had recently gone before the town council a third time. Jaide was named a striker, and Kyle goalkeeper. Jack waited for his name to be called, and forced himself not to be too disappointed when he was listed in the reserves with Tara.

"So that's our team," Mr. Carver concluded, rubbing his hands together eagerly.

"Do we have a mascot?" asked Jaide.

"Of course. The Portcupine. Short for the Portland Porcupine."

All the new students goggled at him.

"I, um, inherited it from the previous teacher," Mr. Carver explained, scratching his neck where the synthetic material of his soccer jersey was making his skin itch. "Let's return to school. It's almost time to sing the Song of Parting. I've added an extra verse and I want us all to practice it."

"Great," said Jack, falling back as the class moved off. Jaide and Kyle were at the front, discussing tactics, while Stefano held court in the center of a large group, describing his favorite moves. Tara didn't seem unhappy about not being selected, but she dawdled with Jack, too.

"Thinks he's the bee's knees, doesn't he?" she said.

"And the ant's elbows." Jack forced a smile. "Grandma hasn't even put him on the dishwashing roster."

"Perhaps you should do that for her." She smiled back at him. "We went to Italy once for vacation. It's really nice. The food is amazing, except for all the stinky cheese . . ."

Jack was only half listening to her story. He had just had a thought: Being on the soccer team would mean training and practice games, which would cut into their studies for the Examination and everything else that was going on. They still didn't know anything concrete about the Catastrophe or the Warden of Last Resort, nor had they made any progress tracking down Lottie's past. While Jaide was off defending Portland's honor on the soccer field, *someone* had to help save the world.

It was a strange and largely silent dinner for Susan that night. Grandma X had the twins and Stefano practice their silent communication, which she called "rapporting," but

Stefano referred to as "teeping." It was common trouble-twister slang, he said. Hadn't they heard of it? No one who was anyone called it *rapporting* anymore.

If Stefano was able to hear the words Jaide directed at him then, he didn't react.

The twins found it very hard to get even a single word through, straining until they were pink in the face. Finally, Jack managed to ask Stefano to pass the salt, and Jaide told Grandma X that she'd like the sauce. As was often the case with their new troubletwister skills, it seemed much better to do things the normal, easier way.

"Sometimes you can't do things the easy way," their mother piped up when they complained out loud. "That's why jobs like mine exist. If doctors didn't learn how to heal people when they were sick because *most of the time* we're perfectly well, where would we be?"

Jack could accept that point, but it didn't help him ask for seconds.

++Alfred tells me you did well this morning,++ said Grandma X. ++I'm pleased. The second Examination will take place tomorrow night. Stefano, you'll be Examined, too.++

The older troubletwister's mental voice was a scratchy whisper on the edge of hearing.

++Do I have to?++

++Yes. You've had extra time, so I expect you'll do well.++

He hung his head.

++What's wrong?++ Jaide tried to ask him. ++What do you know about it?++

Stefano's head snapped up. His expression was furious.

++Nothing,++ he said. ++There's nothing wrong with me.++

++Huh?++ said Jaide. ++That's not what I said.++

++Sometimes our minds reveal things we don't mean to say,++ said Grandma X. ++You must make allowances, and be patient while you learn to control your thoughts.++

Stefano glared at Jaide. Tiny sparks zinged off the cutlery and metal surfaces in the room.

++Stefano,++ warned Grandma X.

He returned his hot gaze back down to his lap and the electric fireworks subsided.

Jaide looked at Jack, who shrugged.

++Beats me what that was all about,++ he teeped to Jaide.

++Eats the what?++ she said back.

++Feast's not hot at all. Mine went cold while I was trying to teep you.++

Grandma X let them struggle on, sparing them the chores while she and Susan cleaned up. Then it was time for her to take Stefano to the blue room for his special lessons. The twins had hoped to spend the rest of the evening searching through the *Compendium*, but Susan had other ideas.

"All this Examining and now soccer practice," she said. "It's time for you to do some homework."

The twins groaned and argued, but there was no defying their mother on this front. She had given ground on a slightly later bedtime, being able to stay over at Tara's on a school night, and even having a phone, but when it came to schoolwork she was absolute. Not even Grandma X could deny her.

So they trudged upstairs and slaved through pages of math problems and English questions, all of which they had to do by hand since they had no computer in their room. By the time they had finished, it was time for bed.

Grumbling, Jack went to check on Cornelia while Jaide brushed her teeth. But when he got to the panel leading to the blue room, he found it locked again.

Jack raised his hand to knock, but stopped to listen first. He was curious about what Grandma X and Stefano were up to in there. What could be so important that he and Jaide weren't allowed in to see it? They had passed the first Examination, hadn't they? It really wasn't fair that they were being excluded.

Whatever was going on in the blue room, it was quiet. Jack held his breath and pressed his ear against the door. The silence was deep and heavy. He could hear his heartbeat, and the clock ticking downstairs, and the creak of floorboards as someone moved in the room below.

Wait, he thought. The room below was Stefano's room. If Stefano was there, then he couldn't be in the blue room, could he? Jack relaxed, laughing at himself. There was nothing going on behind the locked door because there was no one in there at all.

He almost jumped out of his skin when the sound of Cornelia suddenly squawking came loudly through the panel.

"Charlie! Charlie! Look out!"

"Be quiet, Cornelia." The second voice was Grandma X's. "You're not helping."

When Jack's heart had stopped hammering, he pressed his ear back against the door, but the voices subsided back into silence. All he could faintly make out was the sound of movement.

Tentatively, he knocked.

"Oh, is that you, Jack?" his grandmother said without opening the door. "Don't worry about Cornelia tonight. I'll put her to bed."

"O . . . kay," Jack said. "Well, good night."

"Good night."

Jack reluctantly backed away.

In bed after lights-out, he described to Jaide what had happened. She was as mystified and annoyed as he was. If Grandma X wasn't doing something secret with Stefano, what was she doing?

"There must be some way to spy on her," Jaide said.

"I can't think of any. Why don't we just ask her?"

Jaide snorted. "When has that ever worked?"

"I know, but this time, maybe." Jack wasn't ready to let the secret of what Grandma X was up to in the blue room remain unknown forever.

They argued back and forth until Susan came to tell them to settle down. Jaide lay in the dark, trying to feel sleepy but once again utterly failing. She had passed the Examination and got onto the soccer team, but what else had she really accomplished? Lottie was still stuck in the Evil Dimension, Grandma X was back to her old secret self, and Stefano was the new star of school.

She began to drift, her thoughts becoming slow and wandering. At the sound of a distant drumming over and over, she thought she might finally be dreaming. Clocks were chiming too, only they were chiming thirteen. Fourteen. Fifteen . . .

A voice whispered into her mind.

++Help us,++ it said. ++Save us.++

Lottie, she thought, her eyes snapping open. This wasn't a dream. The room was pitch-black and something was tickling the back of her hand. She wiped it away and tried to concentrate on nothing but the voice. Lottie was calling her from the Evil Dimension!

++Hello?++ Jaide teeped. ++Can you hear me?++

++Yes!++ came the immediate reply. ++You can help us!++

++How?++

++Open the way. That's all you have to do.++

++How do I do that?++

++Open the way and we can come through.++

++Yes, but how?++

Jack stirred.

"Voice," he mumbled. "Weird."

There was something on his face.

He opened his dark-sensitive eyes and saw two tiny white eyes staring back at him.

"Eeeurgh!"

It was a weevil. He sat up, wildly brushing his face with both hands. From several rooms away he could hear the chiming of clocks and steady, metallic banging sounds. There was a voice whispering in his mind.

++Open the way and we will come through.++

The sound of Jaide responding to that voice sent a chill straight down his spine.

++Can you tell me anything else?++

"No, Jaide — it's The Evil!" he cried, flinging himself out of bed and crossing to her side of the room in two steps. She was sitting straight upright in bed with her eyes tightly shut. "Jaide, snap out of it!"

Her eyelids opened and she looked at him. Jack almost fainted with relief that her eyes were completely normal.

"It's not The Evil," she said, puzzled by his strange behavior. "It's Lottie."

She frowned and looked down at her hand, where the thing that had been tickling her had returned. It was an earwig, and its eyes were white.

Her expression changed so suddenly Jack almost jumped off the bed.

"It tricked me!" she snarled, squashing the bug and leaping to her feet, sending her duvet flying. Her fists clenched, and a dark disk of air swirled around her head like a crown, shooting out thorny sparks of electricity. The four-poster bed rocked and swayed under her like a ship on stormy seas. *"It tricked me!"*

++So close!++ cried The Evil, all attempt at pretense abandoned now. She could hear the cold absence of anything human in its voice now. ++You are so close — just open the way and we will come to you!++

++Never!++ replied Jaide. To Jack she said, "Where's it coming from? How did it get in here? We can't get rid of it until we know where it *is*."

Jack turned on the lights and looked around for the weevil he had brushed off his hand. He couldn't see it, but he did see an ant on the floor by his feet, a tiny black spider high in one corner, a fly parked on the wall next to the window, and a millipede inching up one bedpost. All had glowing white eyes.

"It's everywhere," he said, raising one bare foot to squish the ant. "We need an exterminator!"

Behind them, the door crashed open. Stefano stood there, framed in bright blue light. His hair was blowing wildly and his expression fierce.

"You called?"

He raised the iron rod he held in his right hand.

But before he could do anything with it, Grandma X pushed him aside, dressed in her nightgown with hair in curlers.

"Not in the house!"

She raised her moonstone ring and pointed palm out at

the spider. Cold white light flashed, and the insect curled up and dropped to the floor.

"But *you* are," said Stefano, red-faced.

"Do as I tell you and don't argue!"

The ant made a run for it, but Jack put his foot down. Jaide bashed the millipede with one curled fist. When Stefano lunged for the fly, it buzzed away from him, right into another white flash from Grandma X.

"What's going on?" asked Susan, stepping on the weevil as she burst into the room. "What's all this racket?"

"The Evil," said Grandma X shortly. "The early warning system went off. I've been searching the house for the source and finally found it in the children's bedroom."

"What was it doing to you?" asked Susan, turning pale and gathering the twins to her.

Jaide struggled, but her mother's arms were too tight.

"Nothing, Mom. Just talking."

"We're okay," Jack assured her. "Did we get all of it?"

They looked around at the walls, ceiling, and floor, wondering if anything was left. From the blue room came the continuing sound of clocks chiming and a mechanical bear banging its drum. Jaide's sudden rage had faded, but she could've kicked herself for not recognizing those sounds. The house had several means of alerting its inhabitants to the presence of The Evil. As well as the clocks and the bear, several special barometers were sure to be showing stormy readings and the weathervane on top of the house would be spinning like mad until The Evil was completely gone.

"There must be a small piece remaining," Grandma X said. "We can't rest until we've rid the house of it."

"What can I do?" asked Susan.

"Get the vacuum cleaner," she said. "I'll call the cats and get Cornelia out of her cage so they can help. You three" — she turned to the troubletwisters — "search the house from top to bottom. Stay in sight of one another, and don't use your Gifts unless it's an absolute emergency. I'm sorry I was sharp with you, Stefano, but there was simply no need to go overboard. Talking is all The Evil can do in such a small form."

The twins nodded. Stefano looked resentful, but nodded, too.

"Words can be enough," she added. "Don't listen to any rapports you might hear, unless you're sure they're from me."

"Grandma," said Jaide, "how is it getting in? The wards are still working, aren't they?"

"They are. Don't worry. It's nothing you're doing."

They split up to pursue their separate tasks, and for the next hour the house was full of the sound of vigorous pursuit, as cockroaches, moths, worms, even a sleepy bee were shaken out of their hiding places, many of them innocent, but some decidedly Evil. Ari took no chances and ate all the bugs he found. Kleo was both more elegant and economical in her Evil-killing, skewering bugs with a single claw as they tried to scurry away. Cornelia snapped her beak with uncanny accuracy at anything flying.

Every now and again, Jack and Jaide caught a hint of The Evil's voice as they went through the house. Mostly it just repeated what it had said earlier, but once, when they had a white-eyed mosquito cornered in the bathroom, it tried a different tack.

++One of you will join us,++ it said. ++One always does. Why do you think *she* isn't trying to rescue the one she calls sister?++

"Be quiet," said Jack, swatting at the insect with a rolled-up towel. "I'm not listening."

++**She knows how it must be.**++ The Evil's mental voice was thin and whiny like a mosquito's buzz, but that didn't make its words any less horrible. ++**You will join us, or *your* sister will. Open the way and I will leave her alone.**++

"He said, be quiet!" Jaide used her Gift to lift herself up so her towel was in range of the whispering bug. One well-timed swat saw it smeared on the ceiling, silenced.

Stefano peered in from the corridor, where he was sweeping cobwebs with his iron rod. He saw her land on the tiled floor in a swirl of air.

"Your grandmother said —"

"I know what she said." Jaide wasn't going to be told off by him. "I barely used it at all. How are you doing with those spiders?"

Gradually, the banging and chiming from the blue room subsided and the house was quiet. The hunters reconvened on the first-floor landing, dusty, tired, and somewhat deflated. Fighting The Evil had never been so . . . tedious.

"To bed," said Grandma X. "Unless anyone has anything to add."

Jaide was tired and tetchy enough to think that Jack's plan from earlier had a lick of sense. Perhaps it was time to be blunt.

"Why aren't you doing anything to rescue your sister?" she asked.

If Grandma X was surprised by this question, she kept that surprise well hidden. "Is that what it said to you?"

"One of the things."

"Well, you know better than to believe anything The Evil tells you."

"Does that mean you *are* trying to rescue her?" asked Jack.

Grandma X turned to him. "I would never disobey Aleksandr or the wishes of the Grand Gathering."

Jaide put her hands in her hair and pulled at her scalp. "So which is it? Is The Evil lying or are you?"

"I think we're all getting a little overexcited," said Susan. "Now's not the time to talk about this."

"Tomorrow?" asked Jaide.

"It already *is* tomorrow," said Stefano, yawning hugely.

"Exactly," said Susan. "To bed, all of us."

Jaide collapsed face-forward into her pillow and went straight to sleep. This time it was Jack's turn to lie awake, thinking about everything their grandmother wasn't telling them. First on the list was Lottie, of course, but there was also Project Thunderclap, what Grandma X was doing with Stefano, and how The Evil was getting through the wards.

After six months of stability and peace, it suddenly felt as though the twins' lives were being turned upside down again. Only this time, Jack suspected, they would have nowhere safe to land.

CHAPTER SEVEN

TROUBLETWISTERING WITH TARA

Tuesdays were never terribly interesting in Portland, except when The Evil was attacking. And even then, if it was a school day, Mr. Carver had a manner that made anything exciting instantly boring or weird. He insisted on reading everyone's poetry homework for them, adopting an overly dramatic voice that bore no resemblance to the way anyone normally spoke. No wonder, Jack thought, there was a rumor going around that Mr. Carver was such a bad actor even the Portland Players wouldn't let him join their group.

Jaide's reward for getting through the day was soccer practice. Jack didn't have that, so he spent the day seeking something to look forward to. The best he could come up with was recruiting Rodeo Dave to help him look for the mysterious Lottie Henschke.

"Where are you going?" Tara called as he headed up Dock Road instead of trailing after the others to watch Stefano show off.

"The Book Herd," he told her. "I, um, need something to read."

"Great, I'll come with you."

"Oh, okay. If you want to."

"I do." She skipped double-time to catch up, pulling on a pair of fashionable purple sunglasses in one smooth motion. Tara's mother ran a gift shop in Scarborough, so she always had the latest accessories in her backpack. "Gum?" she said, offering him a piece.

"No, thanks."

"It's okay," she said. "I know you're not after something to read. You've got that look in your eye. You're troubletwistering."

"Shhh!" Jack looked around, but he should have known that no one was in earshot because she could say the word *troubletwistering* without her mouth slamming shut.

"Will it be dangerous?" she asked.

"I'm just going to look through some old books," he said, figuring there was no point lying since she had already guessed. "Hopefully with Rodeo Dave's help."

"Will he help you? I mean, he's not supposed to remember this stuff anymore."

"I know. But I think we can talk him around. Just keep your fingers crossed Kleo isn't there. She'll tell Grandma for sure."

"So it's a secret?"

"What we're trying to find out is a secret," he said, briefly outlining what he was hoping to find out and why. "Or else everyone's deliberately forgotten it, like Rodeo Dave has."

They turned into Parkhill Street, where an old lady was sweeping the sidewalk. *What was the point of sweeping the* outside, Jack thought. Everything *was dirty.* They dodged her tiny piles of dust, saying hello as they went, and hurried to the next corner. The Book Herd was open — another hurdle avoided, since "irregular" was a kind way of describing the hours Rodeo Dave kept. Kleo wasn't where she usually preferred to nap in the afternoon, in the window on a large and well-thumbed atlas thoroughly softened by age.

"Town records?" asked Rodeo Dave when Jack told him what he was after. He was a big man with a mustache to match, and like Grandma X, his cowboy boots seemed more an extension of him than something he put on every morning. "Of course, my boy, of course. You know where they are. Weren't you digging around in those last month?"

Jack and Jaide had been, but back then they hadn't known Lottie's surname or the year she disappeared. And the mystery hadn't been quite as pressing as it was now.

"Do you think you could help us, this time? We're looking for someone in particular."

Rodeo Dave stood up from the mound of paperbacks he was cataloguing. At least, that's what he had said he was doing. To Jack it looked as though he was simply moving them from one pile to another, perhaps organizing them by color or cover illustration rather than author name or title, just for a change.

"Ah, it's something specific you're looking for," he said with a knowing wink. "I thought you were just curious. A big game hunt is always more exciting than a sightseeing expedition, so you can count me in for certain. What manner of creature are we chasing?"

Jack was pretty sure Dave didn't mean an *actual* creature. His knowledge of Warden business was completely buried, along with his memories of Lottie. Still, it was unnerving to hear him use the word, and for a moment Jack stammered, unsure how best to answer.

"A woman," said Tara brightly. "She'd be about your age. Jack thinks she might be someone in the family who ran away a long time ago. No one will talk about her, so she must've been pretty interesting. We're just curious to know what happened to her."

"A scandal, eh?" Rodeo Dave's bushy eyebrows jiggled

up and down. "Well, let's take a look. Shut the door, Jack, and put out the closed sign. Let's do this properly."

He led them through the shop, room by room, to a chamber filled with books too large to fit on the ordinary shelves at the front. Most of them were in languages Jack couldn't understand, and he was pretty sure none of them were for sale. Most of them were too heavy for one person to lift, and had to be levered out carefully lest they fall apart in a shower of dust. The air was close and stale, and yet somehow deeply invigorating as well. Jack didn't have to imagine all those old words jammed together, jostling for release: He could *smell* them all around him.

"Right-oh," said Dave, heading to one corner of the chamber where the town records were stored. The twins had never asked how he had come to have them, and he had never explained.

"What year are you looking for?" he asked, running a finger along the worn leather spines.

"Forty-five years ago," said Jack. It seemed impossibly distant. Neither of his parents had been born then. Cell phones didn't exist. The Dark Ages, practically.

Out came a ledger the size of a suitcase. It contained handwritten accounts of council meetings, subcommittee reports, and news clippings from the *Portland Post*. The handwriting was tiny and birdlike, but perfectly legible if viewed closely. Rodeo Dave gave Tara and Jack a magnifying glass each, and used a third to examine a random page.

"That's old Miss Ackroyd's hand, that is," he said. "She was secretary for fifty years, and the council wasn't allowed to use a typewriter until she died. Striking woman. Only four-and-half-feet tall, and at least half a foot of that was hair."

Rodeo Dave was like that. He could remember amazingly insignificant details from his years in Portland, and yet nothing at all about the Wardens and huge chunks of his own life.

"We're looking for a woman called Lottie," he said. "Lottie Henschke."

Dave screwed up his face in thought and looked at the ceiling. "Lottie Henschke . . . Lottie Henschke . . . No, doesn't ring a bell. Are you sure she wasn't from Dogton? They're a rowdy bunch and always have been."

But you knew her, Jack wanted to say. *I've seen a photo of the two of you standing next to each other. You even had a crush on her. How can that all be gone?*

"I'm pretty sure," Jack said instead. "She lived on Watchward Lane."

That was a guess. Kleo had told him once that Grandma X's father had built her the house they lived in as a wedding present. Given that the house next door was its twin, didn't it stand to reason that Lottie had lived in that one? She might not have been married, but she was still her father's daughter. Susan and Hector always made sure that their presents to each of the twins matched in size and prestige, in order to avoid fights and hurt feelings.

"Hmmmm." Rodeo Dave thumbed through the ledger, occasionally stopping to put the calloused pad of his index finger on any interesting pages that flicked by. "Watchward Lane, eh? I seem to remember something interesting from around this time. Let's see . . . whaling protests? No . . . wide-brimmed hats? No again, but I remember that argument. . . . Walking dead? Unlikely . . ."

Jack and Tara leaned in close on either side, looking for Ws and studying names and faces as they flashed by. None of them seemed familiar.

"Wait," said Tara, one plastic-ringed finger shooting out. "What's that?"

There was a picture of a house in a newspaper article, and it was clearly Grandma X's house, although the trees around it were much smaller and the garden wall hadn't been built yet. There was no weathervane, and the external door leading to the blue room was hidden.

The picture wasn't just of that house. It also showed the house next door, which had gouts of smoke issuing from the ground-floor windows. Two men in old-fashioned fire uniforms held a nozzle pointed at the house, although no water was coming from it. The hose attached to the nozzle stretched out of the shot, presumably to a fire truck nearby, because there wasn't a hydrant on Watchward Lane that Jack knew of.

"This must be when it happened," said Jack.

"When what happened?" asked Dave.

"When she, um, left. Is there a date?"

The clipping was just a photo, with no story or date. Dave flicked to the pages before and after, and found references to meetings on May 22nd and 24th.

"It would have to be the 23rd, then, you'd guess," he said. "Strange there isn't anything in the minutes about it."

"What's this?" said Tara, pointing again, this time at the edge of the page Dave had just turned. "Looks like there are two pages stuck together."

"Why, Tara, you're right! Let's see if I can separate them without tearing anything."

Dave produced a letter opener from the back pocket of his jeans and inserted the tip into a tiny gap between the pages. Wiggling it gently back and forth, he managed to ease the blade inside, then raised and lowered it so the pages began to separate. When they fell apart, a cloud of dust rose up that made Tara sneeze twice in quick succession.

"Wow," said Jack when he saw what was contained between those pages.

It was the notes from an emergency session of the Portland town council, which didn't sound at all exciting until they started reading. The session had been called to discuss an accident and several casualties on Watchward Lane the night of May 23rd. The hospital was full of injured people, and its morgue contained no less than five bodies, not all of them identified. Several people were still missing. Of most immediate relevance to the council, apart from the tragic nature of events in general, was the death of the deputy mayor, nicknamed "Joe," full name Earl Joseph Henschke, stepfather of one of the missing women.

Jack read with bulging eyes. This was his great-grandfather they were talking about. It had to be. On the day Lottie had disappeared, Joe Henschke had died. And there was more.

The otherwise utterly legible Miss Ackroyd had blotted her record.

She wrote:

> One of Joe's stepdaughters, Lottie, is listed among the missing and feared dead. The other, ▓▓▓▓▓▓▓, is suffering smoke inhalation injuries and being treated in Portland Hospital. She is being attended by her husband, Giles, and is expected to recover fully. Mayor Green called for a whip-round to send flowers. All contributed.

Jack scratched at the inkblot that covered the name, but Rodeo Dave lightly slapped his hand away.

"Don't damage it!"

"I want to see what's under the ink."

"Well, there are other ways." From his other pocket, Dave produced a small flashlight. He lifted the page and held it vertical so he could shine the beam of white light through from one side while they looked from the other.

All they saw was the inkblot.

"Hmmmm," said Rodeo Dave again. "We're not done yet."

He spread the page flat again, and this time shone the light along the surface of the page, so any bump or crease stood out. By this method Jack could faintly make out some letters. There appeared to be eight of them, although one of them might have been a space.

"What does that say?" said Tara, squinting. "I can't quite make it out. Is than an *L*?"

"I'm not sure," said Dave, moving his magnifying glass back and forth. "It could be an *I*."

Jack took the flashlight from Dave and swiveled it back and forth. "I think it is an *L*," he said. "And that's an *M*. I'm pretty sure. And —"

Jack stopped as a sudden pain shot through his right eye. He jerked backward, bumping into Dave, who almost dropped his magnifying glass on Tara's head.

"What is it?" she said. "What's wrong?"

"Nothing," he said, rubbing his eye. It was fine now. "Just a weird feeling, like I was reading something I wasn't supposed to."

"That *is* weird," said Tara.

"Some books aren't supposed to be read," said Dave in hollow tones. "I guess some words are like that, too."

"So what's the point of writing them down?" Tara asked him.

"To keep them safe . . . to lock them up . . ."

"Are you okay?" Jack asked him. Rodeo Dave suddenly seemed not himself. Perhaps he was remembering. "Is it something to do with Lottie?"

Dave suddenly shook himself, as though emerging from slumber.

"With who?" he said, brushing his mustache and smiling at the two of them. "Oh, yes, most likely something to do with the missing girl. This woman was her sister, after all. I hope she liked the flowers."

Dave flicked through the subsequent pages, which contained very little information at all. Joe Henschke was buried elsewhere, cause of death not recorded. Neither was the cause of the accident. Ownership of the damaged property passed to the injured sister, but there was no record of her repairing it.

When it was clear the records weren't going to tell them anything else useful, Jack and Tara thanked Rodeo Dave and left him deep in an account of the building of Founder's Garden, which had been partly funded by his recently deceased friend, Old Master Rourke. He barely looked up as they left, although he did wave.

"Now what?" asked Tara.

"We check the house."

"Where the accident took place?"

He nodded. "We've already found one interesting thing there this week. Why not another?"

"All right," she said, checking her watch. "Dad will be there at five o'clock. He comes by then most days to see how things are going. I'll text to let him know I'm with you. I'll tell him soccer practice was boring, which was probably true, unless you were playing."

Jack felt a tiny pang at the fun his sister was having at

that very moment. If only he had cheated just a *little* bit. Maybe then he wouldn't be sleuthing for clues concerning an accident two generations past with a girl whose only real involvement in the Wardens was that she couldn't talk about them.

But he did enjoy Tara's company, and he would rather have her with him than be on his own, particularly while sneaking around an empty house that was still spooky, even though it had been cleaned up a bit.

And cheating was *wrong*, of course.

CHAPTER EIGHT
THE EXAMINER STRIKES AGAIN

Jaide captured the ball with her left foot and kicked it ahead of her. She had a clear run for the goal. Two more steps and she'd take the shot.

Someone cut across her, moving fast from the blind spot on her right side to take the ball and kick it at the goal. The kick was a good one, curving low and shallow across the grass, past Kyle's clutching hands and into the net.

Everyone on the team cheered, except for Jaide.

"Hey," she said. "That was my shot."

Stefano grinned at her as someone high-fived him.

"I didn't see you making any shot," he said.

"I was about to."

"You weren't quick enough, then."

"But I'm the striker. I had the ball."

"It's not the ball that matters; it's what you do with it."

"Positions, everyone!" called Mr. Carver from the boundary.

"Stupid show-off boys," Jaide muttered to herself. The scrimmage had been going for half an hour, and Stefano had stolen her ball three times already. It was becoming worse than annoying.

"I'll show *you* quick," she said as the teams reformed across the oval. Stefano winked at her from midfield, although she didn't think he had heard her.

There was the usual scramble for the ball when Mr. Carver blew on his flute. Jaide held back patiently as the center midfielders jostled for control, feet and elbows lashing out in moves that were more or less legal, or kept carefully out of Mr. Carver's sight if they weren't. Occasionally the ball would pop free, only to be rounded back in and tangled up once more. Stefano dodged and weaved with easy grace, toying with the ball just as he toyed with his erstwhile teammates.

Not this time, thought Jaide as he gained control and made a dash for empty ground, long, curly hair dancing, grin wide and triumphant.

Jaide was a dozen paces ahead of him. She concentrated, calling up her Gift and sending a brisk, eager breeze back to keep pace with him. Remembering what Alfred the Examiner had told her about the Gift not belonging to her, she talked to it as she would talk to Ari when he didn't want to do something. She guided it, cajoled it, encouraged it to bide its time when it wanted to lash out in full force. There would be time, she told it. Just be patient.

Stefano looked over his shoulder at the kids following him, unable to match his pace, and that moment, Jaide let her Gift strike.

One powerful puff was all it took to push the ball away from Stefano's right foot. To the casual glance it looked as though he had kicked it much harder than he had intended, but Jaide knew the truth. It was actually the wind, suddenly rocketing the ball forward to where she was standing, ready to accept it. She gathered it up, wrapping the jubilant breeze around her, and ran toward the goal.

Stefano knew what had happened.

"Hey!" he shouted after her, but she ignored him. Kyle could see her coming. That was what she needed to concentrate on now.

As she lined up the shot, feinting with her left foot in order to throw a defender off, she felt her Gift suddenly rise up around her.

"No," she hissed through gritted teeth. "Not now!"

But it wasn't going to listen. And she knew why. It wasn't her fault. This happened sometimes, when she and Jack were practicing at home. It was hard enough keeping one Gift in check, but two in tandem were almost impossible. Only this time it wasn't Jack's Gift interfering with hers. It was another troubletwister's, one she had never had to deal with before.

The sky grew dark above the field as she shot for goal, and a tiny purple line flashed between her cleat and the ball just before they made contact. The wind whined in her ears. With a high-pitched whizzing noise, the ball shot forward, trailing feathery sparks. Kyle took one look at it and dived for the turf.

A resounding boom shook the goal. Light flashed. Jaide's Gifts recoiled, as though shocked by the sudden overreaction. When her eyes cleared, the ball was spinning in the air, smoking. With a sad deflating sound, it dropped to the earth, just outside the goal line. Both her and Stefano's Gifts died with it.

"Inside, everyone!" called Mr. Carver, running onto the field and gathering his students like sheep. "I don't know where that storm came from, but it's time we called it quits anyway. Nice pass, Stefano. Excellent teamwork. And good shot, Jaide. Bad luck the lightning got in the way."

Stefano shot Jaide a withering look, which she returned.

"What're you doing?" Kyle hissed to her as they hurried for shelter. "I didn't think using your . . . you know . . . was allowed."

Jaide's indignation ebbed.

"I know, but he just makes me so mad."

"Have you got a crush on him?"

"*What?*"

"That's how it works in movies. Whenever a boy and a girl are mad at each other, they're destined to fall in love."

"Absolutely not," she said with one hundred percent certainty. She wasn't interested in falling in love with anyone, and if she had been, it wouldn't have been *him*. "We just don't like each other."

"Good," Kyle said with surprising force. "It would help, though, if you tried not to blow me up by accident."

She noticed his singed hair and T-shirt and felt shamefaced, even though Stefano shared part of the blame. "I'm sorry. That was an accident."

"It's okay," he said. "Next time I'm trying to light a fire at Scouts, I want you there to help me out."

They slapped hands. "Deal."

Jack and Tara were waiting for Jaide when she returned home early from soccer practice. Stefano had walked separately and silently, glowering at her back. They didn't talk. The storm clouds had vanished as quickly as they had come, but Mr. Carver wasn't taking any chances. He didn't go so far as to say that he had taken the weird weather as an omen, but she knew he was thinking it. People in Portland ignored such signs at their peril.

"What've you two been up to?" Jaide asked Jack and Tara in their bedroom while Stefano made himself a snack downstairs. She could tell just by looking at them that they hadn't been sitting idle while she had been busy dealing with Stefano.

Jack explained what they had found at the house first, since that was the freshest in his mind. There had been only two construction workers on site when they arrived, and both of them had been noisily expanding the hole that would one day be a parking lot, chugging backward and forward with diggers and earthmovers. They were easy to sneak past. Tara had shown Jack how the back door had been removed and replaced with nothing but a blue plastic sheet to keep the weather out. It was useless against two determined twelve-year-olds.

In less than half an hour, they had scoured the house from top to bottom. It had taken so little time because it was immediately clear that there was nothing to find: no dropped items of significance to Wardens, no notes or scrawled messages on the walls, no hints of the house's tragic past. There was no sign of anything they knew *had* been there, such as the Monster of Portland, actually the former Living Ward, which Grandma X had healed in the old house when The Evil had tried to poison it. The house had been thoroughly cleaned out — in preparation, presumably, for its renovation.

That was disappointing, but the search of the house hadn't been in vain. While the construction workers had been out front, waiting for Tara's dad, Jack and Tara had sneaked into the future parking lot in order to hunt for any more buried clues. While peering intently at the rough-hewn walls, Jack had felt a strange, new sensation.

He found it hard to put into words.

"It was weird," he said. "I could see through the dirt like it was air, only I wasn't really seeing, not in the usual way. I could just tell what was in there."

"Was something doing it to you?" asked Jaide. "Something in the earth, wanting you to find it?"

He shook his head. "It didn't feel weird, and that was the weirdest thing of all. It felt *normal*. Like when I dug Stefano out of the ground when he first arrived. Remember? I didn't think about what I was doing. I just did it, and it felt right."

"I reckon it's his second Gift," said Tara.

"You know, like Grandma X's father's?" Jack said. "He had some kind of architectural Gift. Maybe that's what this is. You have Dad's, and I have his."

Jaide nodded. That did make sense. For now, though, she just wanted to know what he had seen in the earth.

"So what did you find?"

"Lots of rocks and roots, of course," he said. "An old spoon, two forks, some broken pottery and rusty coins, a belt buckle, the tip of an umbrella —"

"Anything interesting?" she cut him off, sensing that he could go on for a while.

"Not a thing." Some of the excitement ebbed from him, which she felt bad about even if she was a bit jealous. While she had been putting up with Stefano, he had been having fun with Tara.

"At least you know what your second Gift is now," she made an effort to say. "That's good."

"I guess so," he replied. Even though it wasn't as exciting as lightning, he was quietly pleased to have something that connected him to the great-grandfather he had never met, the man who had built the twin houses right next door to each other. Maybe, he thought, that was why his second Gift had come to him there, where Joe had died. That thought gave him little joy, but it did seem fitting.

"That wasn't the only thing we learned," said Tara, and she told Jaide about the article they had found in Rodeo Dave's shop.

When she reached the part about Grandma X's blotted name, however, Tara suddenly stopped, looked into the distance as though trying to hear something far away, and said in a hollow voice, "It's time for me to go."

"Not yet," said Jaide. "Your dad won't be coming for another half an hour."

"It's time for me to go," Tara repeated. She climbed to her feet and started walking for the door.

"Wait." Jaide followed her down the stairs, with Jack at her heels. "What's going on?"

"It's time for me to go," said Tara a third time, at the front door.

Without stopping to wave or even look behind her, Tara went through the door, across the garden, and out the gate.

"That was weird," said Jack. "Do you think we should let her just go off like that?"

"You have to," said a voice from behind them. "Apparently it was time for her to go."

Stefano was standing in the hallway.

"Did you do that?" asked Jaide, rounding on him with her fists on her hips.

"No," he said. "I don't know how to."

"Well, what's going on, then?"

Jack looked around him, realizing only then just how quiet the house was.

"Did you see Mom and Grandma when you came in?" he asked Jaide.

"No. I thought they might be out shopping."

"What about Ari and Kleo?"

"I didn't see them, either."

"Nor me," said Stefano, going pale.

Jaide looked behind her, as though expecting to see

someone standing there. Jack, too, suddenly felt as though he was being watched.

"Where is he?" he asked.

"Who?" asked Jaide, although she knew very well who Jack meant.

"The Examiner. He must be here somewhere. That's why everyone is gone. Do you know, Stefano?"

Stefano shook his head.

"But you know what's going to happen," said Jaide. "You've done this before, right?"

"Some of it." For the first time she heard an accent in his voice. It made him sound much younger. "I haven't done all of it."

"Why is that?" said Jack. "What stopped you from going all the way?"

Again, he just shook his head.

"Were you afraid?" asked Jaide.

Stefano's eyes flashed. "No, of course not. I —"

Between one word and the next, Stefano vanished. There was no puff of smoke or flash of light. No sound. One second he was there and the next he wasn't.

Jaide instinctively reached out and took Jack's hand. She was sure it wouldn't make any difference to what happened to them. She just needed the comfort of being with him while she could get it.

"Good luck," she said. "See you on the other —"

Then she was gone, too, and Jack was left alone.

Oldest first, thought Jack, the heel of his right foot restlessly tapping the floor. His nervousness was hard to contain. *I'm ready,* he wanted to shout. *Get it over with!*

The light suddenly went out, and he was lying down. The change happened so quickly he was dizzy for a second. He went to raise his hands to touch his face, but they stopped hard against something wooden and solid just inches away from them. He tried to sit up and banged his head.

He tried kicking his feet. The same.

It was either so dark that his Gift couldn't work or his Gift had stopped working entirely. The surface in front of him felt like wood but he couldn't see it to make sure. A box of some kind. He didn't want to think *coffin*.

"Help!" he shouted. His voice echoed back at him, deafeningly loud.

He tried again, this time with his mental voice.

++Help!++

There was no reply.

He imagined the earth pressing in all around him, heavy and dense, smothering his every attempt to call Jaide.

His heart was racing. This time there was no escaping the fear of being buried alive, because it looked very much as though he had been.

Jaide was falling. But she wasn't falling down. She was falling *sideways*.

Tumbled and tossed by the wind, she had trouble working out exactly what was going on. She still had her arms and legs, so they hadn't been transformed in any particular way. She appeared simply to have been moved, but where, and why? It took her several minutes to realize that she was spinning in a circle, as though in the heart of a giant hurricane. She tried reaching out to it with her Gift, but either this storm wasn't talking to her or her Gift had been temporarily muted somehow.

Another one of Alfred's Gifts, she assumed. But where did the Examination come into it?

The bolt of lightning that very nearly hit her provided the answer to that question, closely followed by a second, and a third.

Blinded and half stunned, she tried calling for help, but either the lightning interfered with her mental voice or Jack was tied up elsewhere in his own trials. What form they were taking she couldn't imagine. For now she had to concentrate entirely on her own.

Another trio of lightning bolts left her feeling frazzled and more than a little crispy, like bacon that had been fried for too long.

Survival, she thought. That was Alfred's point this time. The first test had been about finding Jack using her mental voice and getting home. Now it was just about staying alive, if she could. And her new Gift was the only thing she could draw on to help her.

She'd had no opportunity to explore or develop that Gift, though, not properly. Reaching for it now, she found it readily enough, coiled inside her like a part of her she'd never noticed before. It stirred when she called it. It seemed to listen when she spoke to it, albeit at some remove.

She felt the electricity building in the air and knew there was going to be another bolt coming her way soon. Her skin tingled and her hair stood on end.

"Protect me," she said. "Don't let the lightning hit me."

Her Gift *seemed* to agree.

But when the lightning struck, it prompted a chain reaction of flashes and sheets that set the entire storm alight. Her Gift keened with the joy of it, and too late Jaide was reminded of how her first Gift loved more than anything to form storms and whirling dervishes at the slightest provocation. Why would this one be any different?

She curled into a ball and put her arms around her head, riding out the lightning while remembering Alfred's words of warning after the first test: *Your Gifts are not your friends. You think you control them, but you do not. They will fight you at every turn, unless you have . . . wooed them correctly.*

How did one woo lightning, she wondered as the conflagration gradually eased. What could she possibly tell this Gift to make it calm down?

Jack had a mouthful of dirt. His plan had gone spectacularly wrong. His attempt to reach out to the earth around him using his second Gift had resulted in his cage of wood being broken open, but instead of letting him out, it had only let the dirt in. He felt the dirt shifting and wriggling into the coffin around him, inching its way down his limbs. If he didn't think fast he would be completely covered and would suffocate.

But there *was* air down there with him, a bubble of it that had been trapped with him. It was just in the wrong place, squashed around his feet when he needed it at his head, so he could breathe it.

Jack could no longer speak aloud, but he didn't normally speak aloud to use his first Gift. He just willed it to do what he wanted. He attempted this with the dirt while his air lasted, trying not to think about what would happen if he got it wrong.

The dirt obliged, shifting around him so the bubble could move up to his head. When his mouth and nostrils cleared, he took a deep, gasping breath. The air was already a little stale, smelling of earthworms and his own feet, but it was the sweetest breath he had ever drawn.

"Thank you," he said, and the earth wriggled around

him like an excited puppy. That surprised him, since it had come so close to smothering him a moment ago. Perhaps it didn't mean him any actual harm, but simply didn't know him well yet. They were new friends, and it was excited to meet him, but it would take time to understand that being so close to him might actually kill him if it wasn't careful.

"Will you take me up?" he asked it, pushing his arms above his head through the damp soil. "Will you do that for me?"

The earth wriggled again, and slowly, painfully, he began to go upward.

The problem, thought Jaide, wasn't that she had too much lightning. The problem was that it was the wrong kind of lightning. She might not be able to stop her new Gift from being excited and wanting to play, but perhaps she could encourage it to do so in a way that helped her.

"Yes, like that," she said, sweeping her arms around her like a shepherd giving directions to flying sheep. "All the way around . . . that's perfect!"

Crackling and snapping, her new Gift formed a cage of electricity that surrounded her completely. When next the hurricane's lightning struck, it passed through the cage around her, leaving her completely unscathed.

A sense of accomplishment flooded her. She was still tumbling through a hurricane, but at least she was safe. She wasn't going to die any time soon, unless it was of boredom, or starvation. She had befriended her second Gift.

"Is that it?" she asked aloud, assuming the Examiner could hear her somehow, even over the roaring of the storm. "Did I pass?"

After a long second, during which time she experienced a moment of doubt — what if she was wrong? What if she had misjudged the Examination completely? — Alfred's voice spoke to her out of the clouds.

"You have passed," he said, and suddenly she was standing exactly where she had been before, on the porch of Grandma X's house, and Jack was next to her with dirt in his hair and a look of utter relief on his face. Alfred the Examiner was there, too, looking exactly as he had the previous day.

He was smiling and said, "Well done."

CHAPTER NINE

SOMETHING GROWING, SOMEONE DEAD

The twins talked over each other in an attempt to explain what had happened to them and how resourceful they'd been. They had passed the second test and were now two thirds through to being senior troubletwisters! Alfred let them babble, not speaking again until it occurred to them who was missing.

"Where's Stefano?" asked Jack, looking around him. Apart from the twins and Alfred, the house seemed empty.

"He has not yet completed his task," was all Alfred said.

"What happens if he doesn't?" asked Jaide, afraid of what the answer might be. If she or Jack had failed, would they have died underground or in a storm, or would they have been rescued?

"He tries again later."

"Ohhhhhhh," said Jack, feeling that he was understanding something now that should have occurred to him long ago. "That's why he took this test with us but not the first one. He passed the first one the first time he tried. This is his second time at the second one."

"What happened to his brother?" asked Jaide. "Did he pass?"

"That is for Stefano to explain, not me."

Jaide nodded. *Fair enough,* she thought. She wouldn't want people talking about her failures behind her back.

"What do we do until he comes back?" she asked.

"We wait. You may ask me questions, if you like."

"When's the next test?" asked Jack.

"Tomorrow. It will take all day."

"I have soccer practice in the afternoon," said Jaide.

"If you perform well, you will be able to attend."

Jaide nodded, determined to do better than Stefano, at least, in the hope that he might miss out.

"Are the Examinations always the same?" asked Jack. He was wondering if his father had taken the same ones, and Grandma X.

Alfred said, "No and yes. Troubletwisters are always Examined when they obtain a certain degree of proficiency with their Gifts, but it is the Gifts that determine the shape of their Examination."

Jack nodded. That made sense. So far his and Jaide's Examinations had been similar in principle but very different in details. If he had been in his sister's shoes for the last test, he would've died for sure.

"Can you give us any hints about the next one?" asked Jaide.

"Troubletwisters always ask," said Alfred with a slight smile, "and they are always told no. I guarantee that you will be surprised."

All three turned at the sound of a gasp from the hallway. Stefano had returned. He stood with his arms outstretched, his legs so unsteady that he dropped to one knee and almost fell over. Jaide couldn't help rushing to help him. He looked so weak and pale. She took one arm while Jack took the other.

Stefano didn't seem to see them for a moment. Only when he was back on two feet did he look down at them and shrug them off.

"Did I pass?" he asked in a cracked voice.

"Yes," said Alfred. "You have passed."

Stefano let out a shuddering breath.

"What happened?" asked Jack.

"Don't look at me," Stefano said. He turned and hurried up the stairs. A second later, the door to his bedroom slammed shut.

Jaide turned to Alfred to ask him the same question, but the Examiner had already disappeared.

"He really likes to do that, doesn't he?" she said in annoyance.

A car pulled up the lane, and the twins recognized the distinctive decal flames of Grandma X's new car. They waved, and Susan waved back from the passenger seat. The car pulled up on the gravel by the front porch. Susan got out but Grandma X didn't; the car stayed running.

"I hear you did well," Susan told them, giving them both a quick hug. "Your grandmother wants to take you somewhere, so go on and do that while I think about dinner. You've earned a night off from homework."

Jack beamed. "How did you know we passed?"

"The usual way. She always knows everything." There was no bad feeling in Susan's voice. It was just a statement of fact. "Go on. Showers before bed tonight. You look like you've been rolling in dirt, Jack. You, too, Jaide."

"It's called soccer, Mom."

"Either way, we need to get it off you. Where's Stefano?"

"In his room," said Jack. "Being grumpy."

"Go easy on him," said Susan. "You two don't know how lucky you are."

Jaide wanted to ask what she meant. It bothered her that Susan now knew more about certain things to do with Wardens than they did. It had been much easier in some ways when being troubletwisters was a secret they kept from her.

The engine of the Austin revved and the twins took the hint. Both went for the front door and, after a brief tussle that Jaide won, Jack settled into the broad back seat. Jaide loved the Austin even more than the old Hillman. Everything about it was smaller, making it feel more kid-friendly, and there was a compass mounted in the dash that had words in what looked like Latin rather than *East-West-North-South*. There was no rhyme or reason to the direction it pointed — or at least none Jaide could make out.

"Belts on," said Grandma X, and with a quick wave to Susan they were off. "You both did very well. I'm proud of you."

Praise from Grandma X meant a lot. The twins basked in it for a moment before curiosity got the better of them.

"Where are we going, Grandma?" asked Jaide.

"Somewhere very special," she said. "Two somewheres, actually. I think it's time you officially met the remaining wards of Portland."

Jaide glanced excitedly at Jack, who was leaning forward intently. This was big, and it said more clearly than words that Grandma X was impressed by their progress. The first two wards they had only discovered by accident, and they had never been able to confirm what the other two were, although they had their suspicions.

"I bet it's the cactus and the giant at Mermaid Point," said Jack.

"What makes you say that?" asked Grandma X.

"There was that time you took us on a tour when we first arrived, when The Evil was attacking. You looked at the lighthouse, where the Something Read Ward is, then you looked at the cactus in Founder's Park, and you told us about the giant. They must be the Something Growing and Someone Dead wards."

"Is that what you think, too, Jaide?"

Jaide nodded, although something about Grandma X's tone made her doubt. She felt as though she was being tested again.

"Are we wrong?" Jaide asked.

"Have patience. You'll soon find out."

They drove over the iron bridge and down Main Street, through the heart of Portland. It was a short trip. The Austin stopped at Founder's Park and Grandma X killed the engine.

"It must be the cactus," said Jack, unbuckling, and opening the car door. "There's nothing else out here but grass."

"Is it the grass?" asked Jaide.

Grandma X just smiled.

The cactus garden was in the center of the park, and resembled a miniature spiky forest. Some of the cactuses were over twenty feet high. The tallest had pink flowers at the top that always seemed to be in bloom. The twins crossed the grass until they were standing at the forest's edge, within touching distance of the nearest spikes.

"We're here," said Grandma X.

"Which one is it?" asked Jack.

"You tell me."

Jaide had half expected this. They *were* being tested again, but more playfully, she suspected, with no real consequences if they failed. No consequences except for embarrassment, anyway. She was determined to succeed, and before her brother did, too.

The twins split up and circled the cactus garden in

opposite directions. None of the cactuses stood out, except for the largest, and it seemed unlikely that the Wardens would make the Growing Ward something so obvious.

But weirdly, none of the other cactuses stood out as anything unusual, either. Both twins had learned to trust their instincts when it came to things like this, and they were getting no twinges or odd signals that one was different from the others in any significant way.

Jack and Jaide met back where they had started. Grandma X watched them with an amused glint in her gray eyes.

"Give up?" she said.

"No," said Jack. He was as stubborn as Jaide, in his own way, and if nothing had caught his eye on the outside of the cactus garden, then the ward had to be on the inside. Carefully appraising the fleshy branches and their long, tapering needles, he chose a path least likely to snag his clothes or skin and continued his exploration.

It was like a maze inside the garden, and much denser than it seemed from the outside. Jaide took the same way in but made a left turn where Jack had gone right, at a fat-bellied cactus that looked like a prickly snowman. That wasn't the ward, and neither were any of the others they passed, but Jaide and Jack both felt a growing sense of *something* in the forest, something definitely out of the ordinary.

As they spiraled into the center, that feeling grew stronger.

"Ouch," said Jack, catching his left forearm and leaving a tiny drop of blood behind on the thorn that had scratched him. Ahead, through the tall, greenish trunks, he saw what looked like a small clearing, and on the other side of it was

Jaide, trying to find a way in. Throwing caution to the wind, he turned sideways and pushed through.

Jaide had a long, red weal across the back of her right leg, but she wasn't letting that slow her down. She ducked under a curving spiked branch and stepped into the clearing at exactly the same time as Jack.

"I was first," said Jack. It wasn't true but *saying* it first was a kind of victory.

"No way! I'll give you a tie at the very most."

There were more important matters at hand. "What is this place?" Jack asked.

Jaide didn't know, but it *felt* important. The clearing was seven feet across, and roughly circular, with cactuses pressing in on all sides. The floor was covered in fallen needles, and mostly level except for a low mound that crossed the ground between the twins. The feeling of significance radiated from that mound, but Jaide couldn't see any living thing on or near it. Jack looked for mushrooms or, skimming the top with his sneaker to clear away the needles, some other kind of fungus, but there was nothing. Just bare dirt.

"I don't get it," he said. "There's nothing here."

"No," said Jaide. "Nothing growing, anyway."

"Maybe we've got the wrong ward," Jack said. "Maybe it's not the Growing Ward at all."

"You think it's Someone Dead? Here?"

Both twins took a step back from the long, low mound, which, they both realized at the same time, did look a lot like a grave.

"Oh. Sorry," said Jack, feeling a need to apologize to the person buried here, even though he hadn't really done anything wrong. Grandma X would have been sure to stop them if they weren't supposed to be there. It just seemed disrespectful to have been arguing on top of someone's dead body.

"Who do you think it is?" asked Jaide, staring solemnly at the mound. That was definitely the ward. She had no doubt of it. "Could it be Grandma X's father?"

"We can ask when we get back out."

"After you," said Jaide, happy to get moving now that they had a partial answer to the mystery. It creeped her out a little, the idea of a secret grave in the heart of Portland. Like a lot of Portland's secrets, she suspected it had a sad history, and that made her think of Lottie, who was still trapped in the Evil Dimension and likely never to get home, unless her twin sister helped her.

"Is it your father?" Jaide asked Grandma X when they emerged from the cactuses, somewhat scratched and sobered by the experience. "We know his name was Earl Joseph Henschke, but people called him Joe, and he died in the house next door to yours the night Lottie disappeared. I don't remember him being in the Portland graveyard, though, where Grandpa is. Is that him back there?"

If Grandma X was surprised by how much the twins had learned about her family, or by Jaide's challenging tone, it didn't show.

"It's not Father," she said, "but that's a good guess."

"Who is it, then?"

"Hester Bright. She requested to become one of the wards when she died. Such interment is not usual, but it has been granted in special cases, in return for extraordinary service. She was Warden of Portland for seventy years, and died when I was a girl. I remember her clearly. She could turn into three red foxes that each contained part of her, a very rare Gift that made her the terror of chickens for miles around. I'm not aware that she ever ate one, though; she just thought they were stupid and liked giving them a fright."

That was about the longest anecdote Grandma X had ever told about anyone, and the twins waited intently to see if there was any more to come.

Instead, she just indicated the car. "Let's move on to the next ward. I think you'll find it even more interesting than this one."

That was enough to distract Jack. "Oh, yeah — if this is the Someone Dead Ward, that means the last one is Growing!"

"Do you still think we have a giant in Portland?" Grandma X said with a smile.

"I hope so."

Jaide was not so easily deflected. "Why will you talk about Hester Bright but won't you tell us anything about Lottie?"

Grandma X concentrated on driving for a moment, pulling out from the curve and heading up Main Street. When she did speak, she did so without looking at either twin, and her voice had an emotional tremor that Jaide had never heard before.

"The life of a Warden isn't an easy one. On that night, I lost my sister and my father. Later, I lost Harold and your grandfather. Then Harold came back, and I had to let go of him again. The same might happen with Lottie. You can imagine how this must feel — I can't stop you doing that, but I can spare you anything more. You are young, Jaidith and Jackaran. Worry about the future. Leave the old to deal with the past."

At the hospital, they turned into the beach parking lot. Jaide said nothing as Grandma X brought the car to a halt.

The sun was going down, and a family of five with two very young children was packing up picnic gear and heading home from a day on the beach. They looked so amazingly normal. Jack wondered if that was how he and his family looked to other people. Probably not, he thought, given the number of times people's memories had to be tweaked to stop the secret getting out. Jack and Jaide weren't normal. Normal people didn't have to deal with uncles who almost got them killed or great-aunts trapped in an Evil Dimension.

Jaide didn't notice the family of five. She was thinking about Lottie. Grandma X *had* to be doing something to save her sister, or how could she live with herself?

"Come on," said Grandma X, opening her door and swinging her cowboy boots out of the car. "It's time to meet Angel."

In silence, the twins followed their grandmother across the walking trail and onto the rocky promontory named after a mermaid's tail, because that was what it resembled on a map. They had walked here before, but this time, after their exposure to the Someone Dead Ward, their senses were attuned to the presence of anything unusual, and both of them felt a powerful force radiating from the stones underfoot.

Grandma X took them to a particular cluster of rocks that from a distance looked like a woman lying on her side, sleeping. Each stone was larger than a car, and two stones lying on their ends towered over them like monoliths. Jack, with the beginnings of his new Gift making him more sensitive to earth and stone, had never sensed anything like it. He half expected the boulders to leap up and squash him at any moment.

"Giants don't talk like we do," Grandma X said, affectionately patting the side of one of the stones. "If you took a bag and filled it with gravel and scrunched it around a bit, that's what their language sounds like. But they can learn to rapport if a Warden is patient enough to listen. Sometimes they take human names. Thus it is with Angel, who has been a ward of Portland for one hundred and fifty years, a tiny portion of her incredible life. To us, she is sleeping. To Angel, she is merely resting. And growing all the while. Giants start off very small, little more than pebbles. As they grow, they get larger and more dangerous, like avalanches. The really old ones are as big as mountains, but luckily they rarely wake. Many of the world's worst earthquakes are actually giants turning over in their sleep."

Jaide was willing to be impressed. "Have you ever spoken to her?"

"Only once, when your father was fighting in the Pacific. They were dealing with giants, and Angel's advice was critical in turning back The Evil. Then she went back to sleep. Sometimes I can feel her dreaming. The images are . . . unusual."

Jack put his hand next to Grandma X's.

"Nice to meet you, Angel," he said, not feeling the slightest bit awkward about talking to what looked to the naked eye like nothing more than inert stone. "I hope we get to talk one day."

There came a faint creaking sound, as though the mighty boulder had shifted slightly, and a seagull perched on top took off with a squawk. There was no other sign that the giant had heard.

Grandma X looked at Jaide to see if she wanted to say something, but she was happy to let Jack do all the talking.

Her powers came from the wind and the sun. Heavy rocks like these might kill her if ever she lost control and fell on them.

"We should get back," she said. "Mom's off to work in the morning. She's probably got something special planned for dinner."

Jack's stomach growled at the thought of food. It seemed like days since lunch.

"Here's hoping it's takeout again," he said.

"Kyle and Tara are joining us for dinner," Grandma X said. "I think the plan is for Stefano to cook."

"Stefano?" Jaide exclaimed. "But he's —"

"A boy? Too young?" Grandma X seemed to take great pleasure in Jaide's alarm. "You never know; he might be a good cook. And it seems only fair that he does something around the house, since he's not on the dishwashing roster."

Not for the first time Jack wondered if their grandmother also had the Gift of reading minds. They had only been complaining to Tara about Stefano and the dishwashing roster the day before. Maybe she had said something. Maybe that was why she was invited to dinner as well.

Grandma X put an arm around each of them, and together they headed back to the car. Behind them, the boulder shifted again, and from a distance it might have seemed that a great stony head lifted, just for a moment, to regard the troubletwisters as they walked away.

CHAPTER TEN

STEFANO SHOWS THE WAY

On the way past the school they noticed a large tent being erected at one end of the oval.

"That was fast," said Jack. The Portland Council wasn't renowned for moving quickly. It had recently spent three months arguing about the apostrophe on the sign saying FOUNDER'S PARK. "That'll be up days ahead of the soccer match."

"That's not for the match," said Grandma X. "That's Project Thunderclap."

"Here?" asked Jack. "In Portland?"

"Yes. The fabric of our dimension has been greatly weakened here, thanks to the many incursions by The Evil in recent times, plus your own tinkering with a Bifrost Bridge in Rourke Castle. Aleksandr reasons — correctly, I think — that this will make it easier for us to strike the very heart of The Evil."

The twins examined the tent with more interest, craning to look over their shoulders as it receded behind them. There was no sign of Aleksandr or any other Wardens they knew, but that didn't mean anything.

"What is Project Thunderclap?" asked Jaide. "Why's it such a big secret?"

"It's not a secret, except from ordinary people. You were simply absent from the meeting at that point. Project

Thunderclap draws on some of Professor Olafsson's later work, which suggests that the breaches between worlds can be closed by the right application of electricity. What Thunderclap hopes to do is channel enough power into the realm of The Evil so that it will permanently separate from our world, making us safe forever."

"How are they going to get enough power?" asked Jack, fascinated. "With a nuclear reactor?"

Grandma X sniffed disdainfully. "Nothing so ordinary. Aleksandr has recruited every lightning wielder alive today, and a few relics of those who died long ago, to combine forces and put his plan into action."

Jaide felt her skin tingle at the thought. One lightning bolt on its own was the most powerful thing she had ever experienced. She couldn't imagine what many combined would be like. As a potential lightning wielder herself, she wondered if she would be asked to be part of it.

Then she thought of Stefano, and was sure his extra practice was designed to bring his own abilities up to speed for Thunderclap. That she wasn't receiving that tuition suggested she was going to be left out because she was too inexperienced. Unless she could somehow prove herself . . .

"When is it going to happen?" she asked.

"Thursday," said Grandma X.

"*This* Thursday?" said Jack.

"The very one."

"But that's not enough time!" he said. Jaide was thinking exactly the same thing.

"For what, Jackaran?"

"For you to rescue Lottie, of course. You are going to, aren't you?"

"I gave my solemn promise to Aleksandr," Grandma X said. "You heard me tell him that I wouldn't attempt a rescue. And I never break my promises. You should know that by now."

Both twins were puzzled and even somewhat hurt by her continued insistence that she was going to abandon Lottie to her fate. Grandma X put such great store in doing the right thing. What were they supposed to do now, when it seemed like she was doing the wrong thing? Not just her, but all the Wardens.

The Austin 1600 pulled into the lane and delivered the twins to the front step. They climbed out, moping, some of their excitement at being entrusted with the details of the wards of Portland undermined by Lottie's predicament. If only, thought Jack, they could find the cross-continuum conduit constructor and make their own way across. And if Jaide was part of Project Thunderclap, she reasoned, she might learn more about their plans and get the jump on them. Both possibilities seemed incredibly unlikely.

As they stepped into the house, a powerful smell struck them.

"Wow," said Jaide. "What's that?"

"It's food," said Ari, hurrying to greet them. "*Real* food."

Jack's stomach had taken command of his body from his brain and was already leading him into the kitchen.

"It had better be," he said, hoping it wasn't some kind of cruel trick.

In the kitchen they found Stefano and Susan bending over the stove top, stirring a large pot, the source of the incredible smell. Tara and Kyle were sitting at the table, pretending to do homework but actually totally distracted by the cooking taking place nearby. Kleo was watching from the windowsill, eyes following the spoon from side to side as though hypnotized.

"Just like that," Stefano was explaining. "Not too fast, but not too slow, either. The important thing with a risotto is never to walk away. Arborio rice is unforgiving."

Susan looked up as the twins entered. "Oh, hi, kids. Guess what? I'm having a cooking lesson."

"Seriously?" said Jack.

"From . . . *him*?" asked Jaide.

The twins looked from their mother to Stefano in amazement. Stefano raised the spoon and twirled it like a wand. His cheeks were pink, perhaps from bending over the steaming pot for so long.

"It's just something simple we cook at home," he said. "Anyone can learn it."

"Even me," said Susan, "I hope."

Jack hoped so, too, because if the dish tasted as good as it smelled, he never wanted to eat anything else.

"I hope you made a lot," he said.

"It's very filling," Stefano said. "Perfect for a growing boy."

Jack bristled at the suggestion that he was only a boy. Jaide, too, was resentful at Stefano's implied criticism of their mother's cooking. Yes, it was awful, but she was *their* mother and only *they* were allowed to complain about it.

But the smell was so amazing they were able to swallow their pride and willingly set the table in preparation for what they hoped would be an amazing feast.

They weren't disappointed. The risotto was thick and flavorsome, with mushrooms (which Jack normally hated) and lots of pepper (which normally made Jaide sneeze). Ari relentlessly meowed and head-butted everyone's shins until Grandma X relented and dished him a small saucer, which he lapped up in two gulps. Kleo was more dignified, waiting until offered her own dish and then eating it in several small mouthfuls. She licked her lips appreciatively and glanced at the pot as though hoping for seconds.

Everyone had seconds, and Jack might have gone for thirds if he hadn't been so full. He sat back in his chair, fingers laced over his distended stomach, and sighed contentedly. That was the first really wonderful meal he had had since arriving in Portland.

"That was *awesome*," said Kyle, scraping out the last morsel from his bowl.

"*Super* awesome," agreed Tara.

Stefano dismissed their praise and thanks.

"It was nothing," he said. "We eat like this all the time."

Jaide couldn't decide what irked her most: his modesty, the boastful way he professed it, or the hint of criticism behind it — *what*, you *don't eat this way all the time?* But she, too, was lulled into a state of passive irritation by the meal. When Grandma X reminded her that it was her turn to do the dishes, she didn't put up even a token protest. If Stefano could teach their mother to cook like that every night, she was prepared to do her chores in exchange. Besides, it was much easier with Tara and Kyle to help.

While the dishes were being put away, Grandma X gave Jack his own chore.

"Stefano and I will have extra lessons tonight," she said. "Would you like to see to Cornelia now?"

"Sure," he said, not minding at all. It seemed like ages since he'd seen Cornelia. Normally, she'd sit with him while he was doing his homework and try to eat his notebooks. Or she'd interrupt dinner with raucous comments about hard tack and rum.

Hanging up his dish towel he went up the stairs, detouring to his room to retrieve a crust he had saved from lunch to give to Cornelia as a treat.

The door to the blue room was unlocked, and he slipped through with practiced ease.

"Hello, Charlie," Cornelia said as he came down the stairs. She was sitting on top of the cage, walking slowly back and forth.

"I'm not Charlie," he said. "I'm J —"

He stopped dead on the bottom step. There was a glowing woman standing in the center of the blue room. She was young and blond and looking around as though lost. Although he could see her clearly, she seemed slightly fuzzy around the edges. Like a ghost, Jack thought, made of jellyish ectoplasm.

Her pale eyes caught sight of him.

++Help us,++ she said, and her voice was as pale and watery as she was. ++Save us.++

And suddenly he knew her. She was the Woman in Yellow, the subject of the painting from Rourke Castle that he and Jaide had entered using the cross-continuum conduit constructor. She looked exactly like Grandma X did when she cast her spectral form. She was Lottie Henschke, and she was reaching out from the Evil Dimension once more to call for help.

"Grandma!" Jack called. "Come here!"

"Charlie-Charlie-Charlie," said Cornelia in a singsong voice. Her head bobbed up and down in the bird equivalent of excitement.

++Please help us. You must help us.++

Jack instinctively backed up a step as Lottie approached him. Although he was glad to see her, the apparition's appearance made him nervous, and it wasn't just him. The mechanical bear was shifting restlessly on its pedestal, and the barometer needles were twitching. If the way to the Evil Dimension was open, The Evil might not be far behind.

Jack yelled again, putting all his voice into it. "Grandma! Anyone!"

++Don't let us die,++ said Lottie.

"Man overboard!" squawked Cornelia, flapping her wings.

"Grandma, quickly!"

At last Jack heard footsteps on the steps behind him, a thunder of footfalls suggesting that the entire house had come in response to his panicked call.

"What is it, Jack? . . . Oh my."

Grandma X was suddenly next to him, her expression shocked. Lottie's glowing face turned, but her expression was enigmatic, as though she wasn't really seeing them. Jaide felt a small shudder course through her as that ghostly gaze passed across her. The cats leaned heavily against her calves, for solidarity. Kyle and Tara stared with wide eyes at the apparition, while behind them, Susan gasped. For although her children saw and experienced strange things on a regular basis, things far outside normal human experience, she was rarely exposed to them herself.

++Please,++ said the apparition. ++Please save us!++

"How, Charlotte?" said Grandma X in a voice so soft Jack could hardly hear it. *"How?"*

Stefano pushed past Susan, Tara, and Kyle, over Ari, and between Jack and his grandmother.

"Why can't you do it yourself?" he asked the apparition. "You've come this far."

Lottie shook her head and looked mournful.

++Too hard. Too far.++

"It won't be any easier for us, you know."

"Stefano," said Grandma X, putting a hand on his shoulder.

"No," he said, shrugging her off. "She needs to hear this. If she didn't want to be there, she shouldn't have gone!"

++Please . . . please . . .++

"She's putting us all in danger by opening a breach to the realm of The Evil," Stefano said, his mouth a cruel line. "Help yourself, Lottie, or stay away from us!"

++Very well, then . . . We will!++

Lottie's face crumpled — *literally* crumpled, like a statue made of stone dissolving into smaller pebbles. Only these weren't pebbles. They were glowing leeches, and each of them had white eyes. The leeches squirmed, released from their pretense of Lottie, and launched themselves at Stefano like tiny, Evil bullets.

He fell back with a howl, his hands flung over his face. At last, the mechanical drum sounded.

"Behind me!" cried Grandma X, grabbing Stefano by the collar with her left hand and yanking him backward. Her right hand came up and the light of her moonstone ring struck the dissolving apparition. It exploded, sending leeches flying everywhere. Cornelia squawked and took off, flapping around the chandeliers in a startled panic.

"Yaahh!" said Jaide as one hit her cheek with a solid splat. She went to flick it off, but it clung to her with slimy determination, not biting her but sucking at her skin with a powerful force. Inside her mind she felt a tiny thread of The Evil frantically wriggling.

++Open the way! Open the way!++

Susan reached out, gripped the leech firmly between her fingers, and yanked it from her daughter's face. Grabbing a wooden oar from an elephant-foot hatstand at the base of the stairs, Susan swung it like a club, knocking leeches out of the air and squishing them before they could reach her. Tara found something that looked like a squat baseball bat and did the same. Kyle pulled a wooden shield from the wall and hunkered down behind it, inching across the room to where Jack was grimly squashing leeches underfoot.

++Open the way! Open the way!++

Jack pulled two leeches from his neck. Instantly, the voice in his head fell silent. A wind whipped up around them, and Grandma X called over her shoulder to Jaide, "Control your Gifts!"

Grandma X was hunched over Stefano, who was rolling wildly on the floor, glowing leeches stuck to every exposed part of his body — his face, his hands, his back where his shirt had ridden up, his ankles. There were leeches on his eyes and ears, and his fingers scrabbled blindly to get a grip on their squishy bodies.

"Get them off me!" he cried. "Get away from me! Leave me alone!"

Sparks crackled from his hair and discharged into the wooden floorboards, leaving tiny scorch marks.

"Stefano, listen to me!" Grandma X was shouting at him as she played the light of her moonstone ring over him. "You have to control yourself."

"I can't — it wants me to —"

Light from the ring played across his face. The leeches on his eyes curled up and dropped off, smoking. His eyelids flickered open. Terrible whiteness swirled across his pupils.

++The way . . . must be opened.++

"It's trying to trick you," said Grandma X. "Fight it!"

His eyes cleared. "I will! I will fight it!"

Stefano raised his hands and electricity sparked between them. The leeches clinging to his palms burned instantly to ash. He cried out in triumph and the lightning sparked again, running all over his body and sending tendrils out across the room. Grandma X fell back, her hair smoking, and Jaide called out a warning.

"Hey, be careful with that!"

Stefano ignored her. He staggered to his feet, blasting leeches wherever he saw them, not caring who might be standing nearby. The sole of one of Jack's shoes caught fire when he stomped on a leech Stefano had targeted. Jaide narrowly missed a bolt aimed at a clump hanging over her head.

"Yes!" Stefano cried, his eyes turning milky again. ++Yes!++

A particularly powerful bolt illuminated a section of the wall next to an old grandfather clock, which was chiming double time. The wall glowed, and a door the twins had never seen before appeared. The handle turned and the door blew open, revealing a room large enough to contain a plinth. On the plinth was something they immediately recognized — something long and brassy that was drawing every spark of lightning toward it.

"Stefano, no!" Grandma X cried, levering herself upright with the help of a chair shaped like a dragon's mouth. Her right hand came up, moonstone glowing.

Stefano turned to her with arms outstretched and eyes almost fully white. He raised his hands. A tendril of yellow light swirled between him and Grandma X, a rush of energy shooting from her heart into his. The light of the moonstone flickered and went out, and a jagged bolt of lightning stabbed into the center of her chest. She flew backward, skidded across the ground, then lay on her side, completely still.

CHAPTER ELEVEN

THE WIND FROM ANOTHER WORLD

The twins stared at Grandma X's body in horror.

"Is she dead?" asked Jack.

"She can't be dead," Jaide touched Grandma X's temple. Her skin felt warm and vital, but that didn't mean anything. "She *can't* be, Jack!"

Suddenly Susan was beside her, reaching a hand down to take the old woman's pulse.

"She's unconscious. I think she'll be okay. But what are we going to do about *him*?"

Jaide turned to where Stefano stood, now facing the cross-continuum conduit constructor. Her Gifts rose up inside her, even more angry and powerful than they had been when they had attacked Aleksandr. This time she would not lose control of them. This time she would let them attack.

Stefano glanced at her with his Evil white eyes, and the corners of his mouth twitched in a smile. One hand pointed at her. Yellow energy flowed out of her, and all her strength drained with it. She hadn't lost her Gifts, but they could manage no more than a slight breeze to ruffle his hair. She didn't know what The Evil had done, but whatever it was, it was new and terrible.

"Jack!" she called.

Jack whipped around, and saw Stefano gloating over his powerless sister. Darkness swirled at his command and the earth quaked underfoot, but then Stefano turned his gaze to him and with a terrible wrench, all the power drained out of his body, just as it had drained out of Jaide's.

Into Stefano's.

++Thank you,++ said The Evil. **++That is exactly what we needed.++**

He turned back to the cross-continuum conduit constructor and punched the air with both fists. A bolt of lightning leaped to the metal bar, and it was so thick and powerful that for a moment Jack's sensitive eyes were blinded. All he could see was a jagged blue line across his vision. All he could smell was electricity. All he could think was: *Why did The Evil want to destroy the cross-continuum conduit constructor?*

++Yes!++ Stefano cried in The Evil's terrible voice. **++Yes!++**

Then there was a sharp thud and a cry of pain. The lightning went out, and Jack, blinking, saw Stefano slumped on the floor, holding his head, and Tara standing over him with a wooden club in her hand. Kyle stood next to her, protecting her with his shield.

"What happened?" Stefano said, blinking dazedly. "What am I doing?"

"Just you stay where you are," said Tara, hefting the club. "Zap anyone else and you'll get it right between the eyes."

Kyle shoved him with the shield for emphasis. "Wood doesn't conduct electricity, remember?"

"All right, all right," Stefano said, "but what did The Evil make me do?"

"You took our Gifts!" said Jaide.

"I'm sorry, but I didn't mean to!"

Jack looked around and wondered why the slugs had stopped attacking. There were still dozens of them on the loose, glowing and alien-looking, but apparently harmless now. He poked one with the toe of his still-smoldering shoe, and it didn't react. Ari sniffed one and all it did was curl up into a ball.

Jaide felt five tiny points of pain on her calf and looked down.

It was Kleo; her tail was swishing in agitation.

"Look at the Bridge, Jaide!"

"The what?"

Kleo pointed with one paw.

The cross-continuum conduit constructor was shining bright orange. Whatever Stefano and The Evil had done to it, with the combined strength of Grandma X and the twins, it hadn't been destroyed. It was shaking on its plinth as though trying to escape. And it was *bending* in a way that hurt Jaide's eyes. Or perhaps it was the light that was bending. Jaïde couldn't tell. Either way, she didn't think it was a good sign.

"He turned it on," she shouted over a rising hum emanating from the Bridge. "This must be the way The Evil was talking about. It wants to come through!"

They crowded together outside the door to the secret room, Cornelia flapping down to land on Jack's shoulder. The wooden frame was twisting into impossible curves, and the cross-continuum conduit constructor itself was now a brassy circle singing with golden light. In the center of the circle a vortex was forming. To Jack it felt like looking down the mouth of a hurricane. He braced himself and reached for his Gifts automatically, but they were still drained. He could only hope his strength returned in order to resist The Evil when it arrived.

Something wasn't quite right with the vortex, though. It swayed and rippled, and the whiteness at the end of the tunnel wasn't getting any closer. Maybe it hadn't had enough power from Stefano to fully open. Or maybe something was interfering with it. Either way, it didn't look stable at all. And it was *sucking* rather than *blowing*, as it should have been if The Evil was about to come through.

Deep in the heart of the vortex was a point of bright, white light.

"Charlie!" called Cornelia. "Charlie!"

The Evil wasn't trying to invade, Jack realized. It wanted to drag them in.

"Keep back," called Susan, reaching for the twins and Kyle and Tara but not having enough hands to reel them all in. "Don't get too close."

"We have to do *something*," said Jaide, retreating to search the chaos of the blue room. Where was the *Compendium*? Perhaps there was something in there that could close the vortex. Already the wall was bending around the door, and a rising wind was pulling in dust bunnies and flakes of ash.

Jack was looking worriedly at the cats. If the vortex got any stronger, they would be in trouble.

"Ari, Kleo, get out of here," he said. "We'll deal with Grandma."

Kleo nodded, seeing the sense in it immediately, but Ari's fur rose.

"I'm not a coward," he spat.

"I know, and if you had hands instead of paws to help with the lifting, you could stay," said Jack. "Wait for us outside. I'm going to try closing the door."

Ari bristled but obeyed, claws digging into the wood to stop him slipping.

"What can I do?" asked Stefano.

"Keep out of the way and don't cause any more trouble!" Jack said.

While Tara, Susan, and Kyle struggled with Grandma X's unconscious body, Jack picked up the oar his mother had dropped. Inching along the wall, his hair whipping around his face, he reached out with the oar to touch the door. Using both hands, he poked the door with the oar and swung it out from the wall. When it reached halfway, the rising vortex caught it and slammed it shut with such force it broke the door in half and ripped it off its hinges.

With a searing, crackling sound the door vanished into the spinning maelstrom.

As though emboldened by the meal, the vortex snatched the oar out of Jack's hands and might have taken him, too, had he not caught the edge of a bookcase in time and hauled himself back. The wind was so strong that for an instant his feet actually lifted off the ground.

Jaide had found the *Compendium* behind the mahogany desk, which had somehow been tipped over during the chaos. Sheltering behind the desk and gripping the folder tightly with both hands, she concentrated fiercely on the situation for two full seconds, then opened her eyes and the folder to see what it revealed.

Sealer of Bifrost Breach Takes Secret to the Grave

Great Steward Earl Henschke left no notes or sketches concerning the method by which he sealed the rent leading to the realm of The Evil. This was confirmed by his widow, who conducted a thorough search of his office in the weeks following his death. Warden Sally Henschke married the Great

*Steward, her second husband, one year earlier, and
inherited all of his effects. Speculation concerning
his methods have run rampant among the Progress
Party, with Chief Speaker Aleksandr Furmanek . . .*

"Gah!" That was no help at all.

Jaide tried again, concentrating on Professor Olafsson's
theories instead. There had to be something in there that
could help them.

This time the *Compendium* opened on a page entitled
Magical Properties of the Elements. It was written in tiny,
crabbed script that she had to peer closely at to read at all.
One line stood out:

*Copper: This most conductive metal allows the
flow of energies within our world . . . and beyond.
Instruments made of copper can be used to open
and close conduits between continuums, if properly exercised.*

That was the clue Jaide needed, and which Aleksandr
had missed. No one had known that cross-continuum conduit constructors were made of copper until they found the
one in Rourke Castle. This had to be the key.

With the *Compendium* held in one hand, she stood up
in order to shout to Jack.

The wind had risen without her realizing it. It snatched
at her, and it snatched at the *Compendium*, too, almost
ripping it from her hands. She clutched at it and barely
caught it in time. Several pages slipped free and went fluttering into the white center of the vortex.

Jack was trying on his own to drag a heavy bookcase
across the doorway, without much luck. Distantly, over the

roar of the wind, he heard his sister shouting. He glanced behind him. She was on the mezzanine floor, waving her arms.

"What?"

"Look for something made of copper!"

"Why?"

"That's how he must have closed it! She didn't give it to Aleksandr so it must still be here!"

Jack didn't know who "he" or "she" were, but he had to assume that Jaide knew what she was talking about. She had the *Compendium*, after all.

The wind snatched more pages and sucked them into the vortex.

"Stop that!" Jaide shouted, but the wind wasn't responding to her command. Either her Gift was still drained or this was a different kind of wind. *A wind from another world,* she thought with a shiver. The world of The Evil.

Several loose hats and a cloudy crystal ball followed the pages into the vortex, which only made it hungrier. A heavy fur coat flapped in next, then the Oracular Crocodile, its jaws snapping uselessly at the air. Each time the vortex absorbed something, the wind got stronger and it became harder to move around. Each time, the urgency to find a way to close the Bridge increased. What happened if it wasn't closed, wondered Jack as he rummaged through boxes and cupboards for anything made of copper. Would the entire house be sucked into the Evil Dimension? The whole world?

Tara and Kyle had successfully helped carry Grandma X out of the blue room. They returned to look for the missing copper artifact. Through the open panel where she crouched next to Grandma X, Susan urged them all to leave.

"It's not safe!"

"It really isn't," Stefano agreed. He was hanging on to the dragon chair for grim life. "Let me call Hector. He'll fix this."

"It'll take him too long to get here," said Jaide, even though she would have liked nothing more than to see her father walk in at that moment. He would know what to do. "We need to fix this ourselves and we need to do it now!"

"What about this?" Jack held up a roll of copper wire.

"Here," called Tara from the other side, clapping her hands together. "Toss one end across. We'll try to tie it up."

Jack wound one end of the wire around the grandfather clock, unwound several feet more, and tossed the roll to Tara, who did the same on her side, using the bookcase Jack had been struggling with earlier as an anchor. There was just enough to cross the doorway four times. When they'd finished, the wire was singing a series of strange, high notes. Jack stepped back to test the wind. It did seem to him that the vortex was losing some of its strength, and the white heart of the vortex appeared to have receded slightly.

But the wind was fighting back. The grandfather clock and the bookcase shuddered and rocked, yanked by the wires. The high notes became a screech, then a scream, then a series of four piercing twangs as the wire snapped, unable to bear the forces arrayed against it.

Jack and Tara fell back. The storm was more powerful than ever. A silver sword stuck in a block of timber was sucked in next, followed by a trio of flapping umbrellas. The sound of the wind was deafening. They could no longer speak over it.

Jaide could barely stand in front of the doorway, but she was determined to. She had found a large copper bowl in a chest, inscribed with symbols that might have been letters in a language she didn't understand. Hopefully *this* was the Warden artifact they needed. Cupping it with both hands, she held the base against her midriff and pointed the bowl into the vortex.

The wind made it sing, too, but with a low mournful wail, like someone blowing over the top of a giant bottle. The bowl shivered in her grip, and she felt herself being inched toward the door no matter how determinedly she pushed back. The bowl was making it worse! With a cry of frustration, she let go and dropped to the floor.

The bowl tumbled through the door and into the vortex, spinning as it went. When it hit the white heart, a shockwave rippled back up toward them, and suddenly she was hanging on for dear life, scrabbling at the floorboards for the smallest amount of grip.

Something heavy, perhaps a chest of drawers, tumbled past her, which only made the vortex hungrier. Jaide felt her hands and feet slipping on the floor. She closed her eyes and gritted her teeth and willed her Gift to respond. "Help me," she hissed with her face pressed against the floor. "You have to help me!"

Instead of her Gift, she felt a strong hand grip her wrist and pull her firmly back from the hungry doorway.

"Here!" said Stefano, pressing something into her hands. "Try this!"

Jaide looked down and saw a polished copper mirror, stained with age. There was a symbol on the back, a triangle with no equal sides. She nodded. It was worth a shot. Stefano had one elbow hooked into the balustrades of the mezzanine. The other he wrapped around her waist so she wouldn't slide. Gripping the mirror tightly in both hands, she thrust its shiny side right down the throat of the hurricane.

The effect was instantaneous. Confronted with its reflection, the vortex reeled and swayed, losing half its strength in the matter of a second, then half again. Jaide's ears were ringing from the powerful roar, but slowly she became aware of her own gasping. She felt as though she had played a hundred games of soccer in five minutes. But she kept her arms outstretched and the mirror exactly as it was. She put all her faith in it and the triangular symbol, because that was all she could do.

The hurricane became a gale, and then a stiff breeze. The flickering light from the spinning cross-continuum conduit constructor ebbed, too, and after a moment she heard a solid clang as the long, metal rod fell back onto its plinth.

She lowered the mirror and looked around. The blue room was in a state of utter devastation. Broken furniture lay everywhere. One of the chandeliers was gone. The *Compendium* lay open on its back, missing half its pages. But the crisis was over, and she sobbed with relief at the thought of it. They had beaten The Evil once again.

Pushing away from Stefano, grateful for his help but not forgetting his role in recent events, she looked around and said, "Where's Jack?"

Stefano hesitated.

"He's . . . gone."

CHAPTER TWELVE

BREACHED

For a full second, Jaide could only stare at him.

"*What?*"

"Jack was right there, and now he's not," said Stefano, pointing to the left of the now ordinary doorway. "Tara was there and Kyle was over there. The bird was here, too. They're all gone."

"*The bird* has a name," said Jaide, hurrying to the doorway and peering warily through it, into the room that contained the cross-continuum conduit constructor. The room wasn't much bigger than a closet, and apart from the conduit constructor and the plinth, it contained nothing at all. No Tara, no Kyle, no Cornelia, and no Jack.

Jaide spun around.

"Jack, if you're hiding somewhere, come out now," she shouted. "It's not funny!"

There was no reply.

"He must have —" Stefano began.

"Don't say it," she snapped at him. "This is all your fault."

"Me? It was The Evil —"

"Yes, but if you hadn't come here it wouldn't have taken you over and done all this. Jack would still be here. He wouldn't be —"

She put both hands over her mouth, unable to finish the sentence. *Trapped in the Evil Dimension.* Jack would be right here with her, where he belonged. But he wasn't. She felt like crying, screaming, and running all at once.

What if he was dead? How would she go on living?

++Jack?++

The voice in her mind made her jump, but it was only Stefano, not The Evil.

++Jack, can you hear me?++

Jaide kicked herself for not thinking of teeping earlier. Just because they were in different worlds didn't mean their minds couldn't reach out and find each other.

++Jack!++ she shouted. ++Hold on! I'll come and find you!++

She listened as hard as she could, and wondered if she heard a faint reply, right at the edge of her senses.

++. . . aide, stay where . . . dangerous . . .++

The voice was so faint she wasn't sure she was imagining it, and when she called again she heard nothing at all in reply.

Then the door at the top of the stairs was opening and Susan was leading Grandma X inside. The old woman moved slowly and weakly. Her hand shook as she gripped the banister.

The gaping hole in Jaide's chest got even wider. How was she going to tell them?

"We closed the breach," said Stefano, and she almost kicked him for the pride in his voice. This wasn't time for showing off! "It was Jaide's work, really. She found something useful in the *Compendium*. We got lucky."

Grandma X looked at the mess as she came gingerly down the short flight of stairs, leaning heavily on Susan's arm. The cats followed more lightly, exploring the rubble to see what could be salvaged.

"Are you okay?" Jaide asked Grandma X.

"I will recover. How about *you*?" she asked Stefano. "Are you feeling . . . yourself?"

"Who cares about him?" said Jaide. "Jack, Tara, and Kyle are gone and it's all because of him!"

Susan put a hand to her mouth and sat down on a wooden chest as though her legs had lost all strength. "No! They can't be!"

"What's this about Jack?" asked Ari, emerging from a tangle of chess pieces and jewelry.

"He and the others fell through before we could close the hole," Stefano said, straightening his back. Dozens of round red marks dotted his skin like pimples, where the leeches had latched on to him. "It is my fault . . . Jaide's right. The Evil used my Gift. It made me attack you. Warden, I am sorry."

He bowed his head low before Grandma X, and for a second Jaide thought he might go down on one knee. Even as she held herself back from punching him, she had to admire the way he took the blame when called upon to do so. Ari looked like he wanted to scratch the boy's eyes out. Kleo sat straight and still with her ears flat against her head, as though not wanting to hear any more.

Jaide waited to see what Grandma X said. Would she send Stefano to his room, or even farther away? Would she blast him to atoms with her silver ring?

In the end she just nodded.

"Yes, I thought it had to be something like that. You were far stronger than you had any right to be." She patted the burned patches in her hair, as though making sure there was any left. "No permanent damage was done."

"Is that it?" asked Jaide. "What are we going to do about him?"

"Don't blame Stefano because of The Evil's actions,"

Grandma X told her. "We all have moments of . . . not weakness, exactly . . . more a kind of distraction. If The Evil has a way of making us forget what is dangerous, it's only because we insist on believing that things can get better. That despite all evidence we will overcome."

She sighed, and Jaide was compelled to hug her tightly. She had never seen Grandma X looking so old and tired and . . . *defeated*.

"What are we going to do?" asked Susan. "How are we going to get them back?"

"We'll have to use the Bridge," said Stefano, pointing at the inert cross-continuum conduit constructor.

"It's not safe," said Grandma X, letting Jaide go but still keeping her arm around her. "You saw what happened when it's activated. I was charged with keeping it out of harm's way, but even so The Evil found it and used it to its own ends. Controlling it is very difficult. We can only guess what might happen if we try to use it again."

"So we don't do anything?" asked Jaide. "I know Jack's alive. I heard him. We can't leave him there, like —"

She stopped and bit her tongue.

"Like I left Lottie?" Grandma X asked her, with a renewed vigor. "If that is what's best for the world, then yes, we must do exactly that. You saw how The Evil used her against us. That apparition fooled all of us, and it fooled the alarms, too. They thought they recognized my sister and that enabled The Evil to walk right into the heart of the house. Be glad its mission was to trick one of us into opening the way, not to kill us in our sleep."

Susan's fists were clenched.

"I will not leave Jack . . . wherever he is," she said. "I will bring him back if I have to go there myself."

Jaide wanted to cheer.

"That won't be necessary," said Grandma X. "I'll talk to Aleksandr. Project Thunderclap must be testing its own Bridge. That must be what's creating these holes within the wards that The Evil is sneaking in through. At the very least, I can ask him to stop doing that."

"I thought the plan was supposed to make everyone safe," said Susan bitterly.

"It will do that eventually."

Grandma X smiled at all the anxious faces gathered around her. It was a brave effort at restoring calm, but it looked strained.

"First, let's clean up," she said. "I can't think with such a mess around me. Some of these remnants are highly valuable . . . and dangerous if left in one another's company for too long. Let's start at this end and work our way to the other side in a line. We'll also have to call Tara's and Kyle's parents, and tell them that they're staying over. That will buy us a little time."

With heavy hearts, Jaide, Susan, and Stefano helped Grandma X and her Warden Companions sort through the rubble, putting pieces together and restoring what remained to its proper place. A surprising amount was missing, ranging from the very small to the very large, and a lot had been broken. They put all the fragments in the center of the room for dealing with later. Every damaged relic aged Grandma X a little more. None of it was replaceable.

Perhaps most worrying to Jaide was the *Compendium*, which contained barely half as many pages as it had before. Was all that information lost forever? What if it got into the hands of The Evil? She didn't want to ask how bad *that* might be. Things seemed pretty bad as they were.

Then a single peal of thunder sounded outside, and the blue door that led to the front yard opened to admit Hector

Shield, looking scruffy and anxious behind his thick-rimmed glasses and floppy bangs. His jacket was smoking from the violence of his arrival.

"Dad!" Jaide dropped the feathered quills she had been collecting and ran into his arms.

"Jaide, darling girl, don't cry. It'll be all right."

That was exactly what she needed to hear, because suddenly she *was* crying — at the thought that Jack might never make it back, that he might already be dead or absorbed by The Evil, or something too horrible for her to imagine. She had heard so many times that for all troubletwisters one twin always fell, but why did it have to happen to her and Jack? Why so soon, when they had barely begun? It wasn't *fair.*

"How can you say that, Hector?" she heard her mother ask. "This is exactly what I was afraid of."

Wiping her nose, Jaide pulled away from her father.

"It's not his fault," she said. "It's The Evil's."

"But if we hadn't come here . . ." said Susan. "If we had stayed right away from all this . . ."

"It would have followed us," said Hector. "It would have happened anyway, and the kids wouldn't have been ready for it. They were always in danger, but they've learned to fight back. Jaide is still here because of that. We should be grateful for what we have."

"Forgive me for not finding that very comforting." Susan's hands were shaking. "Our son and Tara and Kyle are gone and we don't know how to get them back!"

"Jack is a troubletwister," said Hector. "He's not defenseless. He's smart and powerful. If he keeps his head, he'll be okay."

"He's my grandson," said Grandma X firmly. "Of course he'll keep his head."

Susan didn't look reassured, and neither did Stefano. Jaide felt nothing but doubt, either. Neither Hector nor Grandma X had seen the power of the vortex. No one had ever been to the Evil Dimension and returned. Who knew what it was like over there? It might already be too late.

Stefano had been hanging back from the huddled family, and only now spoke, hesitantly, from the mezzanine where he had been attempting to restore order to the desk.

"I'm sorry I let you down, Hector."

"Don't be." Jaide's father let go of Jaide and stepped up the short flight to take him by the shoulders. "You passed the second test. You fought The Evil and survived. There may be much left to learn and do, yes, but you are still alive and still willing, yes?"

"Yes, sir."

"Then let's put this behind us and move forward. As my father used to say, you don't boil water by staring at the kettle — unless you have a pair of Cuthbert's Superluminary Goggles, in which case you very well might."

Stefano didn't smile, but he nodded and managed to partially wipe the hangdog expression from his face.

"Putting on the kettle is an excellent idea," said Grandma X. "Let's go upstairs and I'll make us all some healing hot chocolate. There's nothing we can do for Jack right now, except have faith in him. I'm sure he's doing everything in his power to keep himself and the others safe."

Susan nodded, although she looked about as happy about it as Jaide felt. Without looking at Hector, she turned and led the way out of the blue room, followed by the cats, Hector, and Grandma X.

Jaide snagged Stefano by the sleeve as he went by.

"Not so fast," she whispered to him. "If Grandma thinks I'm going to sit around while Jack gets himself killed or worse, she doesn't know me *at all*."

"What are you going to do?" he hissed back. "You can't open the Bridge again. It's too dangerous. Besides, I don't know how The Evil did it. You could make things even worse by trying."

"I know," she said. That was a real problem. "But we can get around that."

"*We?*" he repeated weakly.

"That's right," she said. "I know exactly how I'm going to rescue Jack. And you're going to help me do it."

CHAPTER THIRTEEN
SURFING THE HURRICANE

Cornelia was the first to go, snatched from her perch on the cage and sucked with a drawn-out squawk into the vortex. Kyle tried to catch her as she went by, but missed, and the one hand he had wrapped around a table leg wasn't enough to hold him secure. He slipped sideways, lost his grip, and then fell after Cornelia into the whirlwind.

"Jack!" Tara cried, and the vortex, inflamed by the sudden intake of matter, reached out to snatch her next. Jack braced himself against the grandfather clock and kicked out across the doorway, hoping to throw both of them back out of the terrible current. But he wasn't strong enough. Their hands had barely touched when the wind caught them both and pulled them in.

Tumbling head over heels, they whooshed separately down the vortex's spinning throat, followed by the tapestry that hid the door to the inside of the house, a four-drawer bureau, and two oak chests. Jack closed his eyes tightly to stop himself from being sick. Unlike Jaide, he found carnival rides nauseating and had actually thrown up once, although that might have been more because of all the cotton candy and donuts he had eaten beforehand than because of the ride itself. This was much worse than that time. He felt like a bug being swirled down a drain. A very small bug in a very big drain.

The thought of what might be waiting for them at the other end only made him feel sicker. No voices taunted them. The Evil didn't need to bother with that. They were heading right down its throat. If he didn't do something about that soon, they were all going to die.

Jack forced his eyes open. Tara was falling next to him with her eyes tightly shut. He couldn't see Kyle or Cornelia for all the junk from the blue room. He had read a book once about a ship being sucked into a giant whirlpool and broken to pieces. He wondered if it had looked like this on the way to the bottom of the ocean.

This wreckage heading for the Evil Dimension was no ordinary wreckage. Grandma X only collected things imprinted with Warden abilities. There might be something that could help them. But how long did he have? The only other time he had used a Bridge had been to cross from Rourke Castle into the pocket universe where the Card of Translocation was hidden. That journey had been almost instantaneous. Wherever the Evil Dimension was, it was clearly a lot farther away.

Jack snatched a coin out of the swirling wind. It was triangular with a small hole in the center. He didn't recognize the name of the country. Holding it tightly in his palm, he willed it to do something, anything.

All that happened was another coin appearing in the vortex next to him. Jack shrugged and put the first coin in his pocket, thinking it a useful trick even if he couldn't spend the money back home.

He felt a bump against his shoulders and twisted around mid-tumble. It was a small wooden statue with mother-of-pearl eyes. When he captured it, he heard a voice speaking to him in a language he couldn't understand.

The next thing to come within arm's reach was a pair

of sunglasses that enabled him to see the view through the back of his head. Useful in some circumstances, he supposed, but not right then.

A hand clutched his shoulder.

"What are you doing?"

His heart skipped a beat. It was Tara.

"Trying to find something that might help us," he said.

"What about this?" She offered him an umbrella she clutched tightly in one hand. "I grabbed it to hit the things that'll be waiting for us. And in case it's raining."

Jack took it from her and hefted it. The umbrella was old and quite heavy. He sensed something powerful about it, but couldn't immediately work out what that might be. Maybe it brought rain. Or maybe it just rained on the person holding it. Wardens probably loved practical jokes as much as anyone.

He fiddled with the latch. When it swooshed open, the umbrella caught the wind and snapped his arm out straight in front of him. Tara grabbed him before he could be swept away and they were dragged along behind the umbrella like an extreme variation of Mary Poppins.

He considered letting go before his arm came out of its socket. But when he pulled back on the handle, he felt something shift. Not the umbrella itself, but the air around it. It was as though the open umbrella was fixed in the wind, and twitching the handle made the whirlwind change course.

That gave him a thought. If he couldn't stop the vortex, maybe he could change where it was taking them — perhaps somewhere other than right down The Evil's throat.

He wiggled the handle and felt the vortex wiggle in sympathy. But not by much. If he wanted to be sure of avoiding The Evil, he wanted to give himself as wide a margin as possible.

"Hang on tight," he told Tara. She wrapped both her arms around his chest from behind, and he gripped the umbrella with both hands. "Let's see what this does."

He wrenched the handle with all his strength. The vortex howled and bucked, but he felt it shift even more and so he wrenched the handle again, assuming that any change in direction was a good thing.

He knew he was making progress when The Evil broke its silence.

++Do not fight us, troubletwister! It will make no difference to your fate.++

That only made Jack fight harder. As the wreckage shifted around them, Tara braced herself against a chest of drawers and he wrenched the umbrella harder still.

Something squawked "Hard to starboard!" in his ear, and suddenly Cornelia was with them. Kyle wasn't far behind, leapfrogging from one piece of floating furniture to another until he was astride the chest of drawers with them, gripping the handle and adding his weight to the magical wind-steering umbrella.

"How did you know we were here?" asked Jack as they wrestled with the vortex.

"I didn't," Kyle said with a grin. "I was just trying to climb back higher, and there you were."

Jack glanced behind him and saw nothing but darkness. Ahead was nothing but white, growing brighter by the second. He felt the end coming near.

"Pull harder," he said, pushing against the chest of drawers with all his strength.

Cornelia walked up Jack's arm and took up the cry, tugging on the handle with her beak for emphasis. "Heave away! Haul away! Set course for Charlie!"

"Who's Charlie?" asked Tara.

"I'm guessing it must be Lottie," said Jack as he pulled. "Grandma called the thing that looked like her Charlotte, which must be her full name."

++You cannot escape us, troubletwister. You and your friends will join us soon. It is your destiny!++

Jack hoped very much that his destiny was to get back home, and pulled harder than ever to make sure of it.

Around them, the vortex flexed and shook. The umbrella began to smoke. Jack gritted his teeth as the handle grew hot in his hands, but he refused to let go. Stark white light rose up around them. Any second he expected to see the terrible eyes of The Evil surrounding them.

Then suddenly the vortex blew itself out. They tumbled onto a powdery white surface — Jack, Tara, Kyle, Cornelia, and the chest of drawers, all rolling head over heels until they came to a halt, their arms and legs tangled up, and Jack practically upside down, with his back against something soft.

He rolled over and stood up, holding the umbrella in front of him with both hands, ready for anything, or at least hoping he looked as though he might be. Quickly, he took in his immediate surroundings. The soft thing behind him was a dune. The white surface was sand, as pale as day-old snow, but warm. Wreckage from the blue room surrounded them, in shallow craters they'd made upon hitting the sand. Dead gray trees reached for the sky like skeletal hands. Not far from their landing site was the huge, curving rib cage of a beast that had died long ago, bleached as white as chalk.

The sky was yellow. There were two suns hanging high above. The horizon was misty and dark to their left and there were what looked like hills to the right, but Jack didn't dwell on that for longer than a second. Kyle was dancing up and down, waving his hands in the air and scaring Cornelia.

"I don't believe it," Kyle cried.

"What?" said Tara, standing up in a shower of sand. "What is it?"

"We're on an alien planet, that's what!"

"How can you tell?"

"The sky, the suns, the way I can jump heaps higher than I could before —"

"It doesn't matter where we are," said Jack, feeling a surge of alarm that made him want to curl up somewhere shady and cover his head. He could deal with an Evil Dimension; an Evil Planet was something else entirely. "As long as we're all . . . wait, where's Cornelia?"

He jumped as the macaw landed on his shoulder. She rubbed his ear with her feathered head and clucked.

"Charlie," she said.

"Is she here, Cornelia?" Jack asked her. "Can you sense her somehow?"

She cocked her head, then bobbed it twice. Jack didn't know how that was possible, or why it was possible, but at that moment he wasn't worried about an explanation.

"Will you go find her for us?" he asked. "Make sure she's here, then come back and get us?"

Cornelia bobbed twice more, then took off in a startling rush of wings.

"Good luck!" Jack called after her.

Her answering squawk was lost as she flapped off into the distance, flying even faster than usual in the lighter gravity.

"That storm is getting closer," said Kyle. "An *alien* storm. Awesome!"

Jack's eyes were drawn to the dark patch on the horizon. It seemed to be changing shape.

"That's not a storm," he said. "We have to get moving."

"You think that's The Evil?" asked Tara.

"I think that's where we were supposed to land." Jack swallowed, trying not to imagine what that would have been like. He had other things to think about, like Tara and Kyle. He was the troubletwister. He was responsible for them. "We've got to get away while we can. Cornelia will find us like she'll find Lottie."

She has to, he said to himself. *What other hope do we have?*

"What about all this stuff?" asked Kyle. "That umbrella saved us back there. Maybe something else here could, too."

"Yeah, good thinking," said Tara. She started opening the drawers and looking inside. "There are clothes in here. We can take pants and tie up the legs. Then we can use them as sacks to carry the small stuff."

"Neat idea," said Kyle. "And I saw some hats. We'll need them to keep the sun off."

"There's a sword somewhere; I'm sure of it. . . ."

While his friends excitedly rummaged through the wreckage, Jack put a hand to his temple. He could hear a voice calling him from far away.

++Jack? Jack, can you hear me?++

It was Stefano! He had been so busy thinking about survival that he had forgotten about everyone left behind. Jaide hadn't followed him here, so that meant she must have found a way to close the vortex before the entire world was sucked into it. *Good for her,* he thought. Jaide never shied away from a challenge, even if it did mean they were now separated.

Jaide's voice came next.

++Jack! Hold on! I'll come and find you!++

He concentrated on teeping back to her.

++Jaide, stay where you are. Look after Grandma. It's dangerous here. I'll call you back when I can.++

He listened and listened for a reply, but nothing came. Did that mean she had heard him or not?

"Jack? We're ready."

He opened his eyes and gaped at his friends.

Tara was wearing the metal chest plate from a suit of gold armor under a frilly white hat and what Jack initially took to be a cloak, but was in fact a pair of pants tied at the ankles and dangling down her back. The waist of the pants was also tied shut, and it had been filled with all the junk she had managed to scramble out of the sand, so it jingled when it moved. In her left hand she held a sword, point down like a walking stick.

Kyle was wearing a bearskin coat with its head hanging down his back. He had a bulging sweater tied around his waist and a deerstalker cap on his head. The wooden oar Jack's mother had used to hit Stefano on the head was tucked into his sweater-belt. In his other hand he held the umbrella Jack had used to guide the vortex, opened to keep the sun off his head.

"You'd better get a move on, Jack," he said. "That storm's getting closer, and I don't think it's bringing rain. We need shelter, and if this really is a desert, we're going to need water soon. That's what I learned in Scouts. Water first, worry about the monsters later."

He grinned, and Jack couldn't help but grin back. He might be stuck in the realm of The Evil with no obvious way to get home, but at least he wasn't alone.

The black stain now covered much of the horizon. Jack

hurriedly rummaged through the remaining wreckage and found a broad-brimmed cap with a feather sticking out of it, a wickedly curved bone four feet long with a natural handle at one end (he suspected that had been in the ground already and wasn't part of Grandma X's inventory), and an embroidered sack into which he put as many interesting items as he could find, including dozens of loose pages that appeared to have been ripped from the *Compendium.*

In a cigar box he found several small brooches of a type he recognized: Grandma X had stuck them on him and his sister once to protect and hide them from The Evil. The protection wasn't total, but it could make all the difference in this terrible place. He pinned two to his T-shirt, gave three each to Tara and Kyle, and kept another for Cornelia. If he bent the pin far enough, it would go around her leg without being too tight.

As he considered taking the brass bowl to catch any rain that might come their way, he heard a familiar chattering noise coming from under the upside-down dragon chair. Tipping the chair out of the way, he found a long ivory skull staring up at him from the sand with glowing red eyes, its jaws clacking anxiously.

"Don't want to be left behind, eh?" Jack told the Oracular Crocodile. "I'll take you if you tell me everything you know about this place without trying to bite my finger off."

"Realm of The Evil, very dangerous," it chattered.

"I mean something I don't already know."

The chattering stopped for a second, then resumed.

"Run?"

Jack reached around the eager jaws to pick up the skull and put it in his sack. He wasn't going to leave the Oracular

Crocodile behind for The Evil, even if it wasn't being very helpful.

"All right," he said, "I'm ready."

"'Bout time." Tara hefted the sword. "Hills, ho!"

"I don't think they're hills," said Kyle, squinting. "I think that's a city."

Jack also squinted at the horizon, but he couldn't make out any details. Maybe he *did* need glasses, as Susan sometimes told him. But his ears were fine, and they were telling him that the rising rumble coming from the direction of The Evil was definitely something to get away from, and fast.

CHAPTER FOURTEEN

SYMPATHY FOR THE EVIL

Through the open kitchen door, Jaide could hear the adults arguing.

"What does it hurt to ask?" Susan was saying. "I'm sure Aleksandr isn't the monster you make him out to be."

"He's not a monster," said Hector. "He's just determined to do what he thinks is right."

"But how can he not think this is right? There are *children* over there now. Can't you convince him that we have to rescue them before his people cut them off forever?"

"Project Thunderclap will only work if The Evil doesn't get wind of it first. That's how he and the Hawks will see it."

"Then he *is* a monster," said Susan, her voice catching. "They're all monsters, everyone who's working for him. . . ."

"Can I just remind you that *I'm* working for him, too?"

"Aleksandr's thoughts have ever been of the greater good, and nothing else," said Grandma X. It was hard to tell if she was trying to soothe Susan or agreeing with her. "He wouldn't rescue his own daughter if she was in Jack's position."

"So what do we do to help him?" asked Susan.

"He is not helpless," Grandma X said, "and Lottie is there, too. They are both resourceful. Together, I believe they will find a way."

Susan's fist hit the table with a loud bang. "I'm supposed to go to work tomorrow. How can I do that before we get Jack, Tara, and Kyle back? How can I do anything?"

"Yes. I'll be doing everything I can, given the restraints I am under. A Warden's promise is binding. . . ."

"I think that's our cue," whispered Jaide to Stefano. "They could be at this for hours."

She and Stefano inched past the doorway, into the laundry room where the bikes were kept.

"Ahem," said a feline voice from behind them. "Where do you think you're off to?"

"It's okay, Ari," said Jaide, turning. She had the excuse ready. "We're going to check the wards."

"Now? At this time of night?"

"It's not that late. And there's no trace of The Evil at the moment. I just want to make sure that's not how it's getting in."

"I'm going to check with your grandmother."

The sound of raised voices made him pause in mid-step.

"On second thought, I'll just get Kleo."

He scampered off, and Jaide and Stefano continued untangling the bikes. There were just two of them, but until they were separated it seemed like there were eight wheels, five handlebars, and at least six pedals to negotiate.

The two cats returned with Kleo in the lead.

"I understand that you, Jaide, have been inducted into the full knowledge of the wards of Portland," she said. "What about Stefano?"

"Well," said Jaide, "he did pass the second Examination, and you wouldn't want me riding around on my own, would you?"

Kleo was forced to concede that last point.

"If you discover anything at all, you'll call."

"Yes," Jaide said, tapping the pocket containing her phone and tapping her head, too. Thanks to the ability to teep, she would never be out of touch again. "I won't take on anything alone, I promise. My Gifts are still feeling weak."

Kleo studied both troubletwisters with cool, appraising eyes. "Very well. I will inform your grandmother when she is less . . . busy."

"Thank you, Kleo. We just can't stand sitting around doing nothing, that's all."

"I agree," said Ari with a flick of his tail. "Maybe I'll come with you."

"You can't," said Kleo. "Warden Companions are not normally privy to the knowledge of the wards."

"I know, but that doesn't stop me *wanting* to know."

"Ari, you are incorrigible. Did your oath mean anything to you at all?"

Sensing another argument on the way, Jaide took the opportunity to open the back door.

"Bye, Kleo. We'll be back as soon as we can."

Jaide wrestled her uncooperative bike out into the night air, and Stefano followed. He was too big for Jack's bike, and his knees stuck out at an odd angle.

"You make it look easy," he said as they pedaled out of earshot. "I've never tried to talk my way past Hector like that."

Jaide looked both ways and turned onto Parkhill Street. "We don't do it very often. Only when we absolutely have to."

"Even so, Santino wouldn't let me. He's such a goody-goody. His secondary Gift is the same as Aleksandr's — that is, to make people do as they're told. He just hates it when I . . ."

He trailed off with a furious expression. Jaide studied him out of the corner of her eye, while avoiding potholes in the lane.

"What happened in the blue room?" she asked, deciding to take a chance. He *owed* her. "When The Evil drained my Gift, how did it do that?"

His expression turned inward. "That was me," he said. "I mean, I didn't do it, but The Evil was using my secondary Gift. I'm not very strong, not normally, but I can make myself a lot stronger by stealing power from other Wardens. That's how The Evil drained you, Jack, and your grandmother, and punched a full-on hole to its home. It's all my fault."

"Having a Gift isn't your fault," she said. "None of us chose them. And I guess they don't choose us, either. They just happen to us, just like you happened to be there when The Evil needed you. It saw an opportunity, that's all."

He nodded but didn't seem terribly reassured.

"It's still stealing," he said. "And stealing is wrong."

"Lying is wrong, too," she said, "but sometimes you absolutely have to."

"Like back there."

"Yup." She tried to sound nothing but certain as they turned onto Dock Road. They were halfway to the oval. It wasn't too late to go back.

"Sometimes I wonder how different we are from The Evil," Stefano said, his face shadowed and brooding.

That shocked her. "We're nothing *like* The Evil!"

"Sure we are. We keep secrets, we steal people's memories, we don't fit in —"

"Yes, but not because we *want* to. If The Evil wasn't trying to take over the world, we wouldn't need to fight it!"

"What if it's the other way around?" he asked.

She couldn't believe what she was hearing. Surely no one could think that the Wardens were the bad guys after all the terrible things The Evil had done. The *Compendium* was full of them, pages and pages of atrocious tricks and schemes and lives lost trying to push it back. For thousands of years, The Evil had shown itself to be nothing but . . . well . . . *evil*.

Looked at that way, Jaide could totally understand Aleksandr's determination to ensure his plan succeeded. If it wasn't *her* brother and *her* friends trapped in the Evil Dimension, she might have been willing to make a small sacrifice in order to ensure the safety of everyone else.

But it was, and she wasn't. And as they pedaled across the grass to the now fully erected tent, where a Warden disguised as a security guard flagged them down, she knew exactly what to say.

"I'm Jaide Shield and this is Stefano Battaglia," she told the guard. "We're lightning wielders, and we're volunteering for Project Thunderclap."

Aleksandr interviewed them personally, scowling at Jaide like a moody lion from the other side of a metal desk. His office was a tent within the main tent. The entire space had been divided into many different sections. Through the flimsy canvas walls Jaide could hear hammering and Wardens shouting orders. There was a lot going on at a rapid, frenzied pace.

"Why are you here?" Aleksandr asked them.

"Like I told the guy outside," Jaide said, "we want to help you get rid of The Evil. And you need all the help you can get, right? It's not going to be easy."

"We need Wardens, not troubletwisters." His scowl

deepened until his eyes practically disappeared into his eyebrows. "You are not disciplined enough. Have you forgotten what happened during the Grand Gathering?"

"No, but you see, here's the thing." Jaide had known that he would bring up the Grand Gathering, and she hadn't known how to handle that until the conversation with Stefano on the way there. "You don't need me to be disciplined, because you've got Stefano here. He's a year older than me and a lot more disciplined. And he's a lightning wielder, too. *And* he's got a Gift that can take my strength into him. All I have to do is be there and he can do all the work."

"Hmmm." Aleksandr made a steeple out of his fingers. "That is an interesting suggestion. You have been training under Hector Shield, Stefano, is that correct?"

Stefano jumped a little at Jaide's side.

"Yes, sir."

"And it is true that you have this Gift of which Jaide speaks?"

"Yes, sir, it is. I mean, I do."

He shot Jaide a look, as though she had betrayed a confidence. She just shrugged. He hadn't said it was a secret, and besides, lives were at stake.

"Interesting, most interesting." Aleksandr nodded. "Very well. You may consider yourselves members of Project Thunderclap — provisionally, of course, subject to review prior to the event." He indicated an aide-de-camp standing by the doorway. "Marjorie here will provide you with identity tokens and give you the tour. Be sure," he said, with a pointed glare at Jaide, "that you touch nothing and interfere with no one. You will be called upon when needed. That is all."

They stood, and Marjorie, a skinny woman with dark

hair pulled back in a bun, waved them through the flap of canvas that stood in for a door.

Jaide expelled a deep breath. They had made it. So far, her plan was working.

Marjorie led them along a narrow hallway full of bustling people, explaining to them as they went to get their tokens. "The tokens mark you as members of the Project and give you access to the proper interior of the tent. Anyone who's not a Warden or a member will just see a circus tent, a circus tent that's closed so they can't get in. And even if they do get a look somehow, they'll just see sawdust and stuff. The Evil has spies everywhere. We can't be too careful."

She took them to a small room, like a sick bay. The tokens were coin-size metal badges that were permanently affixed to their scalps, so that their hair would fall over them, hiding them from view. Jaide rubbed at hers, unnerved by the new, alien bump. It didn't hurt or even itch, but when she tugged on it a sharp pain went through her skin right into her brain. If there was a traitor in Project Thunderclap, there was no way he or she could remove the token and give it to someone else.

Jaide wondered if she qualified as a traitor. Perhaps she did. She certainly had no intention of letting Aleksandr's plan proceed without a hitch. Stefano didn't say anything, but she could tell by his burning gaze that he was thinking the same thing.

Next came the tour. Marjorie was brisk and perfunctory, showing them through the labyrinthine halls of the tent — which seemed much bigger on the inside than it ought to be — naming each room they passed with very little explanation.

"Mess," she said. "Sick bay. Orderly Room. Quartermaster. Ironmonger."

Jaide did her best to memorize it all, but soon became overwhelmed. This was a much bigger endeavor than she had imagined. Without Marjorie, she would have quickly become lost.

Then, over the banging and clanging of industry, she heard a familiar, strident voice rising up in protest.

"My theories require no explanation at all," it declared, "being perfectly evident in the workings of nature. Your contraptions, on the other hand, are inexplicable to the extreme! Just look at this device. Is it a window or a painting? It cannot decide, and until it does I'm afraid it will not make any kind of sense to me, or to anyone sensible. Take this computational confounder away and bring me a scribe with a reliable quill! Then we will begin to make progress."

Jaide hid a smile. Professor Olafsson hadn't changed one bit.

She stopped and turned her head, using her ears to determine where the sound of his voice came from. There was a door just along the hallway with a four-pointed star painted on the canvas. That was the place.

"What's over here?" she said, pulling away from Marjorie and heading in that direction. If she could just make *sure* it was him, everything would be much simpler.

"Jaidith!" called a voice from behind her. "What are you doing here?"

She stopped and turned on the spot. "Dad?"

Hector was hurrying down the hallway. He looked furious.

"I came as soon as I heard," he said. "Kleo told us you were checking the wards, and then Aleksandr called to get our approval. He says you've volunteered. What on earth are you thinking?"

Jaide cursed Aleksandr. She hadn't thought that he would check with her parents.

"I . . . that is, *we* wanted to do something to help," she said, which was technically true, but she didn't think technicalities would matter if he found out what she was really doing.

"You, too?" Hector asked Stefano.

Stefano swallowed, then nodded. "Yes, sir," he said in exactly the tone he had used with Aleksandr.

Hector took Jaide by the arm, and although her Gifts twitched, she let herself be pulled down the hallway. She didn't want her father to know what she was really thinking, and if he saw the Professor he might guess.

"I understand that you're upset, Jaide, but this isn't going to fix anything."

"Isn't it?" she said for the benefit of the people around them. "Jack is gone. Lottie is gone. How many other people are we going to lose before The Evil is stopped?"

"Yes, that is true, but —"

"And you're helping, too, aren't you, Dad?" she said. "You're a volunteer as well?"

He rubbed at the back of his neck, and she saw clearly through the hair there a token that matched her own.

"Well, that's true, too, but —"

"So what's the problem? You'll be here to keep an eye on me, and together we'll get rid of The Evil forever."

She smiled her most winning smile.

He sagged. Hector could never stay angry at his children for long.

"All right, but you've got to come home now. Your mother is beside herself, as I would be, too, in her shoes. She wants to take you with her to Scarborough tomorrow morning, and it's all I can do to convince her that you'll be much safer here, inside the wards, than you would be out there. You, too, Stefano. Come on. It's been a long day, and you have a long day ahead tomorrow."

For a moment Jaide's mind was empty of anything but the plan.

"Just school and soccer practice, and I can skip those if they need help here."

"You're forgetting the Examination," Hector said. "The third round may be the worst of all, and you're not getting out of it that easily."

Jaide and Stefano exchanged a look of shared surprise.

"The worst of all?" Stefano croaked.

"Seriously?" Jaide said.

"Yes, now get a move on before your mother turns up in the helicopter."

Hector led them out of the tent to where the old family car was waiting for them by the oval, Jaide's Gifts stirring nervously for the first time since Stefano had stolen her power.

CHAPTER FIFTEEN
WHACK-A-JACK

Jack!"

Tara's voice was accompanied by the high-pitched ringing of steel. Jack ducked and the sword swished over his head, missing him by a hair.

"What are you doing?" He spun to face her, raising his improvised bone-scimitar. He didn't want to use it, even if she had been turned Evil, but he had to defend himself somehow.

"Look." She pointed at his feet, where something twitched in the sand, cut neatly in half by the impossibly sharp blade.

He squatted to look at it more closely. It was a bug with six wings and way too many legs. A long stinger curled and uncurled from its head. It had four eyes, and all of them were glowing white. As Jack watched, they flickered and went out. The stinger stopped moving. The thing was dead.

"Yuck," said Kyle. "Where did that come from?"

"It was right above you, Jack," Tara explained. "I thought it was going to bite your neck."

Jack stood up and brushed himself off.

"I'm glad you saw it," he said. "Thanks."

"Do you think there are more out there like that?" asked Kyle, sweeping the sky with a nervous gaze.

"Let's not stick around to find out," said Tara, pointing at the structures ahead. "Onward!"

They resumed their march across the sand. It was less a march and more of a trudge, Jack reflected, even though he did feel slightly less heavy in the realm of The Evil. The sand was too soft to properly walk on, and they were getting tired and very thirsty on top of the dozens of aches and pains caused by their crash landing. But their destination was slowly getting closer. Jack was certain now that the shapes ahead weren't mountains, as Kyle had suggested. They were lumpy and cylindrical, lots of them all joined together and bulging up out of the earth, with dark openings that looked like doors or windows dotting their sides. They could have been buildings, but they could equally have been giant anthills. Jack didn't know which possibility made him more anxious.

Either way, he and the others needed to get out of the bright daylight. One of the suns had set, but a third one, the hottest of them all, had taken its place. The only shade he had was that beneath his hat. The huge number of bones sticking out of the desert sand was testimony to how often things died here. Not all of the bones were of giant beasts. A lot of them were human-size, but nothing at all like human skeletons.

Kyle and Jack fell in behind Tara, who was setting a brisk pace in the lead.

"Did you see the bug's eyes?" asked Kyle. "It was Evil, wasn't it?"

Jack nodded. "That's how it looked to me."

"Do you think everything's Evil here?"

"I guess so. Except for us, and maybe Lottie, if she really is here."

He had begun to wonder about that, now that he had seen the place. If it was all like this, dry and dead, it would be a miracle if anyone had survived for so many years. And thus far there had been no sign of her. Cornelia was still missing. Jack hoped she was faring better than they were.

"Does this mean The Evil knows where we are?" Kyle asked.

Jack hadn't wanted to raise that possibility. Any small part of The Evil was connected to the rest, so whatever the bug had seen, the rest of The Evil knew it now, too.

"I think we should save our breath for keeping up with Tara," he said.

Kyle grunted and put the umbrella up again. As they passed over a stony surface, he reached down and picked up two pebbles.

"Here," he said, giving one of them to Jack. "Suck on it. It'll stop you from feeling so thirsty."

Jack warily put the stone in his mouth. It was hot and tasted like ash.

"You learned that in Scouts, too?" he asked.

"Yes. Here's hoping it'll work on an alien planet."

They killed four more bug things before they reached the base of the "city." Two were Evilflies, as Kyle dubbed them, with scissorlike pincers. He smacked one of them out of the sky with his oar. Jack burned the other. Another consisted of a long wormlike thing with dozens of legs that rose up hissing from the ground in Tara's path and that she squashed before it could bite her. She called it an Evilpede. The last looked like a small tumbleweed that had rolled across their path, and hadn't seemed alive until it had unfolded in front of Kyle and tried to grab hold of his leg with razor-tipped, twiglike legs. Tara sliced the "Evilweed" into bits, revealing two Evil eyes at its heart. Several Evilweed flocks lurked in the distance, shadowing them, but none had approached any closer, perhaps warned off by the death of the first.

Behind them, the black cloud was looming larger and more threateningly than ever.

"We made it," Kyle gasped as they staggered toward the base of the nearest "building." There was one opening at ground level. Jack headed for it without hesitation.

Tara pulled him back. "Shouldn't we at least check to see what's in there first?"

"I can see just fine," he said. "The light's bright enough. There's nothing waiting for us."

"Maybe you can see," said Kyle, "but it's pitch-black to me."

Only then did Jack realize that his Gift had returned, which was a surprise because he was normally least powerful during the daylight, and here, with three suns, there might never be full dark. It was also surprising because he hadn't stopped to wonder if his Gift would even work in the Evil Dimension. If he had, he would have assumed it wouldn't have worked, with the rest of the Wardens so far away.

That was a relief. But his friends would remain in the dark if they went any farther, reliant on him to guide them around.

"Grab some branches," he said, pointing at one of the dead trees they had passed. "They look like they'll burn. I'll light them and then you'll be able to see." One of the items he had retrieved from the sand was a yellowing magnifying glass that focused light much more intensely than a clear one.

His friends did as he suggested, Tara hacking at several thick limbs with her sword, and Kyle putting them in the pockets of his enormous coat. Jack lit two, and when the brands were burning with a crackling, red light, they went inside.

What they found was a vast space crisscrossed by ramps and landings with few level floors. It looked more grown than built, and there were signs that it had once been inhabited by something very much like people . . . so it wasn't a hive for giant ants. There were seats and tables carved into the walls, and several knobby things that might have been tools scattered on the uneven floors. Of the owners, there was no sign.

Several levels up, in the cool heart of the vast structure they found a chamber filled with living plants, where condensation dripped down tall, funnel-like rock chimneys into narrow channels that led from planter to planter. It had once been a garden, perhaps a farm, but now it was a jungle, containing hundreds of drooping, thick-stemmed plants that looked more like cactuses than trees. Some had thorns, some flowers. Bulging, brightly colored fruit hung rotting everywhere they looked.

The smell was awful.

"But water, that's good, right?" said Jack.

"If we can drink it." Tara ran her fingers along one of the gutters and used the droplets she collected to barely dampen her lips. She made a face. "I've tasted worse. But there's not much of it."

"It's all around us." Kyle went scurrying between the planters, looking for a particularly fat stem. "Tara, cut this one, right here."

As Tara approached with her sword, the plant began to twitch and rock, bringing branches down in an attempt to enclose them.

"Stop that!" Kyle bashed it with the burning brand. The tree hissed and growled. "Stop being so Evil!"

"You *are* trying to chop it down," said Jack, unsure why he was defending a plant growing in the realm of The

Evil. Maybe because it was powerless and couldn't help if The Evil had taken it over.

"Not chop it," said Kyle. "*Tap* it."

He put his finger where he wanted Tara to use the sword, and she drew the tip along its skin, revealing thick, green flesh that dripped moisture.

"Now drink," he said.

"Are you sure it's safe?" Tara asked.

"No, but we have to drink, and plants like this filter out all the bad stuff. Who would put plants that didn't in their home, anyway? If you want to, though, we could find a pot and boil it —"

"No, it's okay." Tara bent over and took a deep sip from the weeping plant. "Mmmm, it's sweet."

They took turns, and when the flow began to lessen, they went to another plant. Around them, the jungle clicked and swayed, and Jack knew their presence wasn't welcome. When Tara declared that they had to move on as soon as they were full, Kyle complained about being tired, but Jack knew she was right.

"We've seen plants and bugs," he said. "There could be much worse out there."

"If there is, why hasn't it attacked us?"

"I don't know. Because it's getting ready?"

"I'm not sticking around to find out," said Tara, picking her brand up from where she'd stuck it in a planter's black soil.

"But where are we going to go?" asked Kyle.

"Let's take a look. There must be a window around here somewhere."

They wound their way through the jungle until they saw a gleam of daylight in the distance. It was a window, and they crowded up to it to see what lay across the desert, if anything lay there at all.

"Uh-oh," said Tara.

Jack's stomach sank. An army of Evilweeds, Evilpedes, and Evilflies was massing at the base of the "building," rolling, crawling, and flying in from all directions to form a semicircular wall that was already several yards deep. Sickly white eyes gleamed from every one of them. Many of the creatures had merged to form larger agglomerations — creatures as large as dogs with six legs, shapeless blobs that extruded tentacles to roll themselves along, even two-legged monstrosities with multiple heads and arms. Insect limbs clicked and chattered as the host assembled.

"I'm sorry," Jack said.

"Sorry about what?" said Tara.

"Sorry you're here. You shouldn't be caught up in this. Even if we can escape The Evil here, we've still got to get home before Project Thunderclap does its thing. If Jaide and I hadn't ever come to Portland —"

"We wouldn't be having this much fun," Tara said fiercely, slapping the flat of the sword into the palm of her hand. "Ouch," she added.

Kyle laughed, and said, "Yeah, this is way better than school."

"Do you think it's daytime back home, too?" asked Tara. "That's what I think."

"It's always daytime here. Maybe that means there's always school. No wonder The Evil's so grouchy."

Jack forced a smile. He suspected his friends' jokes were intended to make him feel better, and was grateful for it. Tara might not be faking her new bravado, but he knew

Kyle was as nervous as he was. Kyle's gaze kept flicking back to the window and the view outside.

"Looks like The Evil is going to wait us out," said Jack. "It thinks it has us trapped."

"Doesn't it?" said Kyle. "Eventually we'll need food, and not even my scoutmaster could tell me anything about which alien plants are safe to eat."

"I'm not giving up," said Tara fiercely. "They're only bugs."

"Yes, but there's *lots* of bugs," said Kyle, swallowing. "How are we going to fight a planet full of them?"

"With our brains," said Jack. "We have three heads to The Evil's one . . . err . . . I guess it has a lot more, technically, all joined together. But we've got *smarter* brains."

"And we have all the stuff we collected from the wreckage," said Tara, jingling her sack. "Don't forget that. The Evil will rue the day it messed with us."

Jack had never heard anyone actually use the word *rue* before, although he had read it plenty of times. It made him smile.

Kyle smiled, too, but not from anything either Tara or Jack had said. "And we have her," he said, pointing toward a blue dot flying across the yellow sky toward them.

Cornelia.

Jack felt a rush of relief that the old bird was safe. Maybe, just maybe, she had found Lottie and could tell them where to go.

Cornelia was parched, and needed to drink from a plant before she could do more than croak. Kyle pinned the brooch to her ankle and looked after her while Tara and Jack took the opportunity to quickly sort through the oddments from the blue room. A lot could be discarded instantly, like the necklace that gave Tara a super-deep voice, or the glove with six fingers that magically created an actual sixth finger when Jack put it on. There was a glass rod that gave the holder owl's eyes and the ability to see better in the dark when they were holding it. Tara slipped that into her pocket. Anything with even the slightest potential as a weapon against The Evil, Jack put into his embroidered sack. The trick would be remembering what did what.

Outside, the chittering and chattering of bugs was getting louder. Any second now, Jack bet, The Evil would tire of waiting and storm their shelter. He wasn't in any hurry to meet the army, but if he had to, he wanted to do it on his terms.

Kyle came back with Cornelia, who hopped onto Jack's shoulder and rubbed her feathered head against his cheek.

"Charlie," she said.

"You're talking about Lottie, aren't you?" said Jack. "Charlotte. Grandma's sister."

Cornelia bobbed her head. "Charlie."

"Did you find her?"

Cornelia tugged at Jack's sleeve, pulling him to the window. She stretched out a wing and pointed to a faint shape visible on the horizon. Jack squinted. It looked like a tree, but surely it couldn't be. A tree that far away would have to be enormous.

"So that's where she is?" Jack asked Cornelia. "That's where we have to go?"

Cornelia bobbed again.

"It'd be so much easier if we could fly," said Kyle, peering out the window and swallowing nervously.

"If Jaide was here," said Jack, "we might be able to. But she's not, so we'll have to run."

"Last chance for a drink," said Tara, with a menacing glare at the nearest plant. She had daubed her cheeks in mud and tied her hair back. With the sword in her hand she looked less like a suburban girl from Scarborough and more like a dangerous desert warrior, slaughterer of bugs. Hopefully The Evil would see her that way, too.

When they had taken their fill and checked they hadn't left anything useful behind, they left the window and walked back into darkness, Jack relying on his natural sight and Tara holding the glass owl's-eye rod. Kyle stood between them, one hand on each of their shoulders so he wouldn't trip over anything or get lost. Cornelia clung to Jack's shoulder, rocking gently from side to side.

The plan was to find another way out on the other side of the building, one that wasn't blocked by the Evil Bug Army. That meant being quiet, but the plants weren't having any of that. The first tree they came to shook and clattered its fleshy branches, even when Tara threatened it with decapitation if it wasn't quiet. The next took up the rattling cry, and soon the whole jungle was astir, making a racket that could surely be heard from outside. Abandoning stealth, Tara and Jack broke into a run, with Kyle doing his best to keep up. The sound of him panting was loud in Jack's ear, even over the jungle's hue and cry.

Just when it seemed as though the building had no other side, a glimmer of light appeared ahead. Jack changed course for it, holding his bone-scimitar out in front of him in case anything leaped out at them. They reached the door unscathed and stepped out into a long, narrow space between buildings that might once have been a street, although one with no right angles or straight lines. It was now littered with bones and rubble from collapsing walls. The multiple suns cast complex shadows across their path. Cornelia took off to guide them.

Barely had they gone a hundred yards when Cornelia let out a loud squawk and practically flapped backward in midair.

"Avast! Avast!"

Jack had never entirely understood what that word meant, but from the way Cornelia was acting he guessed she was saying, "Stop! Turn back!"

When, from around the next corner, a vast rolling wave of bugs appeared, sweeping down the street like a slow-motion flood of water, that interpretation was dramatically confirmed.

++We see you, troubletwister!++ cried The Evil. ++We see you!++

"Go back," Jack said to Tara and Kyle, pushing them behind him. "It's me it wants. I'll hold it off while you escape."

"Don't be ridiculous," said Tara, holding the sword in front of her with both hands. "You can't take it on alone."

"Yes, I can. I have all this stuff." He jiggled his embroidered sack. "And I have *this*."

He poked his toe into the nearest shadow, and felt the familiar all-over tingling sensation of becoming Shadow Jack. The world went flat and dark, and Tara and Kyle seemed to tower over him like giants. They spun around, looking for him. He swept along the shadow, crossed over into another one, then popped up ten feet away.

"See?" he said. "I'll be okay. Now, go! Stay inside and I'll catch up with you later."

Kyle pulled at Tara's arm. "He's right. And we don't have time to argue."

Tara looked up at the approaching swarm and nodded. Together, they ran back inside, out of danger.

Jack squared up to face the swarm and narrowed his eyes.

++Yes,++ said The Evil. ++Stay with us, Jackaran Kresimir Shield. We have watched you for so long. We have always known that you would join us. You have always been the one!++

He didn't waste his breath replying. He put his hand inside the embroidered sack and felt around for a small ceramic dog that he and Tara had found in the junk from the blue room. Bringing it out into the light, he breathed on it and set it down on the ground. The Evil rose up and around Jack, insects crawling and merging into shapes too hideous to describe, while the pressure on Jack's mind rose up, too, threatening to subsume him completely.

With a chipper bark, the pottery dog sprang into motion and ran in a cheerful, brainless circle. Jack vanished into the shadow and The Evil crashed down, right where he had been standing. The dog yapped and yapped, but as it was a Warden artifact, The Evil couldn't take it over. The Evil's roar of frustration followed Jack as he fled to the other side of the street, where he popped up again and waved his bone-scimitar over his head.

"You missed me. Over here!"

The grotesque mass of The Evil swept around to face him. It was made of many small, quick-moving parts, but as a whole it was slow and lumbering.

++Do not run from us,++ The Evil hissed into his mind, stopping his legs so he couldn't move. ++It is most unnecessary.++

Jack didn't need his legs to flee through the shadows, and he did so again before the insects could come down on him en masse.

In another spot, legs working again, his questing fingers found another object in the sack. This one was a lump of milky crystal that, when activated, froze everything around it for a minute. He and Tara had discovered its power by accident, and had spent an uncomfortable and terrifying sixty seconds unable to draw breath before the effect had worn off. Jack waited until The Evil found him again before throwing the crystal into the thickest part of the swarm. Then he vanished again, aiming for a shadowed patch closer to the entrance to the building into which Tara and Kyle had fled.

The steady splat of insects dropping to the ground greeted him when he returned. The Evil's wrathful scream filled his ears. A mental fist hit him hard, and this time it wasn't his legs that were affected. His vision snuffed out, and with that went his ability to see what was attacking him, or where he was going. He could only vanish back into the shadows and hope for the best.

He emerged, blinking away the darkness, right in the middle of the billowing swarm.

++We have you now!++

Before he lost all control of his body, Jack threw a handful of blue room items into the air and vanished once more. Behind him, streamers of smoke, showers of duplicate coins, and ghostly, dancing shapes that might have been people dressed in monks' robes kept The Evil swarm momentarily occupied.

Figuring that he had confused The Evil as much as he would be able to, and at sufficient risk to his own life, Jack retreated through the shadows to the entranceway and vanished inside. Darkness led him swiftly to the far side, where Tara and Kyle were anxiously waiting.

They jumped when he appeared beside them, and Cornelia took off. Ahead was nothing but empty desert.

"Okay," said Jack breathlessly. "Let's go."

Following Cornelia's bright blue tail feathers, they ran as fast as they could for the heat-shivering horizon.

CHAPTER SIXTEEN

THE THIRD EXAMINATION

Jaide put her head in her hands and groaned. She wasn't sure how much more she could take.

"Please, let it end soon," begged Stefano beside her, a perfect reflection of her own despair. "If this is what it takes to become a Warden, I don't want to be one!"

"One more minute," said Alfred the Examiner, with relentless patience. Jaide had learned the hard way that this didn't mean "one more minute to go." Instead, it meant that the ornate minute hand on the antique clock sitting between them was put back one mark, so their day became a whole sixty seconds longer.

"Be quiet!" she hissed across the table to Stefano. "You're not helping."

He moaned and returned to his task. They were in the restored blue room, sitting at the mahogany desk. Between them, open wide, were two complete *Compendiums* — special Examination editions, they had been told, containing certain errors and omissions designed to trip up incautious readers. The task for each of them was to follow a trail of accounts back through history in order to identify the first time The Evil had attempted a particular tactic, and then write an essay detailing what had worked then and what had not worked, and how that past practice could be adapted to the present day if The Evil tried that tactic again. Every step had to be recorded. Every conclusion had to be explained — all written by hand, using ancient pens that required them to dip nibs into a bottomless inkwell.

The third Examination was homework. And none of it was multiple choice.

Jaide put her head down and forced herself to press on. She didn't know how long she and Stefano had been at it, but her stomach was gurgling as bad as Jack's did, and her hand was sore from writing so much. Who cared what had happened in Newtown 1664, when The Evil had impersonated a local money merchant and seeded the community with some kind of Evil fungus that looked like tarnished silver coins? How was that ever likely to happen again, in these days of online banking and ATM cards? It was all pointless and confusing. The history of the Wardens was so deep and complicated that it was hard to tell what was real and what was a lie. If this is what life as a full Warden consisted of, as Stefano said, she could do without it. She longed for the day to end so she could concentrate on Project Thunderclap, rescuing Jack and the others, and fighting The Evil for real.

She wanted to ask how much time was left, but she didn't dare. Alfred the Examiner was sitting at the far end of the table, wearing reading glasses and slowly turning the pages of a very large, very old book, which appeared to be completely blank. The slightest hint of rebellion cost both her and Stefano another minute. They were lumped in together, but couldn't help each other. It wasn't fair.

Yes, yes, just like life, Jaide wanted to say. The lesson was so *obvious.* She was beginning to wish she had gone with her mother to Scarborough instead of staying in

Portland for the Examination. Susan had held her twice as tightly and twice as long as normal before leaving that morning, and made her promise to call the second they learned anything about Jack, no matter what that news might be.

Finally, after what felt like a week crammed into one very long day, Alfred closed the book, stood up, and removed the clock from the table.

Stefano glanced up, blinking like someone waking from a very deep sleep. Jaide hoped he hadn't actually been asleep. If he had been, and she failed because of him, she would wring his neck.

"Is that it?" he asked. "Are we done?"

"Let me see your work." Alfred held out his hands. Jaide gathered up her pages in ink-stained fingers and nervously handed them over. She couldn't believe the Examination was over. Part of her had expected to be trapped in it forever.

Her back made popping noises as she stretched. When she went to get up to unkink her knees, Alfred raised one long index finger and, without looking up from their notes, both of which he seemed to be reading simultaneously, said firmly, "Not yet."

Jaide lowered herself back into her seat and exchanged a worried glance with Stefano. What if their work wasn't good enough? Would they have to keep going, perhaps even start all over again? That thought was almost too horrible. She imagined The Evil bursting into the blue room on a tide of glowing, hideous leeches and carrying the Examiner away. Part of her would have been relieved.

"Your handwriting is appalling," Alfred said. "I don't know what you're taught in school these days. Also, you have made several mistakes in your research. Stefano, you should have noted that the black sweat of Pippinedda the Sicilian was a natural exudation. Jaide, a chiliarch is not an ancient refrigerator. On the whole, however, I find your work acceptable. You have passed the third Examination."

Jaide just stared at him, not entirely believing it.

"But," she said, "we made mistakes. . . ."

"Everyone does, Jaide," Alfred said in a kinder voice. "No one is perfect. Not me, not your father, not the *Compendium*, not the Grand Gathering. We all fail sometimes. We all make mistakes, yet you'll notice we are all still here. It's never the end of the world."

"But one day it might be," said Stefano. "The end of the world, I mean. If someone makes a big enough mistake."

"That's why we have the Warden of Last Resort. If called upon, they alone are required not to be in error."

Jaide's ears pricked up.

"I've heard of that," she said. "The Warden of Last Resort. That's Grandma, isn't it?"

Alfred's expression didn't change.

"One day, if you exercise sufficient will," he said, "you will know the truth."

He raised his left hand and snapped his fingers. Something eased in the air, a tension Jaide hadn't been aware of until it was gone. The secret panel leading to the rest of the house opened. It looked starkly functional now, without the tapestry that had once concealed it from view, but its opening seemed wonderful enough as it was. As did the two feline faces that pushed through and ran down to join her.

"It's over?" meowed Ari, tail twitching. He trod a wide

arc around the Examiner to rub his left side against Jaide's elbow. "It's done?"

"Of course it is. Otherwise, why would the door be open?" said Kleo. She gave Jaide a lick on the hand, then stuck her tongue out. Ink had turned the tip of it black.

"We passed," said Stefano, and this time Jaide didn't hear boastfulness in his declaration, just relief.

"Poor Jack," she said.

"He will be Examined upon his return," Alfred said, packing up their copies of the *Compendium* and slipping them into a broad leather case.

"*If* he returns."

"Don't think that way," Kleo told her. "You have to stay positive. He'll know if you give up hope. Twins are always connected, deep down."

Jaide wasn't so sure. She had tried teeping again, but nothing was getting through. It was hard not to wonder if he was dead. That was the one good thing about the Examination: It had kept her mind off what might be going wrong elsewhere.

"There's a feast waiting for you upstairs," said Ari excitedly. "A feast of celebration."

"What if we'd failed?" asked Stefano.

"Then it would have been a feast of consolation. Come on." He scampered down from the table and ran halfway up the stairs to the secret panel, where he stopped and turned to look at them, wondering why they weren't following.

Jaide had started to ask Alfred if he was joining them, but once again the Examiner had disappeared. Resolving never to fall for that again, she followed Stefano and the cats out of the blue room and down to the kitchen.

She had hoped her father might be there, but he had gone away, Grandma X told her, to avoid any complications caused by their Gifts. That made sense, she supposed. The day had been hard enough without having to deal with that possibility. She felt exhausted now, so exhausted she almost wasn't hungry. Only with effort did she force down a plateful of stew she would normally have found delicious, Jaide's favorite, particularly when Grandma X cooked it, followed by ice cream with strawberry sprinkles. Stefano dived in with gusto, while Ari watched in awe. There was very little conversation.

"That so-called teacher of yours called," said Grandma X at one point during the meal. "He wanted to know why you two missed soccer practice. I told him you had more important things to do, but would attend tomorrow."

"Isn't Project Thunderclap tomorrow?" asked Jaide.

"It is. And if it's successful, practice will go ahead the day after."

"And if it's not?" asked Stefano around a huge mouthful.

"Then I suppose very little will change, and practice will also go ahead. Either way, your teacher seemed reassured, despite losing two of his best players."

"And Kyle, too," said Jaide. "How's the story holding up?"

Grandma X had visited both Kyle and Tara's families to explain that their children were staying over for a couple of nights and that there was no need for concern. She brought friendly gifts of chocolate cake to both households, which she had assured Jaide would leave them not forgetful, exactly, but not overly mindful of the deviation from their usual routine. By such means did Wardens move through the complex terrain of everyday life without raising suspicion. One day it would be Jaide's turn to bake cakes like that, or to choose another means of drawing attention away from herself.

All through the meal, Jaide ran the details of the plan over and over in her mind to make sure she knew exactly what she had to do. One of the reasons she wasn't more excited about passing the Examination, besides being so tired, was that Jack was still missing, and would be until she rescued him. But behind that, there was another reason, a question boiling inside her that simply had to be asked.

"Grandma," she finally said, "what's the Warden of Last Resort, and what does it have to do with the end of the world?"

Grandma X studied her with curious gray eyes.

"What did Alfred tell you?"

"Nothing," Jaide said, which was almost the entire truth. "He told me that I'd learn about it one day, if I worked hard enough, or something like that. Why can't I know now?"

"Well, some knowledge is dangerous when given at the wrong time. You know that, Jaide — you remember what happened when you first came here."

Jaide nodded. She did remember. But at the same time, she didn't want to take the word of grown-ups that what she didn't know wasn't good for her. Couldn't she make that decision for herself?

"What's to stop me looking it up in the *Compendium*?" she said, acutely conscious of Stefano watching their battle of wills. "Why can't you just tell me now?"

"For the simple reason that it's a secret. Not a mystery, a secret. Ask the *Compendium*, and it won't tell you anything, because it can't. Only two people know about the

Warden of Last Resort, and that's the Warden himself or herself, and the Examiner, who outranks even the Great Steward in this matter. There is always a Warden of Last Resort, but they don't last forever. They must be replaced, and the Examiner is entrusted with that duty. With it comes knowledge and a great responsibility. That's as much as anyone knows."

Jaide nodded, although she was far from satisfied. Grandma X had a clever knack of supplying information that *seemed* like an answer, but was actually a means of misdirection. Jaide was getting better at spotting it, and was learning how to be more direct in return.

"Do you know who the Warden of Last Resort is?" she asked.

"Yes. All full Wardens know."

"Is it you?"

There was just a tiny flicker of hesitation, a moment in which Grandma X perhaps considered lying, and in her eyes Jaide saw a sudden flash of sadness, as though the answer would change everything, whichever one she chose to give.

"You are not a full Warden" was what she finally said.

Jaide put down her spoon. "I know, but you're my grandma and I have a right to know."

"You have a right to know what you need to know, and you have an obligation to use that knowledge well."

"Are you saying I won't use it well?"

"I'm saying there's a risk. I'm not willing to put you in danger."

"But I'm always in danger."

"There are degrees of danger, Jaide. And there is danger to others if I make the wrong decision."

"Alfred says it's okay to make mistakes. So why can't you take a chance and trust me for once?"

"It's not remotely about trust. It's about you being twelve and still a troubletwister —"

"Almost thirteen! And I've passed three Examinations!"

"But you are not yet a Warden, and definitely still too young. When you're older, I'll tell you, I promise. When you're older, there is much I'd like to share with you. But for now, Jaide, you must be patient. You must trust me in this as you do so many other things."

Jaide glanced at Stefano, who had a wondering look on his face. She knew he was thinking, *Is this part of the plan?* She had started off not thinking that, but now she decided it might as well be.

"If you're not going to trust me, then I don't trust you, either," Jaide shouted, pushing back from the chair in a manufactured huff. "Do your own dishes for once. I want to be alone."

With that, she stomped up the stairs and into her bedroom, putting all her effort into slamming the door and throwing some carefully chosen nonbreakables around for good effect. When she was done, she collapsed onto her bed, feeling a weird mixture of genuine upset and excitement. She loved Grandma X and didn't want her feelings to be hurt, but at the same time, Jaide had to take matters into her own hands. If no one else would rescue Jack, Tara, and Kyle, she would have to do it.

The room felt quiet and empty without Jack in it.

Somehow she nodded off, only waking when Stefano opened the door and slipped through the gap, looking behind him to make sure he wasn't being watched. She sat bolt upright from a dream about Jack battling giant wasps and caterpillars and stared wildly around the room, reminding herself who and where she was.

"Great tantrum," he whispered. "Kleo said something about human hormones, which made Ari hide under a chair. It was put on, wasn't it?"

"Mostly," she said, rubbing her eyes. "You'll keep the cats busy and make sure Grandma doesn't come in here for one of *those* talks?"

He grinned and nodded.

"I will keep her very busy," he said. "That won't be hard. She is supposed to be teaching me, after all, whether she's the Warden of Last Resort or not."

"Thank you," she said, then remembered that she was just as curious about Stefano's lessons as she was about the Warden of Last Resort. "What *is* she teaching you, if you don't mind me asking?"

He blushed and looked down at the floor.

"It's hard," he said, "when your twin is good at everything. You and Jack aren't like that. I could tell straightaway that there are things he's better at and things you're better at, and it all evens out. But Santino . . . well, he's always been the best. So the only way I've ever stood out is by being bad at things."

"Yeah, like soccer," Jaide said sarcastically.

"Santino is better."

"What about cooking? Dinner was amazing."

"Santino is better." He shrugged. "Here I had the chance to be someone different, someone who wasn't in his shadow. And I like that. Then I let The Evil get the better of me, and it turns out I really am not very good at being a troubletwister. That's what your grandmother has been teaching me. Failing the second Examination might have been me not liking my Gift and being unable to control it. But there's more to it than that. I think I have to learn to like myself first, before I do anything else."

Jaide didn't know what to say to that. She hadn't expected such a long and heartfelt explanation — from a boy, or from Stefano especially, even though he had been very talkative lately around her. She didn't know what to say in response. Something profound, probably. She certainly wasn't going to give him a hug.

"Anyway," he said, sparing her the indecision, "the plan! I'll play my part so you can play yours. Wait half an hour to be sure. Teep me when you get back so I know when to give it up."

She nodded. "Thanks, Stefano."

"It's all right. Until Jack is back, I owe you."

The door closed behind him and Jaide slipped off the bed and crossed to her wooden chest. Rummaging through old clothes, throwing them over her shoulder in her determination to get to the very bottom of the pile, she fished out a pair of black tights from a musical at her old school, some black shoes she once wore at a funeral, a black hand-me-down sweater from her mother, and a dark blue beanie (the closest she had to black). She put them on and stared at herself in the mirror. Black was a look that felt wrong on her. It was more Jack's thing, so it seemed fitting that she was wearing it now, in order to get him back.

Waiting was hard, but she forced herself to. At the end of half an hour, she made a pile of pillows under her bedclothes that might at a cursory glance look like her in bed asleep, turned out the bedroom light, and opened the door a crack.

No cats. No Grandma X.

From the blue room came a series of loud crackles and crashes, as though a miniature power generator was having a tantrum.

Jaide pulled the beanie down low over her forehead and tucked her hair up inside. Taking a deep breath, she slipped through the door and tiptoed down the stairs.

It was time to visit an old friend.

CHAPTER SEVENTEEN

ECHOES OF LOTTIE

Jack, Tara, and Kyle made it safely to the tree without being ambushed by The Evil, thanks in part to Cornelia's eagle-eyed scouting from above. It seemed safe to assume that anything moving on the sand below was an Evil spy; they hadn't yet seen a single living thing on the planet that *wasn't* Evil. When she squawked and turned off the path leading to their destination, they knew they had to change course, too, in order to go around the creature ahead.

They were helped by a sudden shift in the weather. Clouds rolled in from their right (Jack couldn't tell if that was north, south, east, west, or some other direction he didn't have a word for), bringing a brief but intense squall of icy rain with it. They huddled around one another with Cornelia tucked safely between them, riding out the pummeling hail and deafening winds until, just as suddenly as it had started, it was over. The clouds swept on across the desert. The two bright suns and yellow skies returned, over a desert smoothed flat by wind and rain. All trace of their footsteps had been erased.

Before the hail completely melted, they stuffed their mouths full of ice and sucked greedily at the moisture. Jack dreamt of Grandma X's hot chocolate, but this would do for now. They pressed on, Cornelia watching from above as before. Behind them, the curved walls of the anthill city faded into the blurry horizon, and their immediate fears of ambush were put to rest. Step by step, mile by mile, the tree Cornelia was leading them to grew steadily closer.

Two things became apparent as they neared it. The first was that the tree was huge. Its rippling, many-limbed trunk was as wide across as a city block, and its uppermost boughs were higher than most buildings. Jack had thought the tree in Grandma X's backyard was big, but it was dwarfed by this one. Portland would easily fit in its shadow. Scarborough, too, probably.

The second thing was that it was dead — very, very dead — and had been for a long time. Its branches were bare of leaves, and in numerous places great rents and tears in the bark were visible where branches had come crashing down through those below, and now lay in drifts of sand around the trunk. Those fallen branches reminded Jack of the bones they had seen all over the desert, only much larger, and black rather than white. It was as though the tree was little more than a skeleton now, one slowly falling in on itself.

"This is where your great-aunt is hiding?" asked Kyle, fanning himself with his hat. His curly black hair lay plastered across his scalp, slick with sweat. The earlier rain had entirely evaporated, leaving the air thick and humid.

"I don't know," said Jack. It did seem unlikely that anyone lived here, let alone for so many years. "But this is where Cornelia is taking us, and it's not as if we have anywhere else to go."

Tara marched on, not wasting energy on doubts or uncertainties. The boys trailed in her wake, eagerly anticipating the shade. They didn't know how long they had been walking. Hours and hours, it felt like. Jack's stomach had given up telling him he was hungry long ago, but that didn't stop him from thinking about food.

Cornelia swooped in and took a perch on one of the outermost branches, so she could watch their approach. When they finally stepped into shadow, Jack breathed a huge sigh of relief. This was where he belonged. It was instantly ten degrees cooler.

Tara waved and Cornelia swooped down to land on her forearm.

"Where to now?" she asked the bird. "Where's Lottie — I mean, Charlie?"

Cornelia swiveled her head nearly all the way around in one direction, then just as far the other way.

"Does that mean you don't know?" asked Jack.

Cornelia bobbed her plumed head.

"But she *was* here?" asked Kyle.

The head bobbed again.

"So I guess we'll just have to look around," said Jack, taking in the enormity of the space before them. From a distance, the fallen branches had looked insignificant, but now, close up, they were big enough to hide whole families.

"We should split up to save time," said Tara.

Jack was loath to agree with that. The deathly silence under the tree was already beginning to creep him out.

"Why don't you just call her, using that telepathy thing of yours?" said Kyle. "If she's here, she'll hear you."

"The Evil might hear me, too," Jack said.

"And it might not."

Jack looked at Tara, who nodded. He got the impression she hadn't been looking forward to splitting up, either. Her brave face was a good one, but it was wearing thin.

"All right," Jack said. "Let's just go in a little farther and I'll give it a try."

They wound their way through fallen dead branches until they found one just the right height for them to sit on. Gray dust puffed up when they did so, making Kyle sneeze. Cornelia took to the branches above, where she sat grooming her feathers and staring at the shadows with her black eyes.

"Okay." Jack closed his eyes and concentrated on what he knew about Lottie. She had looked exactly like Grandma X when she was young and presumably looked just like her now. He had never met her, but they were related by blood, which had to count for something.

++Hello?++

His mental voice vanished into the thick shadows under the long-dead tree.

++You don't know me, but my name is Jack Shield and I'm your great-nephew. My sister and I got your living mail. Are you here somewhere? Can you tell me where you are?++

"Have you started yet?" asked Kyle.

"Shhhh," said Tara. "Don't distract him."

Jack listened a full minute, and when no reply came tried again.

++I want to go home, and I want to take you with me. But we're running out of time. Are you there? Can you answer me? It would really help if you would say something.++

From above came a squawk and a flutter of wings.

"Charlie!"

"Jack," said Kyle. "Open your eyes."

He did and saw standing before them a ghostly green image of the woman he was trying to contact.

"She's trying to say something," said Tara. "Can you hear her?"

Lottie's lips were moving, but no sound was coming out. Jack couldn't hear anything with his mind, either.

"Maybe it's slugs again," said Tara, poking the image with her sword. The blade went right through the image, unhindered.

Cornelia landed on Jack's shoulder. "Charlie?"

The ghostly woman smiled as though she had heard, and reached out one hand to touch Cornelia's gleaming feathers. Her fingers passed right through them, however, and Lottie's face fell.

++Lottie!++ Jack cried with all his strength. ++Tell us where you are and we'll come to you!++

Lottie's lips moved soundlessly again, and she shook her head with frustration. Her image flickered.

"Wait," said Kyle. "Don't go!"

The ghostly image of Lottie disappeared as though it had never been there.

"That really was her this time, wasn't it?" said Tara.

Jack nodded. "I think so, but I couldn't hear her, no matter how hard I tried."

"Well, that means she's here somewhere. All we have to do is find her."

"Cornelia, do you know where to go next?"

The bird managed a very humanlike shrug in answer to Jack's question.

"Great," said Kyle. "What if she's on the other side of the planet?"

"I don't think so," said Tara. "She didn't come to us in the city, but she did just now, which I think means we're getting closer. We just need to know which direction to go."

"Not that way," said Kyle, pointing back the way they had come.

All three stared at a gray cloud that hadn't been there before. It was noticeably growing larger.

"Uh-oh," said Jack. "It heard."

"What do we do now?" said Tara.

"We hide," said Kyle. "Before it sees us."

Kyle led them deeper under the lifeless canopy, leapfrogging over fallen branches or crawling under them where space allowed. They left a wide trail of footprints behind in the dust, which Cornelia tried to brush away with her wings, but Kyle stopped her.

"We're going to create a false trail," he said. "Let's make it look like we climbed the trunk, then we'll double back and take cover . . . there."

He indicated a triangular hollow formed by two fallen limbs, one of them forked in a wide V. Tara kept a worried eye out for The Evil's approach, and suggested every minute or so that it was time to turn back. But Kyle was adamant that they had time to do it properly, if they hurried.

They reached the trunk, where they put some handprints on the rough bark, and then began walking back on their own footprints. It was harder than it looked, and much slower than any of them liked. Already they could hear the humming and clicking of insect wings as The Evil approached. It was growing louder by the second.

Finally, they reached the hollow.

"Okay, you first," Kyle said, pushing Jack ahead of him. "Burrow down deep, and cover yourself with as many twigs as you can find. Don't smother yourself, though.

Leave an air hole. Now you." Tara went next, then Kyle, sweeping the trail behind him with a crooked stick.

The light from the suns outside was turning a deep brown as The Evil encircled the tree. Cornelia landed next to Jack and burrowed down with him. The sound of their rustling seemed terribly loud to him. Surely The Evil would hear and descend on them like a horrible hammerblow? Hopefully the brooch-charms would help. He closed his eyes, held his breath, and kept a tight grip on Cornelia, who was quivering with fear.

The Evil swarmed through the canopy, calling his name.

++Jackaran Kresimir Shield! We heard you and we have come in answer to your call! We are the only way you will ever get home. Join us and we will take you there now, as one of us!++

Jack was immune to its temptations, no matter how badly he wanted to go home. He knew that any bargain he entered into with The Evil would end up with him a glowing-eyed zombie intent on betraying everyone he loved. Mental tendrils reached for him, but he concentrated on thinking thoughts that had nothing to do with him, lest they betray him. The smell of the dust; the feel of petrified twigs digging into his sides; the dry, ashy taste of some dirt that had somehow got into his mouth . . .

Slowly, he became aware of a quite unexpected sensation, something he had experienced before in the second Examination but had never felt so clearly in real life. The ground around him wasn't just dirt. It was a complex environment that spoke to him in a language he could somehow understand. He saw the layers of soil around the tree's massive roots. He saw the pockets where life had once thrived, from catlike creatures who'd lived in tunnels, down to worms and bacteria. It had once been a vital, thriving place, and even though all the living things had long been taken over by The Evil and amalgamated into its ghastly whole, the ground itself remembered, and it knew of one place in the entire realm where life remained.

Jack thought the ground was talking about him and his friends. They were alive, and the ground could sense him just like he could sense it. But that wasn't the case. There was another pocket of life not far away . . . an oasis in the middle of the vast Evil desert. . . .

So excited was he by this discovery that he very nearly exclaimed aloud. It had to be Lottie! Who else could it be? Only with great difficulty did he keep himself still until he felt The Evil swarm pass over him, grumbling and clicking in frustration before heading off.

He didn't move, even though he could feel Kyle beginning to get restless. Jack couldn't feel The Evil through the ground, perhaps because it wasn't life as he knew it. Maybe The Evil was faking going away and was waiting quietly for them to emerge. If they broke cover too soon, they might find themselves surrounded and overwhelmed, and not even Grandma X's brooches would help them then. So he counted to a hundred, and then he counted to a hundred again. Only when he had finished doing that did he risk bringing his head up to see what was going on.

His dark-sensitive eyes saw nothing above or around him but the dead tree and its branches. With a rustle of ancient leaf litter, Tara sat up next to him, sword at the ready, followed by Kyle. Cornelia unfolded herself from Jack's arms and fluffed up her feathers.

"Will you take a look around for us?" Jack asked her in a whisper.

She bobbed her head and took off to circumnavigate the tree.

Jack told the others what he had sensed through the ground.

"Which way?" asked Kyle.

Jack recalled the feeling clearly. "That way," he said, pointing toward the trunk but meaning the desert on the far side. They would have to go around the tree to get where they needed to go.

"And Lottie will be there?" asked Tara.

"I think so," said Jack. "I can't imagine where else she could be. This whole place is dead, like someone sucked the life out of it."

"How can The Evil live here?" asked Kyle. "Don't its bugs need to eat?"

"Maybe they eat each other," said Tara with a quick shudder. "I can't wait to get home."

Cornelia returned.

"Smooth seas and plain sailing," she declared.

They unearthed themselves and brushed down their clothes. It didn't make much difference to their appearance. They remained dirty from head to foot, which was possibly a good thing, Jack thought. Even a small amount of camouflage might help hide them from creatures looking for them across the desert.

"When we get home," Jack said, "I'm going to sleep for a week."

"I'm going to eat a hamburger and drink three thick shakes, each a different flavor," said Kyle.

"I'm going to have a bath and never get out," said Tara. "And I'm never going to wish I was a troubletwister again."

Jack grinned at her, although part of him still felt painfully guilty that she and Kyle had been caught up in this. Grandma X had often warned them about the dangers of involving ordinary people in Warden affairs. He could see the consequences all too clearly now.

Tara raised her sword. "Onward!" she cried, so onward they went.

CHAPTER EIGHTEEN

CAT BURGLARY

Jaide slipped around the back of the Project Thunderclap tent, keeping to where the streetlights were dimmest and where she was sure no guards were patrolling. She had hidden in some bushes and watched for half an hour before making her move. There was a spot near the school buildings where the tent canvas didn't quite reach the ground. If she could get in there without being seen, she would be well on her way to being where she needed.

Breathing quickly and shallowly through her open mouth, she broke cover and made a run for it.

"What are you doing back here?"

She stopped and spun around. A young, round-faced Warden in a security uniform was walking toward her from a spot where she was certain there had been no one before.

Convinced the game was up before it had even started, she could do no more than stammer, "I — uh —"

"The entrance is around the front. That way."

He pointed.

"Right," she said. "I knew that. I was just checking . . . this." She indicated the gap in the tent. "Shoddy workmanship. Doesn't look very secure to me."

"I guess," he said with a shrug. "Nothing'll get past us without a token, though. Don't worry. If The Evil tries anything, it'll get an awful shock. Literally."

"Great," she said, and when it was clear that he wasn't going to wander off until she had left, she added, "Well, thanks. That's good to know."

She sauntered off around the tent in the direction he had indicated. After ten steps, she glanced over her shoulder. The Warden had disappeared. She didn't doubt he was still watching, though. He was right: The tent was very secure.

Still, he hadn't questioned her unusual garb, and when she brazenly walked up to the front flap, no one questioned her there, either. She was a teenager dressed up like a cat burglar late at night, but she had a token so she must be allowed. They had probably seen far stranger things that day.

Feeling slightly foolish for trying to break in the hard way, but no less nervous about being discovered at any second, she walked briskly through the manifold corridors of the giant tent. Perhaps they had been moved, because although she was sure she had memorized them from her visit the previous night, they seemed unfamiliar to her now. There were fewer people, but there was still a great deal of urgency and hustle in the air. When people passed her, they were walking quickly and focused on their tasks. Jaide kept her head down and kept moving, hoping that sooner rather than later something familiar would leap out at her.

When it did, it came from an unexpected direction.

"As speaker for the Portland wards, I implore you to take your 'Project Thunderclap' elsewhere."

That was Rennie's voice, carrying clearly through the canvas walls.

"We have been much weakened by The Evil's recent attacks. The breach you're planning could ruin us forever."

"The breach will only be temporary," said a voice in reply. Jaide recognized Aleksandr's deep, smooth tones. "And if Project Thunderclap is successful, we will no longer need any wards at all. The Evil will be contained to its own realm, unable to menace ours or any other's again."

"That's all very well," Rennie said, tapping the table with her wooden hand for emphasis, "but what if Project Thunderclap fails, and the wards fail with it? Portland will be exposed, and so will the rest of the world. With our best Wardens defeated, who will turn The Evil back then? This plan is too risky to conduct here. Go away and find another town to menace."

A third voice joined the argument, and Jaide ducked quickly into the shadows so she could hear more as two Wardens hustled by.

"I think you're being unreasonable, Rennie. I also know you're worried about Jack and his friends. Don't put those concerns ahead of the rest of the world, I beg you. We need your cooperation if Project Thunderclap is to succeed."

"What price is success, Hector? Would you trade your own son and two innocents for a plan that might not succeed?"

"The plan will succeed, and so I have no choice. It is my duty as a Warden."

Jaide couldn't believe what she was hearing. Their own father, Hector Shield, sounded as dispassionate as Grandma X did about trapping her sister with The Evil for the rest of their lives. What was it about Wardens that made them so coldhearted?

Rennie agreed with her.

"What about your duty as a parent? As a human being? This is how The Evil will defeat you all, if you're not careful: by making you shadows of itself, all emotion eroded away by decisions like this. It's love that makes this fight worth fighting. Not hatred of the enemy, to which all else is sacrificed. You are making a grave mistake and risking too much. I cannot bear to watch it."

"Are you revoking your role as Living Ward of Portland?" Aleksandr asked, and even without seeing his face Jaide understood the question for the challenge it was.

"No," said Rennie. "I would never do that."

Jaide didn't stick around to hear any more. It sounded like the argument would continue all night, and it upset her to think of her father being like this. She was sure it wasn't easy for him to make this decision, but at least he could have tried to argue with Aleksandr. At least he could have sounded sad about it.

She stepped out of her hiding place and moved quickly through the corridors, peering at tent flaps until she found the one she was looking for, decorated with a familiar four-pointed star. It was behind this flap, she was sure, that the professor was hidden. If anyone could teach her how to use the cross-continuum conduit constructor in Grandma X's basement to rescue Jack, it would be him.

Pulling the beanie low over her forehead, she lifted the flap and went inside.

She had feared guards, but all the room contained was a table and several empty chairs arranged in a semicircle. On the table was a metal mesh cage with no door or lock, just bars. Inside the cage, on a wooden frame that looked a bit like an easel, was the death mask she and Jack had found in Rourke Castle, a plaster cast of the face of the real Professor Olafsson, who had died hundreds of years earlier. Along with his face, the plaster retained an impression of his personality and knowledge. He looked exactly the same except for a long crack down the middle of his face, like a jagged scar, that was visible no matter how carefully he had been glued back together. His eyes were closed. Jaide didn't think he slept, but that was exactly what it looked like he was doing at that moment.

She stepped softly into the room. Behind her, the sound of Rennie arguing with Aleksandr and her father rose up above the hum of activity in the tent. That was good, Jaide thought. It would cover any sound she made. Her plan was simply to talk to the professor, but seeing him caged made her want to rescue him. Why would Aleksandr lock him up like that? It wasn't as if the death mask had any means of moving on its own.

Then she realized he was caged for his own protection. The Evil's minions had already stolen him once before. Perhaps they would try again.

She crossed the room and came as close to him as she could without touching the cage. It might have been rigged to sound an alarm.

"Professor?" she whispered. "Professor, wake up!"

"What? Where am I?" The plaster eyelids opened, revealing plaster eyes that darted left and right. "Oh, well. Still here. Haven't you tired of asking me questions to which there are no . . . Wait, you're not him," he said on seeing her. "You're Jaide! Goodness, child, it has been a long time. Not years, though, or else you would be significantly taller, unless your growth has been unnaturally stunted. Has it? What brings you to my dungeon of tedious interrogation?"

"I'm, uh, growing normally," she said. "I'm sorry about this, but I need to ask you some questions, too."

"Well, it's different with you. I *like* you. Perhaps we could move our conversation to a more comfortable environment. Somewhere with a view of the ocean?"

"I'd like to, but you see I'm not really supposed to be here, so I don't know how to open the cage. If I try they might catch me."

"Oh, well, that's easily fixed," he said. "You simply change the metallic structure of the bars by means of Lu Shu's Mental Elemental Transmogrifier, if you have one handy."

"I don't. I'm sorry."

"Ah. How about Aaron Smythe's Invisible Hand?"

"Again . . . and I don't really have time to go back to look for one. . . ."

"Then I must resign myself to continued imprisonment." The professor rolled his eyes in theatrical despair, then froze, staring up at the canvas ceiling. "Oh my!"

Jaide followed the direction of his gaze and saw a shadowy figure drop through a tear in the canvas ceiling. She got out of the way just in time to avoid being landed on. Her Gifts awoke automatically, given the thought still fresh in her mind that The Evil might attempt to steal the professor. The canvas walls flapped in a sudden wind. A cry for help was on the tip of her tongue when Jaide noticed something very strange about this unexpected thief.

She was dressed all in black, just like Jaide, apart from a pair of silver-tipped cowboy boots.

"What are *you* doing here?" they asked at exactly the same moment.

"I should say that's perfectly obvious," said the professor. "Hopefully one of you has the means of extricating me from this tedious predicament."

Grandma X pulled off her black hood, releasing a flood of unruly white hair. With a look that said to Jaide as clearly as words, *We will discuss this later*, Grandma X turned her attention to the cage. Her hands made a complicated gesture, and then she suddenly reached through the metal as though it wasn't there and removed the death mask from its captivity.

"Very nicely done," the professor said with a grin. "I'm grateful to you, my good lady. By what means did you effect the transformation?"

"Tantalo's Telekinetic Pilferer, but let's not stand around discussing the finer details of my technique. Here." She gave the professor to Jaide, then waved her left hand at someone waiting above them. Through the hole in the ceiling dropped an exact replica of the sleeping death mask.

Four reflective eyes peered down from the night sky.

"Hi, Jaide," said Ari. "Nice night for a bit of cat burgling."

"Shush," said Kleo. "This isn't a game."

"No, but you have to give me that one. *Cat* burgling, yes?"

Grandma X placed the fake death mask in the cage, so no one would know the real one had been taken, and slipped the professor into a pouch at the front of her black top.

"Right," she said, turning to Jaide. "I think it best you come home with us. Hector and Rennie are doing their best to distract Aleksandr, but if you're caught, suspicion will immediately fall on them. Put your arms around my waist."

Jaide did as she was told.

"Dad's part of this?" she said, feeling a huge flood of relief. "I knew he wasn't really going to abandon Jack, Tara, and Kyle."

"Of course not." Grandma X pulled the hood back over her face. "Your father is a Shield and therefore stubborn beyond all reason."

Jaide felt that was directed at her, too, and might have been at least partially a compliment, but before she could say anything, a disconcertingly *empty* sensation rose up in her stomach, and she rose up with it, up through the hole in the ceiling and then onto the top of the tent, where a section of the canvas had become as solid as rock, allowing them to walk across its gentle billow and swell without falling through.

The guards didn't see them as they slid down the side and onto the ground. One guard heard a strange noise in the bushes that required investigation, while the other thought he saw a suspicious figure cross the pool of light below a streetlight at the end of the block. By the time they returned to their posts, the two black-clad burglars and their four-footed accomplices had vanished into the night.

Nothing was said until they returned home, where Stefano was slumped over the kitchen table next to a half-drunk mug of hot chocolate. He jerked upright when Grandma X snapped her fingers, and stared first at her, then the sack containing the professor, then Jaide.

"Oh," he said. "I've missed something important, haven't I?"

"Explain," Grandma X said, putting Jaide in the seat next to him and taking one of her own opposite them both, her expression unamused. Kleo sat on the table next to her, and she looked just as stern. Ari, on the other hand, sprawled on the sideboard, head turning from side to side as though he was watching a game of tennis as the words flew back and forth.

"You deceived me and placed yourself in unacceptable risk," Grandma X accused Jaide.

"Yes, well, you deceived me, and if you hadn't, I wouldn't have needed to do anything at all," Jaide retorted.

"What happened to 'no more secrets'? Have you been planning to rescue Jack all along? And Lottie, too?"

"Not Lottie," said Grandma X, shifting in her seat. It wasn't often Jaide saw her grandmother looking caught out. "I promised not to rescue her. But that didn't stop me thinking how someone might *attempt* a rescue . . . someone like Hector, for instance. . . ."

The front door opened and closed, and Jaide turned in her seat, hoping to see her father walking up the hallway into the kitchen.

It was indeed him, and his eyebrows almost jumped off his forehead when he saw his daughter and his mother sitting at the table in almost identical black outfits.

"Jaide, shouldn't you be in bed by now?"

"She should indeed," said Grandma X, folding her hands in front of her. "But great minds think alike, I'm afraid. Seeing she's come this far, we might as well include her — provided she does what she's told from now on."

Jaide beamed. It seemed she wasn't going to get in trouble, after all. In fact, she was going to find out how Grandma X and her father planned to rescue Jack, Tara, and Kyle.

"What about you?" Hector asked Stefano. "Are you volunteering as well?"

"Yes, sir," he said. "Because I want to, not just because it's partly my fault. Because it's the right thing to do."

"That remains to be seen."

Hector came to join them at the table, and another adult stepped into view from behind him. It was Rennie. Of course she was part of the plan, Jaide thought. She and Hector had *actually* been arguing with Aleksandr as a distraction, for Grandma X, not for Jaide.

"Was the mission a success?" Rennie asked.

Grandma X nodded, removing Professor Olafsson from his pouch. He blinked and flexed his plaster features, taking in the new environment.

"Thank you, madam and milady, for retrieving me from that gaggle of ignoramuses," he said. "Not one of them has the slightest speck of curiosity. All they dream of is victory and power. That Aleksandr fellow is a right buffoon."

"He is not without his admirable qualities," said Grandma X. "But we have had our moments, yes."

"Tell us about Aleksandr's plan, Professor," said Hector. "Project Thunderclap: Will it work?"

"I don't see why not, if they follow my blueprint to the letter." The professor's gaze swiveled to take in everyone sitting around the table. "With enough lightning wielders to create a sufficiently energetic megastorm, the cracks between our world and that of The Evil can be erased forever."

"How do you erase a crack?" asked Jaide.

"Take a piece of cheese," said the professor. "Break it in two. Now place the pieces in an oven so they sit next to each other. Close the door. What will happen?"

"The cheese will melt back together," said Stefano.

"Exactly. And so it will be here, when Project Thunderclap is enacted, only with the megastorm instead of the heat of an oven, and dimensions instead of cheese."

"Does anyone else feel like a toasted sandwich?" said Ari.

Kleo's whiskers twitched, but no one else reacted. Jaide was thinking about the word *megastorm*, and how that sounded so much more serious than Project Thunderclap.

"How are we going to stop it?" she asked.

"Stop it?" His eyebrows bolted up the domed forehead so far they looked in danger of falling off the death mask's edge. "Why would you want to do that?"

"We brought you here, professor, because we have some loved ones caught on the other side," said Hector.

"Then you will need to act quickly. Once the cracks are erased, there will be no way to return here from the realm of The Evil — or to go there to rescue them. The way will be completely sealed. They will be trapped forever."

"We suspected as much." Hector looked grim. "Is there any way to rescue them before the megastorm is unleashed?"

"Only one," said the professor. "To do it you'll need a cross-continuum conduit constructor that is turned to the realm of The Evil."

"As a matter of fact, we have just that." Grandma X explained what had been unearthed in the house next door. "We know it works. I have tested it on several occasions, and each time a small amount of The Evil leaked through."

This was news to Jaide, although she supposed she should have guessed. All those small attacks by The Evil had been focused on the house and its surroundings, which made sense if Grandma X was opening the way rather than Aleksandr's Thunderclappers.

"And this is the problem," Rennie was saying. "The Evil always notices when a breach is opened between here and its home. It *wants* the breach to be open so it can come through without running into me and the other wards. It will always be waiting for anyone coming through from our side."

"This was Lottie's downfall, I fear," said Grandma X. "She stole the Bifrost Bridge from the Hawks when they wouldn't let her use it in the hope of making peace. She opened the way, and The Evil was ready for her."

"Jack made it," said Jaide. "Stefano and I heard him calling us, so we know he survived."

"But he didn't tell us what he did to get past The Evil," Stefano added glumly. "And he's been quiet ever since."

"There's a lot we don't know," said Grandma X. "Why was the breach sucking instead of blowing, this time? Is there any way we can control where the breach opens on the other side? Could we somehow disguise the opening so The Evil can't see it? To answer these questions, we need a more complete understanding of the principles involved. Professor, will you help us?"

The death mask's expression was solemn.

"These are difficult questions," he said, "and time is short."

"We know," said Hector. "Will you help us try?"

"Of course," the professor said, "as long as you are aware that the odds are against us."

"We're Wardens," said Grandma X, folding her hands on the table in front of her. "They always are."

CHAPTER NINETEEN

THE IMPOSSIBLE GARDEN

I still can't see anything," said Kyle. "Are you sure Cornelia's taking us the right way?"

Kyle had the sharpest eyesight of the three of them. If he said he couldn't see anything then Jack was happy to assume he wouldn't see anything, either. Tara, however, squinted so hard at the horizon it was amazing she could see anything at all.

"All right, hang on," said Jack. "I'll check."

Setting down his bone-scimitar, he lay out flat on the sand, tilted his head to the side, and closed his eyes. He was reminded of trackers in some of his father's old westerns. They claimed to be able to tell all sorts of things just by listening to the earth. Jack wasn't listening, and he couldn't make out any details like numbers of people or anything like that, but he could sense the life in Lottie's oasis, and he could tell in which direction it lay.

There was no mistake. Cornelia was leading them the right way.

So why couldn't they see anything ahead of them but dead, white desert?

Jack clambered to his feet, brushed the sand out of his ear, and told Tara and Kyle what he thought.

"So we press on," said Tara, although the way she leaned on her sword suggested her enthusiasm was forced.

They were all tired, hungry, and thirsty. It felt as though they had been in the realm of The Evil a lot longer than one day. Not once had all the suns set. Twice more had ice storms swept over them, bringing welcome rain, but never lasting long. The weather always returned to its default state of hot, dry, and boring.

"We press on," Kyle agreed. "But if you and Cornelia are wrong, Jack, I'm going to eat both of you."

"Cornelia would be a bit stringy, I reckon."

"You've never been so hungry you didn't care what you ate?"

Jack thought of his mother's cooking and rubbed his own growling belly. "Sometimes."

They hadn't gone ten feet before Tara said, "Shhh!" and stopped with her left hand held up in the unmistakable *halt* sign.

Kyle and Jack fell in behind her.

"What is it?" asked Jack.

"*Shhh*, I said."

He held his breath and looked all around them, but could see nothing but white sand rolling in waves to a featureless horizon, punctuated by the occasional weird-looking skeleton.

Tara's hand came down.

"I thought I heard something," she said through painfully cracked lips. "Something other than you two big mouths."

"Like what, exactly?" asked Kyle.

"I don't know. Bugs, maybe."

"You're going mad with hunger, just like I am. Let's keep going. We're not actually going anywhere, but that's better than standing around here waiting for something to find us."

"Look at Cornelia," Jack said, pointing upward.

The blue speck was circling over a patch of desert not far from them.

"Is she trying to tell us something?" asked Kyle.

"Maybe she can see something we can't," said Tara.

Jack agreed. "Is she telling us where to go or warning us away?"

"Beats me," said Kyle. "I vote we go find out."

Shouldering his oar, he set off in the lead. Tara looked uneasy but followed. Jack put a hand into his remaining stash of blue-room trinkets before following them, just in case.

"This would make a great beach," said Kyle, "if only there was an ocean."

"I bet there is one, somewhere," said Tara. "All the water in the storms doesn't just vanish."

"Maybe there's an underground ocean." Kyle was excited by this idea. "It'd be cold and dark, and full of eyeless dinosaurs. Maybe that's where Lottie is, Jack, in *The Land That Time Forgot*."

"That was an island," said Jack. "You're thinking of *Journey to the Center of the Earth*."

"Am I? Did that have dinosaurs in it?"

"I think so. The movie did, anyway. But they had eyes."

"That's silly. There wouldn't be any light."

"You think *that's* silly," asked Tara, "but dinosaurs you're okay with?"

Ahead of them, the sand exploded upward, creating a wall of billowing dust directly across their path.

"Uh-oh," cried Kyle, raising his oar. "I don't think this is your great-aunt, Jack."

Jack spun around at the sound of more explosive sand and blooming dust in their wake. To the left and right it was the same. They were surrounded.

"It's a trap!" Tara said, backing up so she, Jack, and Kyle formed a triangle with their weapons facing outward.

Out of the billowing clouds stepped strange figures, alien creatures with too many arms, legs, and heads. At the back was a human, although one that clearly wasn't alive. The figure was composed from Evil bugs, all swarming and squirming in a horrid approximation of a person. The figures, human and alien alike, stepped forward to encircle the three children.

"Stay back!" said Tara, menacing the first to approach with her sword. "I mean it!"

The Evil alien didn't even slow. It came for her with four arms open, and she slashed at it, cutting it in half. There was a ring of steel against bone and the creature fell apart. It was made of bugs swarming a long-dead skeleton.

Another Evil alien instantly took its place.

Jack felt cold sweat trickle down between his shoulder blades. He and the others were tired, hungry, and dehydrated. They were outnumbered many times over. There was no way they were getting out of this one.

++Take me,++ he said. ++I'll give myself up if you let the others go.++

++Too late, troubletwister,++ said The Evil. ++There is no escape now, not for you or your friends. Not now, and not ever!++

Jack slashed his bone-scimitar at the humanoid figure approaching him and felt a sickening squish as it hit home. Two more took its place, reaching for him with squirming, grasping fingers.

Above them, Cornelia was circling and circling, squawking pointlessly. They couldn't move. They were trapped.

Then a ghostly figure appeared in the battlefield, a young woman looking around her as though trying to see her way through a fog.

++Is that you, Jack Shield?++

++Yes!++ Jack cried, relief mingling with desperation. The Evil aliens surrounding them were really pressing in now. One hideous thing with two heads and four mouths snapped entirely too close to his face before he managed to push it away. ++We're in trouble and we need your help!++

++I cannot help you. You must find your own way.++

++I can't! We're surrounded!++

++Do not be afraid. Your Gift is stronger than you think.++

How did you know that? Jack wanted to say. She knew nothing about him. But she had a point. There were very few shadows in a world with three suns, but what there were could be used against the Evil horde. He had to try.

He concentrated and felt his Gift stir in response. He ducked a swipe from a seven-toed paw and pushed up with his bone-scimitar, noting as he did so how it cast a faint shadow across the chest of the thing attacking him. The shadow flexed and darkened, then slid up to wrap itself around the Evil alien's head, where he guessed its eyes should be.

It kept coming, presumably because it was seeing through the eyes of all the Evil bugs at once. Jack ducked another swipe and tried expanding the shadow. If he could blind all of them at once, maybe that would do the trick.

What happened startled him so much he almost lost his concentration entirely.

The shadow spread across the entire alien, which fell back with a chorus of insect squeals, bumping into the creature behind it. Like a contagion, the shadow spread to *that* alien, and to the next one in line, and the one behind that. Within moments, a cloud of shadow was spreading through the entire army like ink through water.

Jack gaped in amazement. He hadn't been trying to do anything like that. But he didn't stop to question it. He pushed harder, encouraging the spread of the shadow to Kyle and Tara's side of the fight. They were still under attack. Kyle's oar was broken in two, and there was only so much he could do to defend himself with the remaining splintered end.

Faster, Jack told the shadow. *Keep going!*

And that was when it happened. The shadow filled the Evil horde and began spreading across the desert, from grain of sand to grain of sand, until everything was black. The sky turned purple, and one by one the suns flickered and went out.

It was suddenly dark, so dark even Jack had trouble seeing.

"What happened?" asked Kyle. "Did we go blind?"

"That was me," said Jack. "I don't know how, but my Gift did that."

"This is our chance," said Tara. She had her owl's eyes again, thanks to the glass rod. "Come on!"

She took Kyle's hand, and Kyle took Jack's. They ducked low under the clutching hands of the alien horde, which was blinded but still trying to attack. Jack kept his Gift working hard to maintain the shadow as they brushed by protesting Evil bug flesh, but really it wasn't that hard at all. All he had to do was keep concentrating and the whole world, it seemed, remained dark.

His head was feeling light when they reached the edge of the horde. Tara seemed to know where she was going, and after a moment Jack realized how. She was following Cornelia's cries. They stumbled across the sand, leaving The Evil horde behind, and ignoring its angry roars.

++Nearly there,++ said Lottie into Jack's mind, her voice little more than a whisper. ++Not much farther. A few more steps. You can do it.++

Jack didn't know what she was talking about. The desert ahead appeared to be as empty as it always was. Just bones and sand all the way to the empty horizon.

But then, without warning, there was suddenly something else.

Jack blinked, not believing his eyes. There was a three-masted ship with ragged sails sitting up proudly in the sand, with trees branching from its decks, hanging low with fruit. Letters carved on its bow declared its name to be *Omega*. Vines crept down its hull to a mat of thick greenery that spread out across the soil. Jack's feet tangled in thick grass, and he almost fell. Kyle pulled him on.

Cornelia swooped down to guide them to the starboard side of the boat, where a ramp led up to the deck. It was steep, and Jack was dizzy. Everything had a strange, dreamlike quality, as though he wasn't quite there. The light was fading in and out, and the shifting shadows made him feel faintly sick. Was the deck moving underneath him, or could that just be his mind playing tricks?

Still holding hands, they came to a large cabin that might once have been the mess. Vegetation crowded the room. They had to push through a wall of foliage just to see what lay at its heart. There, on a bier made from many mattresses sewn together, rested a figure so tiny she looked like a child. She had wispy gray hair and wrinkled features that had collapsed in on themselves, so although it was possible to tell that she had once been beautiful, those days were long behind her. If Jack had had to guess how old she was, he would have said at least a hundred.

"I can't see a thing," said Kyle. "Can you bring the light back, Jack?"

Jack nodded, and the sun returned. White light flooded the cabin, and the old woman blinked up at them.

"Is that really you, Jack Shield?" she said, her voice a rusty wheeze. "You're a little young to be a rescue party. What took you so long?"

"Lottie," said Jack. But it couldn't be her, surely. She was far too old to be Grandma X's sister.

Before the old woman could say a single word, a sudden dizziness rose up in him even more powerfully than before. He clutched at Kyle's shoulder, but missed, and went down on one knee.

"Jack?" called Tara in alarm. "Jack, what's wrong?"

He shook his head, unable to speak. His knee folded beneath him. By the time he hit the floor, he had fainted clean away.

Much later, or so it seemed, the sound of voices drew him slowly back to consciousness.

"It's all about the Gifts," an old woman was saying. "Mine are of growing and concealing. That's how I've been able to survive here so long. They keep my oasis secure and self-sustaining. Once upon a time, there was room here for many people, not just one. But over the years I've grown weaker, and this is all I can manage now."

"Are you the last one?" Jack recognized Kyle's voice. He was talking around something he had in his mouth. It sounded like a bite of apple.

"I am, yes. The others . . . gave much of themselves to

call for help, and when the call wasn't answered their spirits broke and one by one they died."

"What do you mean they gave of themselves?" asked Tara.

"Our life force, our vitality . . . we used some to escape The Evil when we arrived, and the rest to strengthen our living message. It took its toll. They died before their time. Finally, I was the only one left. But I refused to give up. I knew someone would come for me eventually. We gave half our lives to send that message. Our cry for help had to arrive, one day. We knew it would not be ignored."

"Could we send another message now?" asked Kyle.

"No! Not without draining you children of all the life you have. You would end up like me, and I'll not have that, no matter what happens."

A deep sadness filled Lottie's ancient voice, but underneath it was an iron backbone that reminded Jack of Grandma X, and convinced him that this really was his great-aunt.

He opened his eyes and tried to sit up, but his vision was blurry and it was all he could do to raise his head.

"Ah, Jack is awake," Lottie said. "Help him up and give him some food."

Kyle and Tara appeared at Jack's side, and eased him up by the armpits. He blinked and his eyes cleared. He was still in Lottie's cabin, and had been lying on an ancient rug that smelled of dust. He let himself be led to a wooden chair and collapsed gratefully into it. Tara gave him a fruit that looked like an orange banana. Kyle pressed a gourd full of liquid into his other hand. Jack stared at them blankly for a moment. It had been so long since he had eaten or drunk anything that he had almost forgotten how to do it.

"What happened to me?" he asked.

"You overused your Gift," said Lottie from where she lay tucked up in her bed. It looked as though she never moved. Boughs reached over her, all of them laden with produce. All she had to do was reach up and take what she needed. Cornelia sat on one of those boughs, gazing lovingly down at the old woman.

Jack remembered Custer warning him and Jaide about the dangers of using their Gifts too much without eating.

"I didn't mean to make things so dark," he said.

"Our Gifts are much stronger here," Lottie explained. "But the effort of using them still costs you. I'm glad you didn't work that out earlier, or else you might have drained yourself dry. Three of our number did exactly that. They're buried out on the port side."

One thin hand moved slightly, as though to point.

"Are we really in a ship?" asked Jack. He had so many questions, but that was the first one to trip across his lips.

"Yes. We found *Omega* right where it is. Ships go missing sometimes, when The Evil is trying to break through. This could be one of those. Or else it's the remains of a previous expedition. There were no logs for us to check. They had been taken or destroyed long ago, along with the crew. We needed somewhere to live, so we just moved in."

"Try the banana thing," said Tara. "Seriously. It'll make you feel a lot better."

Jack did so, biting numbly until the taste hit him. It tingled like sherbet all along his tongue. Without stopping for breath, he gulped the whole thing down in three bites. Then he sipped from the gourd, which made his parched flesh sing.

"Take it slowly," Lottie warned him with a tiny but warm smile. "Rest, and I'll tell you everything. You're safe here, and that's the first thing you need to know."

The oasis, she explained, was as invisible to The Evil as it had been to Jack. Only when Lottie broke her telepathic silence did The Evil have anything to home in on, so she had tried to call them only twice, once at the dead tree and then a second time when they were right on her doorstep. The Evil had followed her first call to the general area of the oasis, which is how it had known where to lay its trap.

"Does that mean it definitely knows where we are now?" asked Kyle, glancing out one of the cabin windows.

"It has a much better idea now, yes," said Lottie. "But it was worth it. If I had said nothing, you would have died."

"How did Cornelia know?" asked Jack.

The old woman raised her head and smiled at the bird. "David Smeaton used to take me on day-trips to Rourke Castle. I would bring treats for us to eat, but Cornelia always fished them out. It became quite a competition. I soon learned that I could never hide anything from my old friend here, no matter what charms I employed. Her eyes see the world much more clearly than ours — and her ears and nose, too, I suspect. She could always tell when we were coming, even from miles away."

Cornelia bobbed her head and seemed to grin through her beak. "Got you!" she cackled.

"What about those creatures back there?" asked Tara. "Some looked like people, but most of them were . . . weird."

"Everything and everyone The Evil has absorbed is stored in its vast mind," Lottie explained. "We're not the first civilization it has attacked, and we're not likely to be the last."

"Project Thunderclap —" Jack started to say.

"Yes, your friends told me something about that," Lottie said with a roll of her rheumy eyes. "Aleksandr hasn't changed a bit, has he? Only ever thinking of himself, never seeking a permanent solution. His plan might make humanity safe, but what about other people elsewhere, who live on other worlds? Isn't it our responsibility to protect them, too? And what about The Evil itself? Doesn't it have any rights of its own? It's a living thing. We can't blame it for being what it is."

"But what it is," said Tara, "is *evil*."

"Tosh." With a small gesture, Lottie dismissed the remark. "We have to see beyond our version of reality. The Evil is trying to survive, just like we're trying to survive. Just like a lion is trying to survive when it eats an antelope. Is the lion wrong? Is The Evil? Maybe from its point of view, we're the ones who are wrong. That's hard to imagine, I know, but you've got to open your minds. You can't defeat your enemy unless you understand your enemy, and maybe when you understand your enemy you won't want to defeat your enemy anymore."

Jack's still-woozy brain struggled with this. "Do you mean we should just give up?"

"Of course not! But there are other ways. The Evil is an intelligent being — we know this because it's so hard to fight. It can reason and plan and communicate. Why can't we learn to coexist? We owe it to ourselves to try, or else we are no better than monsters ourselves."

The old woman sighed. "Of course, that's what brought me here. *Trying*. I've had so many years to wish I'd done things differently, and so many reasons to feel regret, but I remain certain I did the right thing. No one else has studied The Evil as I have. No one else has the knowledge I have of its nature. I must get home to share what I have learned with everyone."

"We want to take you home," said Kyle firmly.

"We just don't know how," Tara added.

"With your youth and my knowledge," the old woman said, "I'm sure we can find a way. But first, I must ask you something about the world I left behind. I have heard nothing for so long. I want to know more about my family. Jack, you say you're my great-nephew, and you have the look of the Shields about you. You're definitely Giles's grandson. Tell me about your twin. I want to know all about your parents, my nieces or nephews. And my sister! Oh, she was so against me opening the Bridge. We argued something fierce the night before; she actually threatened to tell Father on me. I don't suppose *he* is still alive. Did he ever forgive me? Did he ever live down the shame of a disobedient daughter like me?"

Jack's stomach clenched around his food. Of course: She wouldn't know that her father had died the night of the Catastrophe. How was he going to tell her that? She looked so small and frail. He was afraid it might kill her.

But it didn't. She took the news quietly and silently, offering no more than a nod to confirm that she had heard. Her shining gaze never left Jack's as he stumbled through the words, and when he was done she reached out, with no small amount of effort, and took his hand. Her fingers felt as dry and light as autumn leaves.

"It's all right," she said. "Father was a good man, and a very good Warden. You have something of him in you, I think. Gifts pass down the generations by other means than genes, you know."

Jack nodded, thinking of his secondary Gift.

"And what of Lara Mae?" she asked. "Did she ever forgive me?"

"Who?" he asked.

"Lara Mae. My sister, your grandmother. Don't tell me she died as well?"

"No, she's very much alive. We call her Grandma X. I don't know why. Is Lara Mae her real name? Jaide will have a fit we found out first."

Lottie's grip tightened, then abruptly let go. Her hand flew to her mouth, and pressed there, as though to keep something terrible inside.

"There is only one circumstance under which a Warden will surrender her name," Lottie said. "And that is to become the Warden of Last Resort."

"What does that *mean*?" asked Jack, leaning forward. Lottie was proving to be a veritable fire hose of information. "Why won't anyone talk about it?"

"Only the Examiner knows," Lottie said. "And the Warden herself. People say it is supposed to be horrible, a fate worse than death, and I believe they may be right. . . . Oh, Lara Mae, what have you done?"

"If it's so bad, why would she do it?" asked Tara. She had been sitting contentedly by while Jack and his great-aunt caught up on family and Warden business, but this new mystery had her hooked.

Instead of answering, Lottie held up one wrinkled finger. The tip flashed with a bright, silver light. Jack was immediately drawn to it, and so were Tara and Kyle. The silver light was cool and at the same time oddly penetrating. It seemed to drill through the back of their eyes, right into their brains.

"You will not remember," Lottie said in a soft voice. "I

conceal this information from you, until such time as you have need of it. Until then, it is forgotten."

Her finger curled into her fist and the light went out. The children stayed as they were for a moment, eyes blank as their minds rearranged themselves to tuck away the preceding minutes.

Then Jack blinked. What had they been talking about? His mind had wandered off for a moment. He was clearly more tired than he thought. Lottie was feeling the toll of the excitement, too. She seemed to have aged another ten years.

"We're going to take you home," he said firmly.

"With your youth and my knowledge, I'm sure we'll find a way," the old woman said with a determination that belied her frailty. "Let's gather our strength as we make our plans. We will need both if we hope to succeed."

CHAPTER TWENTY

PROJECT THUNDERCLAP

The sound of a storm-warning siren curled eerily over Portland's tiled roofs and along its deserted streets. It was dawn on Thursday morning, and the Hawks were making their move. The tent was a whirlwind of people coming and going, many of them via lightning. Above the town, thick clouds were gathering, piling higher and higher into the stratosphere. The strange weather had ordinary meteorologists scratching their heads and ordinary citizens boarding up their windows.

But Aleksandr and his Hawks weren't the only conspirators on the move that morning. In the passenger seat of a flame-daubed Austin 1600, with her knees up to her chest, Jaide Shield stared sleepily at the townsfolk passing by. The streets were as packed as she had ever seen them. Traffic on the roads to Scarborough and Dogton was down to a crawl. From above came the steady *whocka-whocka* of her mother's helicopter. Susan's paramedic team was there to lend credence to the fake state of emergency that the mayor had declared overnight. Depending on who heard the news, the warnings were either of a storm front or a chemical spill, or whatever theory sounded most credible to them. Jaide wondered if Kyle's father and his fellow Portland Peregrinators were imagining UFOs, or perhaps a Sasquatch uprising.

School was canceled. The hospital was being evacuated. A pall seemed to fall across Portland as the bruise-colored sky deepened even further to greenish black. Even the cats were evacuating, urged by Kleo and Ari to prowl elsewhere for the day. By midday, the town was expected to be completely empty.

In the meantime, Jaide and Grandma X were parked on the corner of River Road and Station Street. They had been there for an hour.

"What are we waiting for, exactly?" Jaide asked her grandmother. "How big is this thing?"

"Look for a removal truck or something similar," Grandma X said. She was peering through a pair of binoculars at the traffic inching by, lowering the glasses occasionally to wipe the mist off the windshield. "You'll know it when you see it. There's only one lodestone big enough to hold the energy Aleksandr will need. It has to be the one from Avak."

Jaide was a little fuzzy on what the Avak Lodestone was, or how it was going to be used in their plan. It was an ancient meteorite, she gathered, or a large chunk of one, secretly unearthed by Wardens a long time ago. It could store huge amounts of lightning energy, and then release it all at once, at its controller's command. There had been talk about tapping into that power, but that was where Jaide had gotten lost. They had been making plans well into the night, and she had started the night tired after the third Examination. Her father was involved. That was all she was sure of.

Grandma X had made her go to sleep for a few hours, but she didn't think anyone else had stopped to rest. On being woken before dawn, she had found the blue room cleared and the cross-continuum conduit constructor sitting at its center. There was no sign of the professor: Someone had stolen back into the tent and put him where he was supposed to be, so Aleksandr wouldn't know that he had ever gone missing. Grandma X had been a whirlwind of activity . . . but now here they were sitting in the car, waiting for Portland to empty and a big rock to drive by. Stefano got to hang out with Hector.

Jaide wondered what Jack was doing. She had tried teeping him several times as she lay tossing and turning, haunted by the empty bed in her room. He hadn't replied once. She had even tried texting his phone, but the messages had all bounced back, undeliverable. Mentally, and sometimes physically, too, she crossed her fingers and hoped with all her heart that he was safe.

Her wandering gaze caught sight of a familiar face driving by.

"Hey, isn't that Doctor Witworth?" she said, pointing.

"Indeed it is." Grandma X seemed unfazed by the reappearance of the woman who had drugged her and then stolen the professor, six months ago. "The Evil's minions are everywhere. It is not surprising they suspect something. There has never been a gathering of lightning wielders like this, not in all of Warden history."

"Do you think she'll try to stop us?"

"Undoubtedly, if she learns what we're planning." Grandma X sat up higher in her seat. "Ah, here it is, just as I expected."

Jaide saw a big white truck lumbering toward them down the road. It sat low on its rear tires, as though carrying something very heavy. Jaide watched it go by Station Street and signal to turn at Gabriel's Auto Sales. It was definitely heading for the tent.

"Now what?" asked Jaide.

"One moment." Grandma X's eyes were closed. "I am just speaking with Hector."

Jaide waited, with only mild impatience. Ever since she had been inducted into the conspiracy no secrets had been kept from her for long. The answer would come eventually.

Grandma X's eyes opened. She started the car.

"Now we go join your father," she said. "It's time for the lightning wielders to present yourselves at Project Thunderclap."

Hector was waiting for Jaide with Stefano when the Austin 1600 pulled up by the oval. He had something hidden under his pullover — either that, thought Jaide, or he had eaten an astonishingly large breakfast.

"All's ready?" he asked Grandma X. Something passed between them through her open window. It looked like a large, flat black stone, rough on one side, smooth on the other, and Hector's stomach had returned to normal.

"It is now," she said. Glancing behind her to make sure Jaide and Stefano were away from the car, she pulled away from the curb and drove home.

"What was that?" Stefano asked as they headed for the tent.

"A piece of the lodestone," said Hector. "Magnetic meteorites have special properties. We have this small piece here and the large piece in the tent, but for a while it'll be as though they were never separated. What happens to one will happen to the other. And what goes into one we can take out of the other."

It was like an extension cord, Jaide thought. Aleksandr was charging up a giant battery in the tent, and Grandma X could draw from that battery in Watchward Lane. Professor Olafsson had been clear that it would take more than three lightning wielders, two of them troubletwisters, to ensure the safe operation of the Bridge to the realm of The Evil. If they were going to do it safely, they would need to steal from Aleksandr.

At the entrance to the tent, they were greeted by two Warden guards who waved them through. The interior of the tent seemed even bigger than it had been the previous night. Many of the canvas partitions had come down to form a wide central space at the center of which loomed a tall obelisk-like object. The Avak Lodestone, Jaide presumed. Mr. Carver would have approved. It was attached by thick wires to a single metal pole that stuck vertically out of the ground and poked right up through the highest point of the tent. Next to the lodestone was a cross-continuum conduit constructor that Jaide recognized as the one they had found in Rourke Castle, now repaired and shining as new. A crowd of Wardens was assembling around the lodestone and the bass cylinder, some of whom Jaide recognized from the Grand Gathering. Some were in statue form, or paintings, presumably the relics Grandma X had referred to. There was even a tree with a human face carved into the wrinkles and knots of its ancient bark.

Jaide, Hector, and Stefano joined the throng, and moments later Aleksandr stepped up onto a podium to call everyone to order.

"This is a historic day." His deep voice embraced the crowd and drew everyone in it to his bosom. "Today, our long labor, and the labor of our forebears, will end. Today we usher in a new era of peace and security for all of humanity. Today we defeat The Evil once and for all!"

The crowd cheered.

"Famous last words," Stefano whispered in Jaide's ear. "At least, they will be if he's wrong."

Someone shushed him.

"In a moment we will begin," Aleksandr continued. "Your cell leaders have their instructions. You know what to do. I wish only to acknowledge the part you will play in this great endeavor, and to say that you have my undying gratitude and admiration. Do not flag, and do not doubt. Everything we do today is for the good of all."

He waved one arm high above his head and stepped down.

"I'm your cell leader," Hector told Jaide and Stefano. "It's very simple, really. All we have to do is draw the energy out of the storm and into the lodestone. Take my hands. It's starting."

Around them, Wardens lined up behind their cell leaders, linking hands in chains and beginning to concentrate. Jaide could feel a tension growing in the air, like someone was stretching the world out and pressing it flat under a hot iron. Her father's hand was very dry, and it gripped hers tightly. Her Gifts shivered inside her with something like excitement. Neither she nor they had ever been in the presence of so much *power*.

A surge traveled along one chain of Wardens three away from where Jaide was standing. She didn't see all of it, just the aftermath, in which the cell leader flashed white and turned into an X-ray image of himself. She could clearly see his bones and teeth, and he twitched all over as though electrocuted. Then, with a piercing crack, lightning struck the tent's central pole. Energy flowed into the lodestone, the cell leader returned to normal, and the build-up resumed.

"Just like that," said Hector. "Follow my lead."

Jaide concentrated. She could feel her father's Gift linking with hers through their hands. An echo of Stefano's came to her, too. Hector's was stronger and more disciplined than both of theirs combined. It was like a rope, already staunch and safe, made stronger by the two new strands they provided. A lasso, she thought, reaching out to tame the lightning.

Three more bolts hit the pole in quick succession. Jaide barely heard them. She was concentrating on her Gift and marveling at what it could do. The storm looked huge and monolithic from below, but up close it was a wild mess of eddies and sudden surges. How were they supposed to tame *that*? Jaide had no idea, but Hector knew. Through him she saw techniques and tricks she might never have devised on her own. Threads of electricity were drawn in and woven together. Potential began to build.

Her hair stood on end. The soles of her feet left the ground. She felt as though she was breathing in, and in, and in, until she was full of the energy of life itself. Just as she began to wonder if it was too much, it suddenly rushed out of her, into her father, who turned into a horrifying X-ray version of himself, jerked all over — and lightning struck the pole, brought down to earth by the three of them alone.

She dropped back to earth, feeling a mixture of elation and exhaustion.

"Again," said Hector.

And so they did it again.

Jaide soon lost track of time. Each bolt seemed to take an hour, but she knew it couldn't be that long. The air inside the tent was immensely hot, but at the same time bone-dry, like the inside of an oven. Wardens offering water in pitchers came by periodically, provoking the occasional wild spark. Twice, older Wardens were carried off to recover, their strength depleted. Jaide became so used to people becoming skeletons that she didn't even blink when it happened. Her ears were numb from the relentless booming of thunder.

In the center of the tent, the lodestone started to glow a dull cherry red.

It couldn't be much longer now.

"I want to go," she whispered to Hector. "I want to be with Grandma when it happens."

He didn't have any words. When he opened his mouth, only sparks came out, so he simply let go of her hand. Jaide stepped back, feeling every rigid muscle in her legs complain. Stefano opened his eyes, panting with exhaustion, and nodded.

Jaide slipped out of the circle of straining lightning wielders and headed for the exit. Her legs and knees felt like they were held together with pipe cleaners. It was all she could do to walk in a straight line, which explained how she completely failed to see Aleksandr coming.

"Leaving so soon, young Shield?"

"Uh, yes . . . but not because I want to." It took as much effort to lie as it did to stand without falling. "My Gifts . . . too close to Dad, it turns out. I did what I could. Do you mind . . . ?"

"Not at all. Come back in an hour or so to witness the big push. We'll be ready by then." His gaze slid off her, back to the glowing lodestone. He brushed his beard and breathed, "Historic . . ."

Jaide bolted for the exit, not caring if she wobbled, just as long as she got away before anyone else decided to talk to her. The spaces around the central chamber were thankfully empty, and although it took her three tries to find the exit, she breathed a sigh of relief when she saw the light outside again.

Only there wasn't much light. What little there was had been filtered through the heavy sheets of rain that were now lashing Portland. Occasional flashes from the lightning streaming into the tent pole only confused things. Jaide stood on the threshold for a moment, considering her options. She could try calling someone to get a lift, but Grandma X would be busy and Susan had her own tasks to perform. Jaide wasn't sure she wanted her mother looking over her shoulder as they tried to rescue Jack, Tara, and Kyle. It wasn't as if she could do anything, and if things went wrong . . .

Scrunching up her face and tucking her elbows in close to her side, Jaide decided to make a run for it.

Within three paces, she was soaked to the skin. Water streamed down her face, getting into her eyes no matter how furiously she blinked. It was so dark the streetlights had come on, even though it was still morning. The tiny pools of illumination they cast looked relatively warm but were no less cold than everywhere else. Jaide groaned unhappily as she ran up Dock Road. By the time she reached the Parkhill Street intersection, her teeth were chattering.

Before she turned, she glanced behind her and saw a wondrous sight. Bolt after bolt of lightning was striking the top of the tent. The thunder was almost continuous now, and the tent was lit up from within by a bright orange glow. The alternating lightning-blue and orange flashing was almost hypnotic, and she stared at it an instant too long. The toes of her right foot caught the curb and her left foot landed in a slippery puddle. Both legs went in different directions and she came down hard on her backside, crying out in pain and surprise.

Instead of feeling sorry for herself, she told herself to get up and keep going. There were worse things than being covered in mud.

An open hand came down at her from the torrential rain, offering her help. She was startled, but took it with gratitude. The woman — that was all Jaide could make out through the rain at first — leaned back and pulled her upright. Jaide longed for the raincoat the woman was wearing. It was long and dark, with a hood.

"That was quite a fall! Are you all right?"

Jaide brushed wet hair from her eyes, and nodded. The woman looked familiar but Jaide couldn't immediately place her.

"Thanks. I'm all right."

"Are you sure? You should come inside and let me check you over."

"I'm okay, honest."

"It's no trouble. I'm a doctor."

Jaide went so cold she was surprised the water soaking her clothes didn't turn instantly to ice. *That* was where she knew the woman from. She was Dr. Witworth, the Evil minion Jaide had seen entering Portland earlier.

"I have to go," Jaide said.

A strong hand gripped her elbow before she could take a step.

"Don't be foolish, Jaide Shield. The safest place in this storm is with me."

"Yeah, right. I know who you are, and I'm not going anywhere with you."

Dr. Witworth's eyes narrowed and her fingers dug deeply into Jaide's flesh. She had abandoned all pretense now. Her eyes were fully human, but she didn't need to be possessed to be Evil.

"No one can stand up to The Evil's full power on her own. You are arrogant to think you can, or perhaps you're simply stupid. It'll give me great pleasure to see you destroyed like everyone else when the storm strikes."

"You can't fool me," Jaide said, stung by the accusation that she was stupid. "The storm has nothing to do with The Evil. It's —"

She stopped, kicking herself.

"It's what?" asked Dr. Witworth, pulling Jaide close.

"It's . . . nothing," Jaide said. Maybe she *was* stupid for almost blurting out everything about Project Thunderclap. "It's just freaky weather, that's all."

"There is no *all* when this many Wardens gather." Dr. Witworth's expression was nasty. "You may have the old fool back, but now I have you. You'll either tell us everything or we'll use you as leverage. The Great Steward wouldn't abandon one of his own, would he? Your lot is so predictably sentimental. That's why you're going to lose."

Wanna bet? Jaide almost said, but this time she kept the voice in her head still. "I told you once," she said instead, "I'm not going anywhere with you."

Her first Gift came to life at her calling, surrounding Dr. Witworth in a rushing cylinder of air. The woman felt herself being tugged away, but instead of screaming and giving up as Jaide had hoped, she lunged for Jaide and took her into a viselike embrace. Jaide was pulled into the miniature hurricane with her and sent skidding across the sidewalk in a storm of wind and water.

"Let go of me!" Jaide kicked and wriggled, but Dr. Witworth had her arms tightly pinned.

"Call it off!" the woman ordered, her face just millimeters from Jaide's. There was fear in her eyes, a fear that drove her anger. "Call it off, you little witch!"

Jaide was so startled to be called something like that she almost did exactly as she was told. Was that what ordinary people would think of her, if they knew what she could do? Why not, since that was exactly what *she* had thought Grandma X was, before learning the truth? Perhaps that was why some people fell in with The Evil — because they thought the *Wardens* were the Evil ones, witches and warlocks in league with the Devil.

That so obviously wasn't the way it was, but the thought threw her off, regardless. Her concentration faltered, and the whirlwind eased accordingly. Dr. Witworth found her footing first and managed to get one arm around Jaide's throat.

"Now, walk," she hissed in Jaide's ear. "And no more funny business."

Light flared in front of them. Something growled, deeper and louder than a saber-toothed tiger. Then it roared, and the light rushed toward them. Dr. Witworth froze like a rabbit caught in headlights, and Jaide took her chance. She pushed as hard as she could and burst free of the arm around her throat. Then she leaped out of the way as a car as large as a small house ran over the very spot where she had been standing.

Brakes squealed. A door opened.

"Get in!" cried Rodeo Dave. "This is no night to be out walking on your own!"

Jaide didn't need to be told twice. She clambered onto the car's enormous back seat, leaving a trail of water behind. She was breathing hard and her hands were shaking.

"Where did she go? Did you hit her?"

"No." Rennie was in the passenger seat, peering out the window. "She seemed to take off like a rocket when you pushed her away."

"Oh." Jaide remembered her Gift. Who knew what it had done with the woman? She didn't have the stomach to wonder. "How did you know I needed you?"

"We didn't," admitted Rodeo Dave. "We were strongly advised by Officer Haigh to get out of town. She said she wasn't leaving the porch until we did, so we got in the car and drove around the block, hoping she'd be gone when we got back. That was when we saw you."

Rennie smiled and held out her hands. Jaide took them. Of course the Living Ward was never going to leave Portland, on this night or any other. And Rodeo Dave might have lost his memory of being a Warden, but that didn't mean he'd lost his instincts. He'd be there for Portland if it needed him.

"Where has Haigh got to?" he said, peering through the window at the front of his shop. "Why isn't she chasing kidnappers and looters instead of kicking honest folk out into the storm?"

His mustache bristled and his nose turned a deep shade of purple. He looked like he had a lot more to say on that subject, but then he remembered Jaide in the backseat and visibly calmed down.

"Let's get you home," he said. "Then we'll see about all that."

"Good idea, Dave," said Rennie. "And then perhaps you can drop me at Mermaid Point. I know someone who will be able to help keep Portland safe."

CHAPTER TWENTY-ONE
HERE BE DRAGONS

Something was stirring. Jack could feel it. He was sitting on the deck of the ship, concentrating exactly as Lottie had told him to, while the others were in the cabin, supposedly searching through the remains of the *Compendium* and trying to get the Oracular Crocodile to say something useful without eating anyone's finger. In truth, they were mainly arguing. Their angry words washed over him, distracting him and making him tense.

"You can tell just by looking at this world that The Evil has sucked it dry," Lottie said. "I was the only thing bigger than a bug left until you arrived. That's why it was so desperate to draw you in. The Evil is starving."

"What's wrong with that?" Kyle asked. "It tried to eat *me*. Let it starve, I say!"

"And I say that it is a unique creature on the edge of extinction. It would be wrong to kill it out of hand. How do we know that it can't learn to change? Has anyone asked it?"

"Have you?" asked Tara.

"No," Lottie conceded with a sigh. "It tried to eat me, too. Many times."

It was all theoretical, Jack thought. No one was trying to kill The Evil, were they? They just wanted to cut it off from Earth, so no more people would die. *Human* people, anyway . . .

He tried not to think about that part. The meditation was difficult enough as it was, without his conscience niggling at him. What if The Evil only wanted to come to Earth because there was nowhere else left to go? What if the success of Aleksandr's plan meant that it would starve to death? Was that the murder of an intelligent being or the cold hard cost of survival?

Concentrate!

The Evil, Lottie had told him, exploited cracks in reality to cross between worlds. It couldn't make its own cracks, the way Wardens did, but it could collect them and hold on to them, creating a kind of Grand Central Station leading to all the worlds it had taken over. She called it the Inward Facing Mandala, which Jack didn't really understand. It was something Buddhist, she said. All that mattered was finding its location. Finding it, and then getting to it. And then getting home, *if* they beat Project Thunderclap to the punch.

At any moment he expected the sky to light up with lightning. If that happened, all possibility of escape would slip away. He didn't know what time it was back home, but he suspected they didn't have much left.

That feeling was reinforced by strange rumblings and murmurs in the bedrock of the realm of The Evil, conveyed to him via his secondary Gift, which he was using to seek the way out of the world. He could sense life through the ground, so why couldn't he sense life through cracks as well? That was Lottie's argument. The world was full of life, so it should be clearly visible via his Gift, if he looked in the right direction. But it was confusing. There was so much rock in the world beneath him, and it cast reflections and mirages that led him in circles or down dead ends. He could feel the opening he was looking for, just out of reach, but every time he thought he was getting close it slipped away from him.

"Nom nom nom nom," said the Oracular Crocodile, followed by a sharp yelp from Kyle.

Jack closed his eyes more tightly than ever. His friends were doing everything they could. He should do the same. The Mandala had to be somewhere!

It was no use. The world's bedrock didn't show any holes or tunnels leading anywhere.

Jack felt a movement at his side. It was Tara, squatting down next to him. There was a sheet of paper in her hand, possibly one from the *Compendium*. On it was a mess of diagrams and sketches of things so strange it hurt Jack's eyes just to glance at them.

"Some of your Warden friends were crazy," she said. "I mean really crazy. This guy lived in a barrel and never cut his hair, ever. They found him smothered one day when they came to bring him his breakfast, his hair had grown so long. Anyway, Lottie says his Gift was seeing things far away. He drew the first maps of Antarctica, hundreds of years before it was discovered. And he drew maps of a place that doesn't seem to exist. I think it's this place, where The Evil lives."

"Cool," Jack said, although the business about the barrel certainly wasn't. "Did he say where the Mandala was?"

She held up the paper and pointed at a place where dozens of lines converged.

"Look for a mountain," she said. "That's the best we've got."

He nodded and squinted at the picture.

"What's that he drew coiled around the mountain? A snake?"

"We don't know, and neither did the crocodile skull. I guess we'll have to find that out the hard way."

Jack took a deep breath. "Thanks, I think. It didn't occur to me to look anywhere *high*."

He closed his eyes again and forced his mind to settle. The ground was even more restless now than it had been before, as though something was worrying it. Huge echoes rolled back and forth like ripples on a giant pond, but instead of water it was the stone moving. It made him feel like he was moving, too, rocking up and down on a sluggish sea. He tried to put it out of his mind in case he started to feel seasick. He wasn't very good with boats.

Across the surface of the world his mind went, seeking the source of the vibrations. They did seem to be converging on one spot, and it was indeed a mountain, conical like a volcano, but old and cold and riddled with empty chambers where lava had once flowed. Jack explored those chambers with his mind, and found spaces he couldn't comprehend, including passages that were infinite and holes that looped back on themselves. None of those were helpful, but he kept looking, hoping against hope that he'd find a flicker of life.

Deep in the heart of the mountain, he found something tiny but detectable. It made his heart race and his mouth water. He could practically smell the air of Earth in his nostrils.

Jack opened his eyes.

"That's it," he cried. "I've got it!"

"Where?" asked Tara excitedly. "How far? Kyle has built a sled thing for Lottie. It'll slide over the sand and we can take turns pulling her."

That was the bad news. "It's a long way from here. We'll never make it on foot."

"Uh," she said, falling back on her heels. "So what do we do?"

Jack sat in silence for a minute, possibilities turning in his mind. It didn't seem fair that they could have found the way out but weren't able to get there in time. There had to be a way. They had one Warden, one troubletwister, two resourceful children, and a very wise Hyacinth Macaw, not to mention a bloodthirsty skull and some random pages from the *Compendium*. There was nothing they couldn't do back home, if they put their minds to it. Why not here as well?

"My Gifts are stronger here," he said, an idea slowly occurring to him. "Lottie never explained why. But maybe we can use that to our advantage."

"You're not seriously thinking of bringing the mountain to us, are you?" said Tara.

"Wouldn't that be amazing?" He grinned at the thought. "But not quite. Let's go tell Kyle and Lottie that we found it. And then you can tell me if I'm crazy or not."

"I don't care about crazy," said Tara, helping him to his feet. "Just as long as it works."

The deck was really shaking underfoot by the time they were ready to leave. Jack was the only one who could feel it, which amazed him. It was like an earthquake, rising and falling in waves. There were times he had to stop and hold on to something until it passed. No one else felt it, though. It was just him, thanks to his second Gift.

"I'm going to miss this place," said Lottie softly. They'd

propped her up on Kyle's sled and put her on the foredeck. "It's been my home all these years."

"Wait until you see what's waiting for you," said Tara. "There's the Internet and HDTV and cell phones and . . ."

"All I want is a bath, dear. And a cup of really *hot* tea that I don't have to coax out of the plants by force of will."

Kyle came up the ramp with a double armload of fruit. "That's the last of it. Do you think it'll be enough?"

Lottie nodded. "Put some here and the rest where Jack can reach it. He'll need every calorie he can get."

Jack was standing on the bow, trying not to feel nervous. The circle of greenery surrounding *Omega* seemed very small, and the distance they had to travel was very large. The horde of Evil aliens that had chased them appeared to have dispersed, but that didn't mean they weren't hiding somewhere, waiting to pounce.

It was going to work, he told himself. It *had* to work. Tara had declared herself captain and ordered him to not do it wrong.

Said captain was making one last inspection to ensure nothing had been forgotten. When she was done, she stood behind Jack and put her hands on her hips. With her sword tucked into an old belt she had found belowdeck, and Cornelia on her shoulder, she looked like a young but very fierce pirate.

"Let's go," she said.

Jack closed his eyes and woke his Gifts. They came easily, rushing out of him in an explosion of energy. The sunlight flickered, but that was just a passing glitch from his first Gift. It was his second that he needed, the one he had inherited from his step-grandfather, Joe Henschke.

There was a long, drawn-out creak. The deck shifted under him. He braced himself and pushed harder.

With a great ripping and tearing of roots, the ship began to move. Only it wasn't really the ship that was moving, but the ground under it, rising like a wave, carrying the *Omega* high on its back.

"Anchors aweigh!" Cornelia squawked in triumph.

"Yee-ha!" shouted Kyle. "It's working!"

It was indeed. The ship was moving, carried along on the crest of a slowly building wave of soil, bringing a large number of trees and lots of tangled vines along for the ride. The wave, and the ship surfing with it, was heading in a straight line across the desert, aiming more or less at one of the suns hanging low over the horizon. That was the direction the mountain lay. But the ship needed to move much faster than this if it was to reach the mountain in time.

Jack's stomach growled.

"Don't forget what she said." Kyle thrust an orange banana into his hand. "Eat it or you'll burn yourself up."

Jack didn't argue. He knew Lottie was doing the same. It was her job to keep the ship hidden as it traveled across the sand. He stuffed the fruit into his mouth, swallowed, and felt a tingling sensation down his throat as the pulpy flesh was instantly absorbed.

He felt a new surge of energy, and the wave of soil responded to his urging. The ship ran down ahead of it a little, and Jack heard things clattering below deck. Another fruit and the wave accelerated again. He opened his eyes and saw great plumes of sand spouting in high arcs on either side of the ship, like water spray from a speedboat. He turned his head and gasped at the vast wall of swift-moving dirt he had raised up. It was at least a hundred feet high, but it was surprisingly narrow, only thirty or forty feet wider than the ship itself.

"Woo-hoo!" shouted Tara, waving the sword above her head. "Here we go!"

Jack bared his teeth and reached for another orange banana.

The sun ahead began to set. Jack had no idea how fast they were going, but he sensed the mountain coming steadily closer. With both wave and ship hidden safely within the bubble of invisibility Lottie provided, they passed several outcroppings of The Evil at work in its realm. Huge swarms of bugs tilled the soil, searching grain by grain for anything living. Vast gray honeycombs housed the eggs the Evil bugs hatched from. Overhead, occasional flocks of Evil birds scoured the land. Jack wondered if they were looking for the escapees. The Evil must surely have noticed the empty oasis by now.

Jack ate constantly, absorbing energy contained in the fruit directly into his Gift. The pile beside him grew steadily smaller. Just as he was beginning to wonder if there would be enough, the horizon ahead changed from a perfectly straight line to a line with a slight blip in it. Silhouetted against the setting sun, which turned a muddy orange that was only slightly eye watering to look at, the mountain looked like a single tooth in an aging alligator's bottom jaw.

"Is that it?" asked Kyle, who was sitting next to him, holding the umbrella above Jack's head to keep the burning light of the other suns from him.

Jack nodded. His mouth was too full to talk.

"Land ahoy!" Kyle shouted back to Tara. It seemed appropriate, even though they were surrounded by nothing but land. The mountain rose as the sun inched below the horizon, uncannily like an island rising into view from an endless sea. Jack pulled mentally on the wave, making it shift course slightly. The hint of life was coming from the other side of the mountain, to the left.

"No sign of that snake thing," said Tara.

"Maybe it lives inside," Kyle said.

Jack wished he hadn't said that. The sides of the mountain were pockmarked with holes, like gaping mouths. If the mountain was hollow, it could house a very big snake indeed.

The far side of the mountain came into view. It was strangely lopsided, and there weren't any holes that he could see. Perhaps there had been a landslide, Jack thought, although that didn't make sense, either. The rear of the mountain was a different color to the front, too. The stone on the near side was reddish-orange, whereas the landslide was gray-white. It was the same color as the insects, in fact. . . .

A queasy feeling swept through Jack. He let the wave get smaller, earth tumbling away to either side, the ship slowing as he did so. It was much quieter now, with less soil being displaced.

"How's Lottie doing?" Jack whispered to Kyle.

"Fine, I think."

"Go check, and be quiet about it. Tell Tara we need to be absolutely invisible. Everything depends on it."

"Why? What's happening?"

"See that entire side of the mountain? Where it looks like someone poured wax down the side of a model? That's all bugs, and we really don't want them to know we're here."

Kyle gulped.

"No," he said. "I'll pass that on."

Weirdly, it was harder to keep the smaller, slower wave going than it had been to go fast, and Jack's brow was soon covered with sweat. He let Kyle steer: one tap on the right shoulder to go right, one tap on the left to go left. It worked well enough until they reached a shoal of bones at the base of the mountain, a huge mass of bones that Jack simply couldn't raise up. Unlike the soil, it resisted his power. The wave petered out and the ship slowly came to rest, as if it had truly been beached upon an alien shore.

The sound of the swarming mass of Evil bugs on the mountain was like a waterfall, unceasingly busy and full of the hint of violence.

"Is our way out under there?" Tara had come forward to whisper in Jack's ear.

Jack nodded. Of course it was. That was where The Evil most wanted to be. "I think I can get us up there, but I don't know what to do about the bugs. Trying to use both of my Gifts at once might break my brain, and I'm almost out of fuel as well."

He had been trying to go easy, and was already feeling woozy as a result.

"What does Lottie think?"

"She's pretty sure she can't get us through all of that without The Evil noticing," Tara said, confirming his fears. "We need a distraction."

"What kind of distraction?"

"For The Evil to be interested, it'd have to be something living. . . ."

They both turned to look at Cornelia, and they both shook their heads at the same time.

"What about the vines?" asked Kyle. "They're alive, and it would be easy to make a kind of planter for them. It wouldn't have to last long. If we stopped the ship, Jack could send them one way, and we could go the other when The Evil pounces on it."

"Brilliant!" said Tara. "That's exactly what we'll do. Jack, get around this reef and take a rest. I'll see if Lottie can keep us invisible for a while longer. Kyle, you get started on that planter and I'll join you in a sec."

Jack nodded wearily and raised a new wave. It was much smaller, but it did propel the *Omega* around the tangled boneyard to a sandy inlet at the base of the mountain. There he brought *Omega* around in case they needed to make a quick getaway, let the wave of soil go, and eased himself back until he was stretched out flat on the deck, with his hands folded across his stomach. He was exhausted. If he just closed his eyes for a moment he was sure he'd feel much better. . . .

"Jack, Jack, wake up." Kyle was whispering, but he was doing it right into Jack's ear, so it seemed very loud.

Jack sat up, blinking. How long had he been out? There was an entirely different sun in the sky above him, and the ground was booming and rocking like the *Titanic* ride at MovieWorld.

"We're ready." Kyle pointed over the side, where a strange craft awaited its launch. It was little more than four barrels tied together, from which protruded an enormous tangle of vines and branches. They hadn't uprooted everything — there were still plenty of trees remaining on the ship — but nothing easily movable had been spared. The resulting miniature forest had the same shape as a chef's hat, but many, many times larger.

"Okay," said Jack, reaching for more fruit. He felt hollow with exhaustion, but if Lottie was still hanging in there so would he.

"Go that way," said Tara, giving him what seemed like a random direction. "Lottie will protect the raft as far as she can. When it pops up on The Evil's radar, get ready to move. . . . You're *sure* you can take us where we need to be?"

"One hundred percent," he said, although he thought it was actually about seventy percent. He'd never tried anything like this before. Who knew what would work and what wouldn't? But there was no point worrying anyone when they had no other options.

Jack lifted the ground under the vine-raft and sent it moving out across the sand. It wobbled a bit, but another lift set it straight and back on course. He watched it go, farther and farther, and at the last minute thought to lift the wave that propelled it higher before it passed out of the range of his Gift.

Cornelia flapped down next to them, sent by Lottie.

"All hands on deck," she squawked softly.

There was no visible change to the raft, but what happened on the mountain left no doubt that The Evil had seen it. A whirring shriek rose up from the mass of insects as millions of wings started to flap. Bugs tumbled and rolled, clutching at one another to form new shapes, new configurations. At first it was like watching an avalanche from directly underneath. The middle section slumped downward in one rolling mass, while two flanks separated and began a more leisurely outward descent.

The avalanche kept changing. The flanks got longer and broader, while the middle began to bulge outward. It looked almost as though the avalanche was trying to imitate one single thing, Jack thought. Could The Evil ever have absorbed something so big? It wasn't impossible, he supposed, given it was old and had probably invaded lots of worlds. There must be creatures as big as mountains somewhere . . . creatures with solid, muscular bodies, long tails, and wings. . . .

Jack gaped as a giant Evil dragon took shape, poised to leap, then took off directly above him.

A shadow swept over *Omega*.

"Get ready," said Tara.

The dragon flapped its wings once, then arched its long neck, pointed its nose down toward the raft, and dived.

"Now!" Tara cried.

Jack needed no encouragement. The sand was already rising beneath the ship, curling up the side of the mountain. He encouraged it on its way, raising not a wave but more a thick tongue of soil that carried *Omega* where it needed to go. The hole leading to Earth was up there somewhere. All Jack had to do was follow the instincts of his second Gift and keep eating.

They passed several tunnel entrances, but none of them were the right ones.

"Are we close?" asked Kyle.

"Very," said Jack, swinging his head from side to side. *That way.* The ship turned and kept going up. "Almost . . . almost . . ."

Two more holes swept by.

"There!"

Jack felt the presence of Earth like a ray of light shining through heavy clouds. It pulled at him, and the ship rose faster than ever, riding its long, thin tsunami of sand until it was level with the hole they were looking for. It was black and shadowed, but that looked welcoming to Jack after so much sunlight. He wanted to curl up in the dark and sleep for a month.

Omega eased inside the hole, losing the tip of its tallest mast in the process. Jack guided it forward, and the tunnel narrowed around them. Soon the keel was scraping on the bottom, and several of the spars snapped, raining splinters down upon them. When the sides of the boat came under threat, Jack brought the ship to a creaking halt.

"This is how it works, isn't it?" he said in puzzlement. "The tunnel takes us home?"

"Beats me," said Kyle. "I've never done this before."

Jack peered ahead, his first Gift piercing the gloom and revealing his worst fear: The tunnel was a dead end.

"But I can smell it!"

His sensitive eyes searched the rough cave wall ahead. There had to be some way through. . . .

All he saw was a single tiny flower growing in a puddle of sand, watered by the merest drips of moisture falling from the ceiling. A lone forget-me-not, almost impossibly fragile, its blue the blue of Earth's skies and Earth's oceans, grown from a seed that had dropped there and gone unnoticed by The Evil.

There *had* been a way, but it was denied to them now. Blocked, perhaps, by all of the Wardens' most powerful wards. Or perhaps it had never been there at all.

The only direction they could go was back, and try to find another way through.

Jack reached for another fruit, but his hand found only empty deck.

There were no more orange bananas.

"Lottie's out, too," said Tara. "The Evil can see us now."

"What are we going to do?" asked Kyle.

Everyone turned to look up the throat of the tunnel, where the Evil dragon was rising to face them, its immense wings and jaws opening wide.

CHAPTER TWENTY-TWO

The Way Is Blocked!

Jaide and Grandma X confronted the glowing cross-continuum conduit constructor. It and the fragment of the Avak Lodestone it was connected to were doing everything the professor had told them they should be doing by now, except for the critical part of opening a doorway to the Evil Dimension.

"What are we doing wrong?" Jaide asked. She had to shout over the loud humming the device made. It sounded like a very large and very angry bee.

"I don't think we *are* doing anything wrong," said Grandma X. "The way is blocked."

"Could it be Project Thunderclap?"

"I can think of no other explanation."

Jaide had lost track of the time since she had left the tent, but at least an hour must have passed. Aleksandr's "big push" was therefore due any moment. It made her feel sick that they might be just moments too late.

"Let's pay them a visit," said Grandma X. "Here, take my hand."

Jaide gripped her grandmother's strong fingers with all her strength. The light of the moonstone ring flared, and suddenly they were somewhere else. The blue room had transformed into the big tent, with its crowd of lightning wielders and the glowing lodestone at its heart. Only they weren't *really* there: Grandma X had transformed into the glowing ghost of her former self, and Jaide didn't appear to have a body at all.

Jaide searched the crowd. There was her father, linked by his hands to the Wardens on either side of him. Instead of individual cells, the mass of people had now lined up in one long spiral, sending their power in a chain from one to another, all the way to the person at the center. Jaide expected to see Aleksandr there, but instead it was Stefano. The air around him fairly roared with power. Between him and the bright orange lodestone, the tent looked about ready to explode.

"Not long now," crowed Aleksandr, walking along the spiral, patting Wardens on their shoulders and bolstering the connections between them. He didn't notice Grandma X and Jaide. Perhaps they were invisible to his eyes, Jaide thought. Or perhaps he only had eyes for the Project. "Ten seconds!"

Grandma X hurried her along the spiral to where Hector stood, chest heaving and long hair stuck in damp ribbons to his forehead. Jaide had never seen him looking like this, even after The Evil had first attacked them, almost a year ago. He was on the verge of collapse.

++Hector,++ she said.

His eyes flickered open.

"Mother," he breathed. "Is Jack . . . ?"

++We need a small amount of time,++ she told him. ++I will create the opportunity, if you can give me just a few seconds.++

He nodded wearily, and let himself fall.

Strange surges rippled through the tent. Aleksandr's triumphant mood turned to alarm.

The chain was broken.

Grandma X tugged Jaide away. They moved through space once more, jumping to the lighthouse, then to the cactus garden, then to Mermaid Point. There they found Rennie, braced against the full fury of the storm. She was staring out to sea, not minding the icy rain, her teeth exposed in something that might have been a grin.

"I must ask for one last favor of you," Grandma X told her, shouting over the howling wind. "The road home is closed. Jack needs a way through. Can you help us?"

"You are asking me to deliberately break the wards. I, the Living Ward of Portland."

"Yes, just for a moment."

"Has such a thing been done before?"

"Never, as far as is known."

Rennie looked down at her feet, then up at the roiling sky.

"It is truly a night for miracles," she said. "Miracles, or terrible mistakes."

"Only time will reveal which is which."

Rennie bared her teeth again, only this time it was definitely a grimace, and gazed once more out to sea.

"It is done."

Jaide felt a fluttering in her chest, and suddenly they were back in the blue room. It was weird to be out of the elements and back in her body, especially as it was freshly dried and in fresh clothes after the soaking she had just received. Grandma X was dry, too. Jaide had never wondered what happened to Wardens' spectral bodies in bad weather. Now she knew.

The fluttering continued. It had nothing to do with the return to her body. She had felt this twice before, when something had happened to the wards of Portland. They were faltering.

Grandma X's fingers didn't release her. The moonstone flashed once again, and the lodestone fragment flared. This time the cross-continuum conduit constructor began to bend space as it was supposed to. The floor, walls, and ceiling bulged out around it, while the corners of the room drew closer, creating a warped sphere. Everything in the blue room flattened and smeared into two-dimensional wallpaper. The only solid things left were Jaide and her grandmother, and the conduit constructor itself, now a spinning, golden circle.

"Seek him," said Grandma X over a rising sound of rushing wind. "We must find him, and quickly!"

But Jaide didn't need to. Even as the Bridge opened, Jack's voice came clearly to her, out of the vortex.

++Jaide, can you hear me? We need your help. It's an emergency!++

"Don't reply," said Grandma X sharply. "We don't want to lead The Evil to us."

"But he's in trouble!"

"And getting ourselves killed won't help him." Grandma X indicated the vortex unfolding right in front of them. "Go through and explain in person. Just don't let go of my hand, whatever you do."

Jaide didn't see how that was possible. Wouldn't she be stretched between two worlds like spaghetti until she snapped?

"Trust me," said Grandma X, nudging her toward the vortex. "And don't let go!"

Jaide remained uncertain, but she knew better than to doubt her grandmother. It didn't matter what people called her: the Warden of Portland, the Warden of Last Resort, the crazy old witch who lived on Watchward Lane. Grandma X was her father's mother, and in a little less than a year, Jaide had learned to love her. If anyone could bring her back from the Evil Dimension, it would be Grandma X.

They would do it *together.*

Jaide took one step and leaped into the vortex. She spun and tumbled, and the blue room vanished behind her, but she could still feel Grandma X's fingers tightly gripping her. Her arm trailed behind her as though tied by rope. Was there a hint of a ghostly hand in hers, glowing faintly silver?

She didn't have time to worry about that. The vortex was wild and fast, and she shrieked as she fell. It was like the most terrifying carnival ride she had ever been on, only much worse because there were no safety bars and she didn't know how long it would last.

++Jaide, answer me! We really need you!++

She closed her eyes and concentrated on Jack's voice. If she ever needed to be there for her brother, it was right now.

Jack stood with Kyle and Tara on the deck of *Omega* and watched helplessly as the Evil dragon flapped mightily toward their tunnel. The circle of visible sky was shrinking rapidly. Soon it would all be teeth and ripping claws. That those teeth and claws were made from dead bone and Evil bugs didn't make any of them feel better. The end result would be the same.

++Jaide, if you can hear me, do something now!++

He felt as though his words were falling into a bottomless pit from which nothing seemed to emerge, not even echoes. What if Earth was already blocked by Project Thunderclap? He hadn't seen any lightning. Maybe he had missed it, from inside the tunnel.

"It was a valiant try," said Lottie. "Come here, children. We'll wait together."

They gathered around her sled and Lottie held out her hands. Tara took one and Kyle took the other. Cornelia nestled in Lottie's neck, cooing softly. Jack stood opposite his great-aunt, between the best friends he had made in Portland. He tried not to notice the light getting dimmer or to think about what that meant. He ignored the sound of the Evil bugs and their many wings. He concentrated instead on the faded floral pattern on Lottie's smock. It reminded him of one of Mr. Carver's ties. If only they'd met.

If only lots of things. He didn't want to think of those things because it would only make him angry. Tara was crying and Kyle's face was blank with shock. It wasn't fair that they hadn't made it home.

The light went out. He could still see, thanks to his first Gift, but he was weak to the point of exhaustion, and it wasn't a blessing. He could hear the swarm filling the tunnel. There was absolutely nowhere left to hide, and no hope of shadow-walking anyone to safety.

The terrible influence of The Evil began to creep over him, like a slow tide consuming a beach.

++Jaide!++ he shouted. ++This is absolutely your last chance! Don't let The Evil be right and me be the one who falls!++

"No need to shout," said a voice from behind them. "I'm not letting The Evil do anything to you."

Jack spun around. Jaide was standing on the deck right behind him. She looked as though she'd been through a clothes dryer and there was something silver glowing in her right hand, but it was definitely her. He had never been so glad to see his sister before. He broke free of Tara and Kyle and hugged her before he could think twice about it. Two hugs in one week — a new record.

"Why is it so dark in here?" she said, hugging him back and then letting him go. "Wow, Tara, what happened to your eyes? No, wait, tell me later. Let's get us all home, first."

Jack agreed. Evil bugs were already buzzing around them. The dragon's roar was deafening as it crashed into the side of the mountain.

++*Two* troubletwisters!++ crowed The Evil. ++You are welcome, most welcome!++

Jaide ignored the eerie voice in her head.

++Grandma, can you hear me? I've found them.++

++I hear you,++ came the instant reply. ++Hold tight. I'll bring you all back now.++

Jack felt the vortex take hold of him, and suddenly they were moving, spinning, and tumbling their way back to Earth. Cornelia took off with a piercing, triumphant cry and flapped around them, bright feathers flashing.

"Are we really going home?" asked Kyle.

"Looks like it," said Tara, flicking an Evil bug out of his hair. "The ship, too. Is that going to work?"

Jack looked down at his feet, which were still planted on *Omega*'s wooden deck.

"Uh, Jaide?"

"What?" She was staring at a very old woman in an ancient hippieish dress who seemed to be sleeping through the whole thing. That couldn't be Lottie, could it? She looked like Grandma X's grandma.

"Where's the other end of this thing, exactly?" Jack asked her. "How much space is there?"

"It's in the blue room. . . . Oh, that's not going to work. We'll blow the house up!"

"We have to change course," said Kyle.

"I don't know if Grandma can do that. . . ."

"Jack can." Kyle handed him the umbrella he had used to deflect the vortex on the way out. "Here."

"Perfect!" Jack unfurled it, while Jaide watched in puzzlement.

Once the open umbrella was magically locked in the vortex and Jack started pulling on it, she understood. Standing on the bow of the ship, peering through the vortex at the glimpses of Portland ahead — it was like staring the wrong way through a telescope, a telescope that someone was swinging wildly about — she called out directions.

"Left . . . more left — no, that's the Rock!" It was hard to see what was going on. There was so much cloud and rain, and so little light. "To the right! To the right!"

++What's happening, Jaide?++ The voice of her grandmother faded in and out. The ghostly hand flickered and disappeared. ++. . . losing you . . .++

++Don't worry, Grandma,++ Jaide called. ++We're almost home!++

She hoped that was true. The vortex made everything difficult. Glimpses of Portland came and went, growing larger by the second. There was the tent, glowing yellow now with the heat of the lodestone. There was the lighthouse. There was the iron bridge.

"Down a bit — no, the other way! *Down*, not up!"

She was aiming for the swamp. That was the softest place she could think of within the wards.

Jack wrestled with the umbrella. Tara and Kyle added their strength and weight. Maybe it was the ship that was making everything more difficult than it had been going the other way. It kept pulling him off course, almost as though it had a mind of its own.

The open end of the vortex rushed by around them. For a terrifying moment they were in free fall, dropping with their stomachs in their mouths. Jaide smelled rain and electricity and salty sea air. Jack gasped at the shock of icy rain striking his skin and the return of his proper weight. With a descending whistle, they dropped out of the bottom of a cloud rippling with sheet lightning, and splashed down hard in the churning water of Portland harbor.

Omega took water over the gunwales and rocked wildly from side to side. But she stayed upright and at least for the time being stayed afloat, though there were ominous gurgling noises belowdeck. Lottie woke with a gasp.

"Cold! And wet!" she cried. "I forgot what that feels like. How wonderful!"

"This is my sister," said Jack, pulling Jaide closer. "She rescued us."

The old woman on the sled smiled and reached for her. "You're a brave girl. Thank you, troubletwisters, from the bottom of my heart. I had almost stopped dreaming that I'd come home, but here I am, at last, where I belong."

Jaide didn't know what to say. She had done what she had to do, that was all — and she realized now that it was exactly what Grandma X would have done for her sister a long time ago, had she only known Lottie was alive.

Lottie was staring at Portland with shining eyes. She might have been crying, but it was impossible to tell through the rain.

"It's changed," she said. "The old swimming pool is gone. Is that a marina? Looks like they've extended the hospital, making it uglier than ever. And what on earth has happened to Mermaid Point?"

++Jaide? Can you hear me?++

Guiltily, Jaide remembered that she hadn't let Grandma X know that they had arrived.

++We're here,++ she teeped back. ++It worked! We landed in the harbor. I have Jack and Kyle and Tara and Cornelia . . . and Lottie, too, Grandma. Jack found her. Isn't that wonderful?++

++It is wonderful, dear, but I need you to come home as quickly as possible.++

++Sure, once we work out how to steer this boat.++

++ Use your Gift, Jaide, and do it now.++

She sounded impatient, but Jaide couldn't imagine why.

++Okay. But aren't you happy? We have your sister.++

++I'll deal with Charlotte later,++ said Grandma X. ++The Bridge is still open. Look up.++

Jaide did so. At first it was hard to make out what she was seeing. A dark cloud was spreading across the sky, eclipsing the sheet lightning and soaking up the rain. Only when it unfurled its wings did she recognize its shape.

The dragon had followed them to Portland.

CHAPTER TWENTY-THREE

PORTLAND IN PERIL

Jack heard Jaide's gasp and felt the *Omega* shift underneath him. A powerful wind had sprung up out of nowhere, pushing the ship sideways to the shore, the tattered, useless sails streaming overhead.

"What is it?" he asked her.

"That thing up there . . . it came with us!"

Only then did he hear the familiar sound of thousands of Evil bugs roaring in one voice. He groaned, too exhausted to call on his Gifts for help. He could do nothing but watch as Jaide tried her best to outrun The Evil.

At first that looked impossible. The Evil dragon's giant wings were fully outstretched. All it had to do was swoop down on them and they would be finished.

But something was wrong. The dragon's body was slumping and crumbling down the middle. Its wings flapped once but didn't come back up again. The dragonish shape was losing definition around the edges. A rain of bugs began to fall into the sea, wings whirring in desperation.

Jack grinned. Of course! The gravity of Earth was slightly higher than the place the bugs had come from. Here they couldn't fly. They could only fall. And being desert creatures, maybe, just maybe, they would all drown.

A small tsunami spread out from the swarm's point of impact, making the boat tip forward and then back again.

Jaide brought them around the breakwater and headed them sideways toward the marina, the sea breaking over the starboard side. It wasn't going to be elegant, but it would do the job, if she was quick. The *Omega* was heavy and sluggish, clearly taking water. Although she doubted The Evil would let them live long enough to drown, Jaide was reluctant to put that to the test.

The *Omega* shouldered several fishing boats out of the way, but was caught in a wild current driven by the thrashing dragon. The ship groaned and began to spin about to head in almost the opposite direction.

"No, no!" said Jaide. "Wrong way!"

The ship was now heading for the sand flats, where they'd get bogged for sure. If that happened they'd have to swim to the shore, and Jaide didn't think frail, ancient-looking Lottie would survive that experience.

"Hold on," she warned the others. She would have to let her Gift really go for it. That made her nervous after everything Alfred the Examiner had told her, not to mention the many times things had gone wrong when she had lost control. But she had no choice. She would trust her Gift this time. If it behaved, well and good.

If not . . . she would deal with that afterward.

"All I want to do is get there," she said, pointing to where a dredge bobbed and swayed, tied to its own private dock. "I don't care how you do it. Have fun, if you like. Just don't kill anyone, please, and if you can avoid damaging too much property, that would be great."

The wind responded, spinning up around her in giddy triumph. She could feel its energy, its freedom, its almost gleeful desire to cause trouble. But it didn't make any moves to pick up the ship and smash it against the rocks, as she feared it might. Instead, it swept away from the ship and began sucking at the ocean.

"What are you doing?" Jaide said, trying not to sound too frustrated. "Making a whirlpool doesn't help us."

But then she felt the tug of the current pulling the ship in a wide arc around the eye of the waterspout, angling in to the shore.

She grinned with excitement. *So this was how you did it,* she thought. You gave your Gifts enough freedom to do something they enjoyed, but you traded it off against something you *needed* in turn. She could tell her Gift was having fun: Great gouts of water were shooting in all directions, playing havoc with the clouds. The spout itself was doing something that looked like a belly dance. It didn't care about The Evil or Project Thunderclap. It just wanted to play.

Jaide gave it the thumbs-up as the *Omega* smashed alongside the dredge's pier — and stayed there.

"Thank you!"

The whirlwind gave one last jig, sucked up an unmoored boat, and spat it to the other side of the harbor, then evaporated.

"Nicely done," said Lottie from her sled as Kyle and Jack lifted her toward the side of the boat. "How advanced are you through your training?"

"I've passed the Third Examination," she said proudly.

"What?" said Jack. "You did it without me?"

"I didn't have any choice. Grandma wouldn't listen."

Headlights swept across them, which surprised all of them because the town looked deserted. Jack recognized the longhorn bumper bar and sheer size of Zebediah, Rodeo Dave's car. The tootling of its musical horn greeted them.

"Quickly!" he shouted at them through the open window. "I don't know what you're doing playing around on that old boat, but you've got to get out of this weather now!"

No one argued. Most cars wouldn't fit all of them at once, but Zebediah had room to spare. Tara let go of the glass rod so her owl eyes disappeared. The sword she kept. As they came down the gangplank, Jack glanced behind him, looking for any sign of The Evil. The dragon was completely gone; all the bugs had fallen into the water. But he had learned from hard experience not to assume anything until Grandma X said it was safe.

Kyle and Jack put Lottie in the middle of the back seat, between the two of them. As they wrapped the seat belt around her, Lottie chuckled.

"I can't believe you're still driving this old thing, David," she said to Rodeo Dave. "Couldn't you have found a more zippy Companion by now?"

He stared at her via the rearview mirror, brow deeply furrowed.

"I'm sorry," he said. "Do I know you?"

Lottie looked puzzled and hurt. Jack could almost see her thinking how much she must have changed. But he couldn't explain without breaking their promise to Rodeo Dave: to let him forget his past as a Warden, and the loss of Lottie, long ago. But maybe that promise was invalid now that Lottie was back. Didn't that make everything else irrelevant?

"Dave doesn't have any memories of you because he asked Grandma to take them away," Jack ended up saying. "It's a long story. We'll explain later."

Dave frowned even harder. "I asked your grandmother to do what, now?"

Jaide slammed the door to distract him. Rough handling made the car grouchy, Dave said, although soaking wet passengers had had little effect in the past.

"That's all of us," she said, holding a damp and bedraggled Cornelia on her lap. "Let's go. Where are you taking us?"

"Home, I guess," he started to say. "Or perhaps Scarborough. It's getting a bit too blowy out there even for me."

++I will await you at Project Thunderclap,++ said Grandma X. **++Make haste.++**

Jaide jumped. The spectral form of her grandmother had appeared in one of the side mirrors. She still looked very grim.

"Can you take us to the tent?" Jaide asked Dave. "There's . . . uh . . . an emergency town meeting there, for the people who are left. I reckon Grandma will be there. But we might miss her unless we go quickly."

"Right you are." Dave shrugged off the matter of his missing memory as though he had already forgotten it. And maybe he had, Jaide thought. That was probably the key to making a deception like this work: not allowing people to know what they no longer knew.

Jack's cell phone rang as the big car's wheels spun in the mud and they accelerated away from the sea.

"Hello?"

"Oh, Jack, I'm so glad you're safe!"

It was his mother. She was calling from somewhere very noisy. The helicopter — judging by the familiar *whop-whop* sound of spinning blades in the background.

"Everything's okay," he reassured her. "We're all home now."

"Don't go home," she said. "You have to get out of there, fast."

"It's just a storm, Mom."

"We both know it's much more than a storm. And I'm flying in it right now so I can see what's going on better than you. Whatever that thing was that fell out of the sky, it just started coming out of the ocean, and it looks mean."

Jack craned around to look behind him. Something big and black was crawling over the *Omega* and sending tentacles to the shore. It was dotted with thousands of tiny, glowing white eyes.

"Uh, that's not good," he said. "We're going!"

"If you see Hector, tell him . . . just tell him to answer his rotten phone. I've been trying to call him for hours!"

Susan hung up and Jack suggested that everyone look behind them.

"Reminds me of that big storm the week you two arrived," Rodeo Dave told the twins. "We were cleaning seaweed out of our gutters for a month. Good for the gardens."

He seemed almost cheerful about the prospect, but his boot went down hard on the gas pedal.

The tent was lit up like a nightclub as Zebediah skidded around the corner from Main Street to River Road. Instead of parking, Rodeo Dave jumped the curb and drove through the school grounds, right up to the front entrance of the tent. Jack winced at the sound of the broad tires crunching the trellises, on which the class was being forced to grow sickly looking organic vegetables. Mr. Carver would be complaining about hooligans for weeks.

"Wait here," Jaide told Kyle, Tara, Rodeo Dave, Cornelia, and Lottie. "We'll be quick."

Jack scrambled out after her. "Is this where Dad is?"

"Everyone's here," she said, running through the entrance. A lone guard, sheltering himself from the storm, waved them through. "This way, I think."

Jack gaped at the Warden assembly. There must have been a hundred of them, and the lodestone in the center of the room held so much energy it was shining like molten gold. If everyone put their heads together, they could repel The Evil easily.

"The appearance of The Evil is most unfortunate," boomed Aleksandr over the crowd, as though responding to Jack's thought. "We can defeat the incursion or we can continue with our plan. We can't do both."

The twins looked around for their grandmother, and saw her on the fringe, ushering them toward her. When Jack was within reach she hugged him quickly and fiercely, but then let go to concentrate on what the other Wardens were saying.

"The threat is here and now," said one. "Deal with it and try Thunderclap another day."

"But The Evil will be ready," protested another. "This is our one and only chance."

"There's no point succeeding if The Evil is over here now," agonized a third.

"We have the means of containing it," said Grandma X in a firm voice that carried clear across the crowd. "Continue with the Project. Leave the rest to me."

Aleksandr straightened and puffed out his chest, as though he was about to argue with her.

"Do as she says," said a glowing figure who appeared right next to him and swept a cool gaze around the room. Lottie. "If you stand around arguing with the Warden of Last Resort, then you deserve what's coming for you."

A shocked murmur spread through the crowd, and Jack felt a twinge of something lost and forgotten at the back of his brain. Lottie was confirming what he and Jaide had suspected, that Grandma X was the Warden of Last Resort, but was there something else he should be thinking right now? Something about what that role meant?

"Very well, Charlotte," said Aleksandr, deciding in the moment not to argue with the ghost of the woman he had abandoned to the Evil Dimension more than forty years ago. He didn't look happy about it, though. This was supposed to be *his* moment. "We will finish what we started. The megastorm is prepared. All we must do now is unleash it."

The lightning wielders rebuilt their spiral, with Stefano at the center, and the sense of power building resumed. Lottie's spectral form vanished, and Grandma X guided the twins back toward the exit.

"What did Lottie mean?" asked Jaide. "What are you going to do?"

"You mustn't concern yourself with that," she said in a firm voice, putting one hand on each of their shoulders. "Go with David. Rennie has prepared a sanctuary on the Rourke Estate — a bubble of safety where the people of Portland have been evacuated. Go there and wait with him. The megastorm will take some time to reach its full effect. You must stay out of harm's way until it's over."

"And you'll come join us afterward? With Dad?" asked Jack. His sense that something bad was going to happen was rising.

"I will do everything in my power."

Both twins noticed that Grandma X, as she so often did, had avoided answering the question.

"Now go," she said, "and tell the guards to do their best. The tent must not be breached."

There was no disobeying that tone. The twins found their legs moving almost of their own volition, out of the heart of the tent and to the exit, where a gaggle of guards had formed to stare out at the stormy world.

Dark shapes were swarming over the school, difficult to make out but moving steadily and greedily toward the oval.

"We've got to hold it back," Jaide said to Jack. "If she thinks we're leaving, she's crazy. How are your Gifts?"

Jack tested them. They responded, but were still weak.

"So are mine," she confessed. "What are we going to do? There's so much of it."

"There sure is . . . and you know what? That's its greatest weakness." Jack felt a germ of an idea wriggling excitedly, wanting to be brought out into the light. "It's huge and everywhere, but it's only one thing. It's just *it*. One mind, one intelligence. It can be distracted, all at once."

Jaide stared at him excitedly. "Are you thinking what I'm thinking?"

"That we can use ourselves as bait and draw it away from the others?"

"Exactly! Good thinking, little brother."

Jack didn't object to being called that — he was only four minutes younger, after all — because she had complimented him at the same time. They ran back to the car, where Kyle and Tara were nervously looking out the rear window at the looming shapes The Evil made against the town lights. Lottie had nodded off again after the exertion of sending her spirit form to the meeting. Rodeo Dave was sitting restlessly behind the wheel, looking at her in the rearview mirror and frowning again.

He brightened when the twins jumped in.

"Where to now, troubletwisters?"

Jack and Jaide glanced at each other. He never called them that. Maybe the memory block was failing.

"Grandma wants us to get out of town," said Jaide, "but we think we'll be of more use here. How fast can Zebediah go?"

He winked. "You'd be surprised."

"As long as The Evil's surprised, that's the main thing," said Jack. "We're going to lead it away from the tent."

"How?" asked Kyle.

"It's tried to catch us so many times now," said Jaide, "and we keep getting away. This is its big chance. It's not going to pass that up — not if we remind it, anyway."

Rodeo Dave nodded. "Like a bullfight, then. We'll enrage it while the others deliver the final blow."

"Sounds like fun," said Tara. "Let's go!"

Kyle and Jack put their fists up in the air and Cornelia flapped with excitement, all of which took Jaide slightly by surprise. It was Jack's idea and she had proposed it. How did Tara get to be the one who made the decision? Probably it had something to do with what had happened to them in the Evil Dimension, she told herself, and what difference did it make anyway, since they all wanted the same thing?

Zebediah roared and surged around in a wide circle, spraying mud. The car bumped back onto the road and accelerated toward the oncoming mass of bugs.

Jack closed his eyes. He had never tried to start a conversation with The Evil before. Normally, it was The Evil trying to talk to him.

++Go home,++ Jack told it. ++Why won't you just leave us alone?++

++Join us, troubletwisters,++ it responded, ++and you will understand that we have no home. We need no home. We have only us. We need only you.++

Rodeo Dave eased off the gas pedal and swung the wheel so they headed down a line between the oncoming blackness and the tent. As the headlights swept across The Evil, they provided a glimpse of squirming Earthly bugs and slimy seaweed, with larger creatures mixed in, such as fish, eels, and the occasional stray dog. At the fore stood Dr. Witworth, with arms outstretched. Her hands had far too many fingers, thanks to the bugs she had absorbed, and she rode high, thanks to the buzzing of dozens of insect wings sprouting out of her back. Her sickly white eyes tracked the path of the car.

++You and us, together at last,++ The Evil chanted. ++You and us, you and us.++

++We'll never join you,++ said Jaide. ++Never!++

"Is it following?" asked Tara.

"Looks that way," said Kyle.

Jack agreed. The leading fringes of The Evil were swaying and changing course. Like a plague of mice trailing a piper, or a really big block of cheese, the black mass turned to follow them.

"Let it think it's keeping up," Jaide told Rodeo Dave. "We don't want it to give up."

"Don't worry. I'll save something for when we most need it." He patted the dash. The car was rumbling happily down Dock Road, heading for the old cemetery.

Behind them, a single bolt of lightning fired up from the tent into the clouds, sending fierce tendrils lashing like whips in all directions. It didn't die as ordinary lightning did. It crackled on, sending powerful booms of thunder rolling across the town. Jaide imagined the lodestone releasing all its pent-up energy, through the Wardens, through Stefano. She thought she heard him cry out in something that might have been triumph but might equally have been pain. The megastorm had begun.

Got to keep The Evil distracted, she thought.

++Do you recognize this place?++ she asked as the lighthouse came into view. The Something Read Ward shone with a bright, golden light near where the actual lighthouse globe was housed. ++This is where we first beat you.++

++You will never defeat us,++ it said. ++We are forever. You will join us or die.++

++How old *are* you, exactly?++ Jack asked. ++Isn't it time you retired?++

++We have been here forever. We will always be here. Join us and live with us in eternity.++

Jack imagined The Evil spreading across the universe like some terrible, all-encompassing disease, sucking up life and leaving nothing but death behind. It truly might live forever, if it could find enough to absorb.

Zebediah bumped off-road again, swinging around the tiny church next to the Rock and paralleling South Beach. The hulking mass of The Evil followed, swarming over everything in its path.

++Everything dies,++ said Jaide. ++Even you, sooner or later.++

++Never,++ it said. ++Only those who reject us will die — humans, Wardens, and troubletwisters alike.++

Something large crashed down in front of them, as though from a great height. Mud splattered everywhere. Rodeo Dave spun the wheel, barely avoiding a collision.

"That's the clock of the church steeple," said Tara in amazement as the object went by. It was little more than tangled stone and metal now. "The Evil must have ripped it off and thrown it at us!"

Jack and Jaide looked at each other and wondered if they had gone too far. They didn't want to antagonize The Evil into killing them.

++Tell us again why we should join you,++ Jack said. ++What do we get out of it, exactly?++

But The Evil didn't answer. Something else crashed heavily in front of them, this time a giant chunk of dripping granite uprooted from the breakwater. Rodeo Dave spun the wheel again, and Jaide realized with a sick feeling what The Evil was doing.

It was herding them, forcing them to come around so they had no choice but to drive right into its waiting mass.

"Go around the Rock," she told Rodeo Dave. "That might stop it from throwing more things at us."

"Right-o," he said. "Hold on tight!"

They bounced and jolted across the terrain, narrowly avoiding the Cutting, a slice of hillside that had been removed to make way for Crescent Street.

++Running only delays the inevitable,++ The Evil said. ++Join us and know an end to fear.++

"Look!" cried Kyle, pointing out the side window, up to the slope.

The Evil had swarmed up to the very top of the Rock and rose over it like the mutant child of King Kong and Godzilla. Projectiles came thundering down on them, and only a sudden burst of speed spared Zebediah from a crippling impact right through the engine. As it was, the near misses were very near, and it was clear that with The Evil holding the higher ground, their luck was bound to run out eventually.

Grandma X's house on Watchward Lane came into view, and Rodeo Dave made for it. The weathervane was pointing straight at them, and at The Evil rising up behind them.

The bench that sat at the top of the Rock crashed down in front of them, followed by a thick tree trunk and two large boulders. Zebediah skidded, but there was no way to go around the obstacles. The Evil had blocked their path completely.

Zebediah jerked to a halt. Rodeo Dave put the car in reverse and twisted to look behind him. He revved the engine, but didn't go anywhere.

Jack could see why. The Evil was rushing down the side of the Rock like an avalanche. If they went that way, the end would only come sooner.

"We could lock the doors," Tara said, looking up the hill. "Will that help?"

"For about a second," said Kyle, swallowing.

They sat frozen for a moment, out of ideas.

Then the sound of something smashing made them whip their heads around to the front. The old stone bench had been turned to rubble, and as they watched, two heavy stone fists lifted the tree trunk, snapped it in two, and threw it away. A broad, stony face leaned down to peer into the car.

++EVIL BAD,++ boomed a mental voice that sounded like two mountains clashing. ++TROUBLETWISTERS RUN NOW RUN RUN RUN.++

"Angel!" exclaimed Lottie, blinking in sleepy surprise through the windshield. "I thought I was dreaming. What's she doing awake?"

Jaide gaped at her, then turned back to the giant. The Something Growing Ward lifted one of the boulders and threw it at The Evil so hard that it trailed red fire before it hit Dr. Witworth square on. Bugs flew in all directions.

"I think we'd better do what that thing says," said Rodeo Dave, putting his foot down as far as it would go. "Have we distracted The Evil enough?"

Jaide looked for the tent through the trees. It wasn't hard to find, although its bright yellow glow had faded to a simmering red. The lightning flickered and went out.

"I hope so," she said. "Get us out of here!"

CHAPTER TWENTY-FOUR

THE WARDEN OF LAST RESORT

Zebediah sped through the streets of Portland, leaving the giant and The Evil to duke it out. There were signs of devastation everywhere. Trees had come down. Roofs were caved where The Evil had passed. Dead and dying bugs were everywhere.

A voice filled all their heads, but this time it wasn't The Evil's.

++Project Thunderclap is a success,++ said Aleksandr. **++The Earth is safe forever from the realm of The Evil. All remaining Wardens and troubletwisters have one minute to evacuate.++**

"What's going on?" asked Jack. "Evacuate why?"

Lottie was still awake, completely recuperated thanks to her nap.

"The realm of The Evil may be closed to us," she said, "but so much of it managed to escape here first, across the Bridge that brought us home. Thankfully, it's contained by the wards for the moment. If it ever got out, though, if the wards were ever to fail even slightly, it would turn Earth into that desert I lived in for so long. They have to get rid of it before the world will be safe."

"But they can't send it back," said Jaide, "because the Bridge is closed. No, it's more than closed — it can never be opened again."

"That's right."

"What are they going to do?" asked Jack in a quiet voice. He was imagining terrible things, all involving the destruction of Portland.

"What needs to be done, I guess," Lottie said, which was no more reassuring than what Grandma X liked to say in similar moments. For the first time, Jaide could see the resemblance. "David, take us to the lookout. Do you remember the place? It's just on the border of the town. We went there once, a long time ago."

"I . . . I do remember it," he said, eyes blinking furiously as he drove. "I *do*. How could I have forgotten?"

"Because I left you," she said. "Sometimes it's easier that way."

"You're back now," he said.

"I am, and I'm never going anywhere ever again."

Zebediah turned left onto Rourke Road and followed it out of town, engine surging as the land rose beneath it. Jack knew the lookout Lottie was referring to: It was not a particularly high vantage point, but it did show the town in a good aspect, from the Rock all the way to Mermaid Point. There was a plaque there, acknowledging the whalers who had founded the town and the many whales that had died to ensure its early prosperity. Mr. Carver had insisted on the latter part, and for once Jack fully agreed.

The twins had only ever gone to the lookout with their mother, because it was just outside the wards of Portland, somewhere Grandma X couldn't go. As they drove up the increasingly curving road, they saw Wardens traveling in various guises. There was Custer in his saber-toothed tiger form. There was a wolf, a lion, a flock of sparrows, a boa constrictor, and a fierce-looking bird that Jack thought might be a cassowary. Some ran at incredible speeds. One glided like Jaide did, following the air currents above the treetops. Jack caught a glimpse of a shadow-walker flitting in and out of existence alongside the ride. Tara and Kyle stared at them with amazed expressions.

The only thing missing was lightning. The exhausted creators of the megastorm drove or were driven. As Zebediah neared the lookout, they saw a large number of cabs and minivans scattered higgledy-piggledy through the parking lot. Wardens didn't like right angles very much, it seemed, or staying within the lines. Jaide wasn't surprised.

"What are they doing up here?" Kyle asked Lottie. "How did you know they'd be here?"

She shrugged. "It's an old place, important to Portland even though it's not really part of it anymore. This is where the founder sketched the first plan. It's also where the first ward was created by the first Warden of Portland. History is important."

Rodeo Dave carefully drove the big car into the only spot large enough to hold it. The kids jumped out, and Cornelia took the opportunity to spread her wings and fly. The rain had fallen away, although the clouds remained, heavy and brooding above. Rodeo Dave insisted on carrying Lottie, although the boys tried to take her from him. She hardly weighed anything, he said. That wasn't entirely true, Jack knew, but he suspected it was more than just gallantry that made Rodeo Dave say it. They had a history of their own.

Jaide and Tara hurried ahead to where two distinct shocks of hair, one black and the other white, revealed the presence of Hector and Grandma X. What they hadn't seen from the road were the limp rotors of a helicopter in the lower parking lot. The pilot sat behind the controls with a glazed expression, not really doing anything — and possibly not seeing anything, either — while Susan stood with her husband, watching the assembly.

Susan saw the twins and performed a strange but utterly heartfelt leap of delight and relief. They ran toward one another with arms wide. Jack overtook Jaide and was the first to meet her. The three stood in a tight embrace until Hector joined in and made them four.

"It's over," Susan said. "Thank goodness it's finally over."

"It is not over," said Aleksandr, his voice trembling with repressed rage. "Today did not go *at all* to plan, thanks to the willful disobedience of the Shield family. Were it within my power to strip you of your Gifts, I would seriously consider doing so. You have left us with an exceedingly serious problem on our hands."

As one, the gathering turned to look toward Portland, above which a dark cloud of The Evil was gathering, made of birds and any terrestrial insect that could fly. The dragon form was returning, and with it a sense of questing menace. It was looking for Wardens. It was looking for revenge. Most important, it was looking for a way out.

"The wards are sealed," said Grandma X. She stood on her own, slightly apart from the rest of the gathering. "The Evil is contained, for the moment."

"Exactly," said Aleksandr. "*For the moment.* We cannot keep it here forever — you know how hard it is to deal with even a tiny excision — and we cannot send it back. There is no known way to actually kill The Evil, so what do you propose we do? Call in a nuclear strike and hope for the best?"

That was the worst of Jaide's fantasies, and she hoped that wasn't seriously on the table.

"Why can't you kill it?" said Kyle. "That doesn't make sense!"

"Because it is not truly alive," said Grandma X. "It is a facsimile of life, a vampire that has no blood of its own, no matter how much it drinks of the blood of others. It is the yearning to be, without the means to be. It is the most tragic creature in the universe."

Lottie nodded, and so did Stefano. He was standing behind Aleksandr, looking distinctly singed around the edges.

"It's a parasite," Stefano said, "but even parasites deserve to live."

Aleksandr looked like he was about to explode. His mood wasn't improved by the sudden appearance of Alfred the Examiner, who emerged from the wooden deck of the lookout not far from where Aleksandr was standing, making him jump.

"What do you suggest we do, then?" Aleksandr asked. "Set it free so it can grow fat and happy on the people we have sworn to protect?"

"Of course not," said Grandma X. "There is another way."

"A secret way," said Lottie from her cradle in Rodeo Dave's arms, "kept secret for a very important reason. It undermines the very purpose and existence of the Wardens."

All eyes turned to her. None looked more surprised than Alfred's.

"You cannot know this," he said.

"I can," she said. "Remember where I have been. I've watched The Evil every day for over forty years. I've studied its ways, and my own ways, too. I've learned some things . . . things that shocked me at first, but they had to be true because there was no other explanation. Jack, tell them what you experienced when you were in the realm of The Evil."

Jack had never expected to be addressed in such a highly charged moment.

"Uh . . . I don't know what you mean."

"What happened to your Gift?"

"It was strong. Way stronger than it is here."

"Why do you think that is?"

He remembered Kyle jumping up and down excitedly. "Because we were on a different planet and things work differently there?"

"That's what I thought at first, too," she said, "which made me wonder what it was about our Gifts that could make them change that way. I experimented. I did what I could with what little I had. In the end, I came to the conclusion that the change had nothing to do with me at all, or the planet I was living on. The Evil was what mattered."

"Your Gifts got bigger because they could tell it was closer?" asked Jaide. "Because they wanted to fight?"

Lottie shook her head. "Not because they wanted to fight, but because The Evil is the *source* of our Gifts."

A startled murmur rose up from the crowd.

"Think about it." She shouted to be heard. It was amazing that such a strong voice could emerge from such a frail body. "Where do you think our powers come from? Out of the ether, like magic? Not likely. And haven't you ever wondered why we can do so many of the same things that The Evil can — talk with our minds, defy the normal laws of this universe, change our forms? We exist to fight The Evil, but without The Evil we would have nothing to fight *with*. Our Gifts, you see, ultimately belong to The Evil. We who have the ability have stolen them and used them against it. We have passed them from parent to child for thousands of years, without truly understanding what they are. And the more we use them, the more like it we become.

Our blessing is also our curse. We are the parasites, as surely as it is."

The twins were staring at Grandma X, who nodded slowly.

"It's true?" Jack said.

"You've known this all along?" said Jaide. Her skin crawled at the thought that inside her was part of The Evil — a part that she had thought was becoming her friend, even as it rebelled against her.

"I have known only so long as I have been the Warden of Last Resort," Grandma X said, addressing not just the twins but the entire crowd. "I was selected by Alfred when my predecessor died. It takes a Warden of exceptionally strong will, in case he or she is ever called upon to act. In all our history, none of them have ever been called. But now I have been. And I am here."

She looked down at her feet, and the twins realized that she was standing alone for a very important reason. Everyone else was outside the wards. She alone was inside.

"Grandma," said Jaide, "you've got to get out of there. The Evil is coming."

And indeed it was. It boiled up over Portland, a dragon in shape and intent, flapping its mighty wings and baring its teeth, flying at all speed to where Grandma X stood on a lonely hilltop with an excellent view of the town.

"I can't leave, Jaide. I am the Warden of Portland. If I take one more step, the wards will fail and The Evil will escape into the world."

"But you can't stay there," said Jack. "It'll kill you!"

"No, it won't." Grandma X smiled.

"That remains to be seen," said Lottie. "This is what it means to be the Warden of Last Resort — to take this chance, if required to. When everything else has failed."

"Is it, Mother?" asked Hector. The twins were surprised to see tears running down his cheeks. "Is there no other way?"

"This is how it must be, dear boy," she said. "Not least because everything Aleksandr said is true. I made decisions today that put the world in danger. This is how I will make amends. Let me put everything right . . . if I can."

The twins looked to Aleksandr, hoping he would find a way to talk her out of it. He looked at Alfred, who shook his head.

"I don't understand," whispered Kyle to Jack. "Is she going to kill The Evil or not?"

"She can't do that," said Tara, "because that would destroy everyone's powers. Who would want that?"

Grandma X smiled at them. "It's good that you are here, children. We have fought for so long to save the people of the world. You are witnesses to all we have done, for good and evil. You must understand what we sacrifice. You will remember."

Her moonstone ring flashed once. Kyle and Tara stiffened and their eyes opened wide. They blinked, but only with an effort, and they couldn't look away.

Grandma X turned to face the dragon.

"No!" the twins cried. They would have run to her but for their mother's hands holding them back.

The dragon grew large and furious before the assembled Wardens. Although they knew it couldn't get through the invisible barrier the wards created to keep it out of the world, it was still difficult to stand unmoving during its approach. Long years of hard training — or perhaps it was a sense of recognition, many Wardens now thought, given everything Grandma X had just told them — prompted their Gifts to stir. Tendrils of smoke and flame curled out of thin air. Patches of grass bloomed suddenly from solid concrete. The daylight turned orange, then green, then returned to its former listless gray. A chill wind swept through the gathering, whistling mournfully.

"We like to say that The Evil is so evil we don't have a word for it." Grandma X stood firm before the dragon, even as it rose up above her, mouth and clawed feet opening to engulf her. "That's not entirely true. We may not have a word, but we do have something much more powerful. We have . . ."

The Evil struck her with all its force. She disappeared under the sheer weight of the dragon, and Jaide cried out in horror. The vast mass of The Evil crashed into the wards, too, spreading out as though against an invisible glass wall. Jack turned away, unable to bear the sight of all the squashed bugs. The air was suddenly full of the smell of them.

++We have you now,++ gloated The Evil. ++We have you at last, Warden of Portland. You will thwart us no more! We have . . . We have . . .++

Its voice changed, becoming higher pitched.

++We have . . . we have. . . a *name*?++ it said, only it didn't sound like an *it* anymore. The voice sounded exactly like Grandma X's.

The mass of dead bugs parted and she stepped through the invisible wall, into clear air. Her eyes shone a bright, lifeless white. The Wardens backed away from her. The wards shivered. She took five steps and stopped. She didn't seem to see anyone or anything around her. She looked down at her hands and shook her head.

The wards collapsed, prompting a flood of dead bugs that reached almost as far as the heels of Grandma X's cowboy boots. Nothing living stirred in that terrible mass. The dragon was dead.

++We are . . .++ she said. ++I am . . .++

The whiteness in her eyes swirled furiously, spinning in ever-tightening circles. Her hands clenched and unclenched into fists, leaving tiny half-moons in her palms where her fingernails dug in. Strange forces swirled around her, twisting her hair into strange streamers and whorls.

"Lara Mae," said Lottie. "Come back to us."

Grandma X jerked as though struck. Her eyes closed, then opened.

The whiteness was gone.

"Thank you, Charlotte," she said in her normal voice.

Then she collapsed.

The twins pulled away from their mother and were instantly at her side.

"Will she be all right?" Jaide asked. The old woman was unconscious but breathing. Jaide touched her neck where she had seen her mother do it the other day, and felt a rapid but steady pulse.

"What happened to her?" asked Jack.

Rodeo Dave knelt down beside them, with Lottie still in his arms.

"She became The Evil," Lottie said. "But not the usual way. Instead of being taken over by it, she took *it* over. I bet it wasn't expecting that."

"That is what she meant about needing extraordinary willpower." Alfred had joined them and was manipulating one of Grandma X's hands as though testing to see if the joints still worked. "The Evil is still here, but it's part of her now, bound up with her, under the name she surrendered until she needed it again."

"So it's not The Evil anymore?" said Jaide. "It's . . . *Lara Mae*?"

"It's still The Evil," said Lottie, "but it's Lara Mae as

well. Names have power. They are bound together now. It can never escape."

"What will she be like when she wakes up?" asked Jack. "She *will* wake up, won't she? Will she be herself?"

"Time will tell," said Lottie, mopping her sister's brow. It was hot. "Time will tell."

Susan forced her way into the huddle.

"Until then, I think it's best we get her to a hospital," she said. Behind the crowd, the rotors of the helicopter were already starting to turn. "Jack, Jaide, you can fly with me, if you want. You, too," she said to Alfred, "in case something weird happens on the way. Hector, go with David and make sure Tara and Kyle are okay. The rest of you" — Susan looked around at the gathered Wardens — "you can start cleaning up some of this mess."

For once, the twins were grateful for their mother's bossy tone, and it seemed Aleksandr and the others were, too. As Susan and Alfred carefully lifted the old woman off the ground and placed her on a collapsible stretcher, a babble of voices rose up around them. The shocked silence was over. The questioning had begun.

"Lara Mae," said Jaide. "I never would've guessed that."

"She said her middle name was Prudence, once," said Jack. "It sounds right."

"My middle name is Patience," said Lottie with a wry smile. "Our mother named us well, don't you think?"

The old woman looked so small in Rodeo Dave's arms, so frail. Jaide was moved to hug her, experiencing a sudden sense of kinship that she hadn't felt before. This woman was her great-aunt, her grandma's twin sister. She had been gone for a long time, and now she was home. Whatever else happened, that was an amazing, wonderful thing.

"Jack, Jaide, are you coming or not?"

Jack tugged at his sister. This was their chance to finally ride with their mother in the helicopter, something they had wanted *forever*.

Jaide wasn't ready.

"You go," she told him, letting go of Lottie but finding the old woman's hand and feeling it grip hers tightly. "I'll stay here and make sure Dad's okay."

Jack hesitated, then nodded. This wasn't like being sent to the Evil Dimension. They wouldn't be apart for long.

"Hang on tight," called Rodeo Dave after him as he ran for the helicopter. "Don't ever let go!"

Jack looked back over his shoulder, waved, and kept running.

THE GAME GOES ON

The sky was blue and the air was warm. The oval was soaked, but that wasn't enough to delay the soccer game. Portland had survived the freak storm, the mayor had declared, and Mr. Carver had agreed with him, for once. The chance to beat Dogton's under-15s could not be lost!

Jaide was running on the left side of the pack, concentrating just as much on her footing as on where the ball was. She had fallen twice already and was covered in mud from head to toe. But in that regard she was no different from anyone else on either team. The game looked like two gangs of rival swamp creatures having a rumble, only with slightly better manners, thanks to the umpire's habit of sending anyone who misbehaved even slightly to the bench.

The ball was coming her way. Jaide started running, staying just ahead of the huddle of kids struggling to get their boots into the fray. Miralda was in there, and so was Stefano. He was easily the best soccer player on the field, but there were two on the Dogton team who were nearly his equal. One, a girl with spiky blond hair, had scored two goals already. The game was currently tied.

Back and forth went the ball inside the forest of muddy legs. Jaide moved back and forth with it, waiting for an opportunity to come her way. Helpful — and some not-so-helpful — calls came from the sidelines, where parents and spectators stood clutching coffees and bags of French fries. The sky was clear, but the wind remained unsettled with a hint of rain.

Stefano pulled free of the pack. Cries of encouragement and annoyance followed him, but he noticed neither. Jaide put on a burst of speed to keep up, watching not just the ball but Dogton's defensive positions as well. Stefano dodged the right fullback with a quick drag and push, neatly double touched past the center back, but was cut off by the sweeper and almost went offside.

Jaide was in a good position. She didn't call Stefano's name, figuring he had the moves to get himself out of the jam and maybe even put the ball in the net as well. He didn't need to pass to her. But suddenly the ball was coming her way, and she dodged the stopper to get to it first, put the toe of her left cleat firmly into the synthetic leather cover, and watched with pleased amazement as the ball curved through the defending positions, passed just over the goalie's fingertips, and went into the goal.

She whooped with excitement. Stefano ran up and high-fived her.

"No Gifts?" he whispered to her under the cover of the cheering crowd.

"Not at all," she said. "We're definitely even now."

He grinned and jogged off, letting her teammates gather her up in a celebratory hug. The Portland Portcupine, dressed in a tatty costume, waved his arms and kicked his legs in excitement.

Jack cheered from the bench, where he and Tara sat dressed in the uniform of the Portland under-15s, although Jack didn't really expect to play. It was nicer, and much less muddy, to watch from the sidelines. Behind the bench sat

Rodeo Dave, who seemed to be still deciding which memories he would remember and which he would let remain forgotten. Lottie was with him, bundled up so deeply in a thick scarf and coat that she was almost invisible (or perhaps that was deliberate, Jack wondered, given her Gift for hiding). Susan was helping with the cleanup, and Hector was pacing the sideline, shouting not-entirely-helpful things like "The squeaky wheel gets the worm!" At that moment, he was simply cheering Jaide's scoring kick. Kyle was doing handstands in the goal. Cornelia was soaring above, screeching "Offside! Offside!" even though she didn't really understand that rule. It was just a word people were shouting a lot.

"Look," said Tara. "Isn't that your grandma?"

Jack turned his attention away from the field to a striking figure in a bright red overcoat walking across River Road, past the wreckage of the school, to the oval. It did look like her, with that shock of white hair and the gleaming buckles of those cowboy boots, not to mention the two cats keeping pace with her, tails high in the air.

He stood, feeling nervous, although he wasn't sure of what, exactly. No one in the family had seen her since the previous night, when she had checked herself out of the hospital in Scarborough and effectively vanished. Weirdly, the Wardens hadn't panicked about it. That more than anything suggested to the twins that they were involved.

Jack waved at Jaide. She saw him, saw Grandma X, and began hopping up and down on one foot, clutching the other with a feigned expression of agony.

"What's wrong?" said Mr. Carver, running up to her. "You'll be all right, won't you?"

"I think I pulled something with that kick," she said. "I just need to take it easy for a bit."

"Are you sure it's not a sprain, something that will work itself out, perhaps with another kick just like that one? Well, if you're absolutely sure." He patted her on the back in a way that was probably supposed to be reassuring but instead almost tipped her off-balance. "Tara, come on. You're up!"

Tara was off the bench like a rocket, running onto the field as though about to do battle with The Evil.

The twins converged on their grandmother, who looked up and changed course, not to avoid them, but so they would meet near the bundles of canvas and disconnected framework that was all that remained of Project Thunderclap's tent. The cats fell back and stayed some distance away, giving them privacy but remaining within feline earshot.

"Hello, my troubletwisters," said Grandma X.

They stood slightly apart from one another, uncertain how to behave. Grandma X's eyes were perfectly clear, but their Gifts knew there was something new and strange about her. It took all the twins' effort to keep them in line.

"What do we call you now?" Jack asked.

"What you always have, if you like," she said. "I am still in here."

"With . . . *Lara Mae*?" said Jaide.

That prompted a laugh. "Oh, it hates being called that, believe me, almost as much as it hates being human. Don't worry about the names. They only matter to us. To you it's still The Evil and I'm still Grandma X. And that's the way it will remain, if you want it to: Everything can stay the same, even though everything is *actually* different now."

Confusing though that was, the twins relaxed slightly. This sounded just like her. Grandma X never made much sense when she was talking about something important.

She guided them to some nearby crates, where they sat down together, Jack on one side, Jaide on the other, their grandmother between them.

"Here's what was decided last night," she told them. "I'm no longer the Warden of Portland. I'm technically not a Warden at all anymore, which is understandable. Until Aleksandr and the others are completely sure what my relationship with The Evil is — and I'm not entirely clear on that yet, either — I'll be watched closely but at the same time kept at arm's length. Like I'm under house arrest, except I will be able to leave the house."

"But there must be a Warden of Portland," said Jack. "We felt the wards come back on this morning, and Rennie called to say that she'd be too busy to come to the game."

"And there's been no sign of Angel," said Jaide. "All the rocks on Mermaid Point are back where they used to be."

"The wards are in place, yes," Grandma X confirmed. "I'm glad you noticed. Custer is the Warden of Portland for now. David turned it down, of course, although he would have made a very good protector of the town."

"But why have the wards at all?" asked Jack. "The Evil is finished now, isn't it?"

"Perhaps. But I'm not. The wards are in place to stop me from leaving. I may have spent the night outside the town borders, but I'm back again, and this time it's really for good."

"You're under *town* arrest?" said Jaide.

"Yes, and it's fortunate that I like it here, very much." She looked around as though seeing everything for the first time. "All I have to do is keep The Evil under control and I'll be allowed to stay as I am."

"So how does it work?" said Jack. This question had been keeping him awake all night. "If The Evil is in you, we and all the Wardens get to keep our Gifts."

"Yes."

"You, too? Or do you have *all* the Gifts?"

"That's an interesting question. I don't know. I'm still discovering what I do and don't have."

"Okay. So what happens to the rest of The Evil, back on the other world? Will it die?"

"Possibly, unless it can find another food supply."

"But it can't come back here, can it?"

"Not unless it comes via another world, no."

"And what happens when *you* die? Will The Evil die, too?"

"Jack," said Jaide, appalled that he would ask a question like that, right to her face.

"It's okay, Jaidith," said Grandma X with a smile. "I've been wondering that, too. And believe me, I'm not the only one. Someone last night actually raised the possibility of putting it to the test."

The twins were shocked.

"They would kill you," Jaide said, "because that might kill The Evil as well?"

"Indeed. Only the threat that it might release The Evil instead made them back down."

They sat in silence for a long time, Jaide wondering if maybe it was true that over the course of one's life a Warden's Gifts made them more and more like The Evil. That was what had kept *her* up all night.

"What happens to *us*?" Jack asked. "Are we going to stay here?"

"If you'd like to. And if we can convince your mother."

"Will you still teach us how to use our Gifts?" asked Jaide.

"That's also your decision. Is that what you want?"

They looked at each other. It wasn't something they had talked about, but now that they were with their grandmother and she didn't seem any different, the decision was easy.

"Yes," they both said at the same time.

She smiled. "Good. I'm pleased. And there are two others who will be glad to hear it, too."

She crooked her finger and the cats came running up.

"Is it decided?" said Kleo, jumping into her lap and staring up at Jaide with her ears back. "The troubletwisters are to remain?"

"It seems so," said Grandma X.

"Brilliant," said Ari, hopping up onto the crate next to Jack and leaning into his side.

"But Grandma's not a Warden anymore," Jack said. "How can you be Warden Companions anymore?"

"We'll be regular companions now," said Kleo, "although we retain certain privileges."

"Visiting rights, most importantly," said Ari. "For snacks. Speaking of which, what's happening to Stefano? As long as he's on the cooking roster, I say he can stay as long as he wants."

"He will remain in Portland until he passes his final Examination," said Grandma X. "Speaking of which, Jackaran, we must arrange for you to take the third Examination as soon as possible."

"It's the worst," said Jaide with relish. "You'll just die."

"Great," said Jack, rolling his eyes. "If you'd just tell me why it's so bad, then I could be ready for it."

"She won't," said Grandma X with a warning look. "And when you're all ready, all three of you will take the fourth and final Examination. I've spoken to Alfred. He believes you will have no difficulty passing. The three of you have already achieved much more than some Wardens do in a lifetime."

She smiled, and the pride they saw in that smile was like the sun breaking through the clouds. Neither of them could believe that she was remotely Evil. They didn't understand how it worked, but this they knew in their hearts, where it really mattered.

"You'd better get back to the game, Jaide," she said. "Dogton just scored and that so-called teacher of yours looks like he's going to have a stroke, or possibly explode."

Jaide leaped up, sending Kleo tumbling, and saw the opposing team hugging one another in celebration. Kyle and the Portland Portcupine looked glum. Hector was waving frantically at her, and she waved back.

"I suppose I have to," she said. "But it's really Stefano who's winning the game for us."

"No, it's not," said Grandma X. "It's teamwork. And never giving up, not ever."

Jaide knew she was talking about something far more important than soccer, but wasn't in the mood for a lesson.

"Wish me luck!" she said, running to join the team.

Jack watched her go, idly scratching Ari behind the ear but not really thinking about either Jaide or Ari. There was one question he hadn't asked.

"What will the Wardens do now that The Evil is gone?"

"What would you *like* them to do?"

That was an easy question.

"Help people," he said, thinking of how Tara had once believed him and his sister to be superheroes. "But not because we want to be famous or anything. I'd keep it just the way it is, a secret, with no one really knowing what we do."

"That's a noble plan, Jack," she said. "I wonder what Aleksandr would say to it."

"I don't know," he said. "He's not a bad person. He just likes telling people what to do . . . maybe too much. And maybe that would be a bad thing, given how much spare time he's going to have now."

"Don't you worry about that," said Grandma X, picking up Kleo. "I'll find ways to keep him busy."

Kleo purred.

"Humans should work harder at doing the right thing on their own," she said.

"Yeah," sniffed Ari. "And they think *we're* hard work."

"Maybe it's true," said Grandma X. "We should be more like cats. They always land on their feet, for one."

"Don't worry, Grandma," said Jack. "We'll look after you."

Grandma X took his hand in a very tight grip, and smiled.